CONSEQUENCES *of* NORMAL

CONSEQUENCES *of* NORMAL

a novel

ELLE BAADE

This is a work of fiction. Names, characters, organizations, places, events, and incidents are either products of the author's imagination or are used fictitiously. Otherwise, any resemblance to actual persons, living or dead, is purely coincidental.

Published by Lake Union Publishing, Seattle

www.apub.com

EU product safety contact:
Amazon Media EU S. à r.l.
38, avenue John F. Kennedy, L-1855 Luxembourg
amazonpublishing-gpsr@amazon.com

ISBN-13: 9781662532450 (paperback)
ISBN-13: 9781662532467 (digital)

Cover design by Lisa Amoroso
Cover images: © PasSaKorn22 / Shutterstock; © stanley45 / Getty

Printed in the United States of America

This book is dedicated to the moms who find their voices and the kids who don't have one yet

Chapter One

I mutter to myself, yanking the casserole out of the oven. It'll burn if I leave it cooking while I'm gone. My phone buzzes on the kitchen counter with texts from my husband, Matt.

> Jane. Where are you? I thought you were picking us up an hour ago.
> Have you left yet?

My ten-month-old, Henrietta, is in her hand-me-down Exersaucer, so I scoop her up.

"So much for picking up your poor daddy and sister, or having dinner ready on time," I say softly to my daughter. "Charles, we need to go pick up Daddy and Louisa. We're late!" I yell across the house.

Charles floats into the room as if the whole world waits on him. "We're always late, Mama," he says casually, slowly taking crackers out of a bag one at a time to eat them.

"Don't I know it? You can bring your snack. Please grab some shoes," I beg. "Just get in the van and get buckled."

He's just about to turn six, so I'm trying not to be impatient with his glacial pace.

"How come Daddy doesn't have a car?" Charles asks as we climb into the van.

"It . . . costs too much money. So me and Daddy share. It's nice to share." Charles doesn't reply. He looks out the window silently while we drive the few minutes to the school.

Tall, old trees line its long, picturesque driveway. The light shines through the gaps in the dreamy leaves, adding to the charm and beauty. The elite Browning School keeps its massive grounds impeccable.

The academic year has just ended, and only a handful of accelerated summer classes are in session. Most students and staff from the boarding school are gone for the season.

The tree-lined drive opens into a big circular driveway adjacent to the main building and the great lawn. As we get closer, I can see balloons and tables on the property with at least a hundred people milling about, with still more coming from the direction of the athletic fields.

"Welcome, Prospective Students and Families" reads the banner across the courtyard.

"Great," I mumble so Charles can't hear me. "I don't remember Matt mentioning it was open house today." Seeing all the Browning people out in force was not on my bingo card this morning.

We hang back in the security of the trees while I pick at my cuticles and contemplate making my husband and daughter walk the extra few minutes across the big circular drive to find me.

Hiding out in the trees seems suspicious, though, so I barely enter the main circle and stay as far from the action as possible without making my family hike out to us. I send a quick text to Matt so he knows I'm waiting.

"Just when I thought it was safe to return to Browning," I mutter, biting my fingernails and looking around.

"There's Daddy's building," Charles chimes in proudly, and I follow his small pointing finger to the manicured lawn stretching to the stately middle school building. Matt has taught here for five years now. He got his PhD, hoping to become an administrator, but the Browning School hasn't gotten him anywhere closer to his dream.

Even though I texted Matt, he's nowhere to be seen. I imagine a sniper in every tree, ready to laser in on all my imperfections in front of my husband, the only person in the world who is nice to me.

I wish I'd showered today.

"Mom, I'm hot," Charles complains. He's right. It's unbearably hot, even in June—another reason to hate Texas.

"I know, sweetie. Me too. The air conditioner isn't working again. The windows are open. We need to hope for a breeze." The fan is set to high but only circulates hot air.

My anxious thoughts start to slow as I see my daughter Louisa coming out from the main building, but as soon as she heads my way, I notice Katherine James watching her, then changing her focus to me in my van.

Katherine James is the "Queen Mom" of Browning School and is undoubtedly involved in the open house. She heads my way as if she's on a mission. Katherine is joined by one of the moms in her squad whose name I've never bothered learning because, from day one, they all seemed to dislike me. At this point, the feeling is mutual.

My heart starts to race again as they walk toward us on the outer edge of the circle. I press the button to open the van door to let Louisa in, and somehow, both doors begin to open. I begin frantically pushing buttons to close them as if it will protect us.

"Mom, it's Mrs. Katherine," Charles yells as the van doors open. I turn back to look at him, only now realizing he's wearing a chocolate milk mustache and his sister's old pink princess dress. His long brown curls stick to his sweaty face.

"Shit," I whisper. We rushed out of the house, and I never looked at him.

"Jane," Katherine says in a tense voice without looking at me, as if I once drowned a sack of her kittens or something. She leans into my open passenger window to speak to me in a tone reserved for stupid dogs. "The Browning School is holding an event right now, so it's not the time to . . . loiter."

Katherine's friend laughs aloud as a gust of wind comes through the open doors and tosses some trash from my van onto the sidewalk at their feet. The laughter dies quickly.

Charles, who, along with his older sister, is always trying to save the planet, starts yelling, "Get the garbage! You're littering, and it could fall in lakes or rivers."

I sigh, unbuckling my seat belt and getting out to clean up the garbage. "I got it, Charles. I've got it." My hands shake as I pick up a bag of days-old fast food. Katherine and her crony shrink away from the van like I am handling some biohazard. Charles is still chattering away about the dangers of littering.

As if things couldn't get any worse, I notice Dr. Hawthorne observing the whole scene outside my van. Dr. Hawthorne is the school's headmaster. She's also the woman who has denied my husband four promotions since we arrived here. He's up for another this week, and I stare at her through my sunglasses, willing her to give him a chance.

As if she can smell my general disdain for all things Browning, Dr. Hawthorne walks our way, joining us all in the mess at the passenger side.

My van is still startlingly full of fast food and snack wrappers, sippy cups and bottles, clothing, and shoes. Dr. Hawthorne has a front-row view because she's hanging into the open door.

"Well, hello, Zander family," she says. Her voice sounds fake, stopping silent when she surveys the mess. Her impeccable gray suit probably cost more than our ridiculously overpriced mortgage payment. Her red hair is cast into flawless curls with copious amounts of hairspray. Her makeup is seamless. I couldn't begin to tell you how one achieves being so put together.

"What on earth do we have going on in this van? Do you live in here?" She laughs, but I don't see how mocking us is funny. Witnessing Dr. Hawthorne's perfection, I realize I have a grape juice stain on a shirt that is already too big for my slight frame. I'm painfully aware my shaggy brown hair is unbrushed. On my best day, I'm plain and too ordinary to notice. Today, I'm a hot mess.

I am not cool enough to shrug off the whole situation with a joke or some quip about how I "embrace the mess." Instead, all I feel is judged, and my heart beats in my ears.

I start mumbling, "I'm so sorry. We've been so busy . . ." as I wipe the sweat off my face. She waves a hand at me to stop talking, and I do.

She turns her attention from me to the kids in the back seat as Louisa climbs in. Dr. Hawthorne leans in farther and surveys Charles and his pink, frilly dress.

"My goodness," she says to Charles. "You look, um, lovely. What is the occasion to look so lovely?" I almost think she's being sincere with her sickeningly sweet voice. Charles glows and tells her he's going to wear it for his birthday party tomorrow. Katherine snickers with her friend, which turns into laughter. Dr. Hawthorne leans out of the van. She pulls her sunglasses down to look at them both with a scowl. They run off, giggling, back toward the party.

Why did I come into the main circle? It's full of everyone I don't want to see, even in summer.

"It's almost his birthday and—" I start to say, but she cuts me off. She leans in close to me as if she has a secret.

"Do be mindful with what you allow. You are the parent, and you should have the control. If you aren't careful, you'll confuse the poor dear and he'll be painting his own nails. And that would not go well at Browning, would it?"

She looks at me to find my mouth hanging open, with no reply or rebuttal.

Just then, Matt walks up to the van and saves us.

Matt is one of those handsome hometown guys. He isn't Brad Pitt or Tom Cruise but could be their cousin: tall, dreamy, brown hair, bright-green eyes. He's too thin right now, and his clothes hang off him enough that he could use at least a size down. Still, I've always thought him so handsome.

"Dr. Hawthorne," he says politely, looking perplexed. The doctor and I aren't known for chatting after school. I didn't know if she could pick me out of a lineup until today.

"Mr. Zander. It's always so nice to see you and your . . . colorful family. Happy birthday to your son. It *is* your *son*, right?" Her laugh comes out as more of a cackle. With a nonchalant wave, she's gone.

Matt picks up the rest of the trash with me, looking amused but confused. I roll my eyes in response. Matt tosses the last few bags into the back and sees Charles. He gives me a look as he climbs into the passenger side.

"Charles is wearing dresses for running errands now?" he asks with a smile that his tone doesn't match.

"Mom was arguing with Katherine and Dr. Hawthorne," Louisa chimes in.

"We weren't arguing, Louisa. We were just talking," I tell her.

"That was the kind of arguing adults do that sounds like they are being nice, but they are not being nice."

I turn my attention to Matt.

"I'm sorry for being late and letting Charles come out when he's such a mess. And then a bunch of garbage flew out of the car when I opened the door. And how was I supposed to know Hawthorne would practically get into our van? I had no idea today was open house. It's been too hot to clean this van out . . . I'm failing at life today," I say with defeat, and Matt says nothing, so I keep on rambling.

"And then, of course, it all happens in front of my ex-friends . . ."

"Can we call them 'ex-friends' if you only hung out once or twice?" I wince, but Matt doesn't notice. He has a way of saying things to be funny without realizing they might be painful. Also, Matt is the person who suggested I become friends with Katherine.

"Katherine and I had two playdates with our girls, which went perfectly fine, but she has barely spoken to me since," I answer, my voice flat. "Except for today, when she came to tell me to go away. So I don't know. I don't get past one or two hangouts with friends before they disappear."

"What about Tracy? You two are friends."

I shrug. Tracy is another Browning misfit, and I get the impression that Matt isn't thrilled that I'm friends with her. Her family has very little money, and their daughter is on a scholarship at Browning in Louisa's class. They live in a trailer in the next town over, and Tracy has about as many friends at the school as I do.

"She only answers my texts, like, half the time. We aren't exactly close." I take a breath and turn to my husband. "I swear to you, Matt, I'm trying so hard *every day* just to keep everyone fed and in one piece."

Matt's face softens, and he reaches for my shaky hand and intertwines our fingers.

"It's okay. We all have rough days. Anyway, didn't I tell you Hawthorne has it in for me? Did you hear her call me 'mister'? She never calls me 'Dr. Zander.' God forbid she imply that we are equals. She claims to call all the teachers 'mister' or 'miss,' regardless of their degrees, because it's *easier for the kids*. And yet she instructs the kids to call *her* 'doctor.' This place is so frustrating. I'm just nervous because of the interview." Matt tucks a piece of my hair back as I put my seat belt on. When I turn around to look at him, his face is serious.

"I know you're trying. It's never been more important just to fit in, especially if I get this promotion, by some miracle. We are behind on the mortgage, and we've got twenty-four dollars in the bank until payday." He's whispering so the kids can't hear.

"Correction. We have seven dollars. I had to buy the last few things for Charles's party tomorrow. And yes, I will try harder," I say, silently hoping he believes me.

Matt takes a deep breath and nods, letting go of the stress and sliding back into his mellow self despite my reducing our last cash to less than a third of what it was this morning. He's good at that. Me? I can't turn down the anxiety at all.

Matt turns to face the back seat and asks Charles about his day, reaching out and tickling him until I hear his adorable and aggravating little shriek. I put the van in gear, and we head home.

Chapter Two

Matt is supposed to come home any minute to help me with Charles's birthday party when I get his text. He's at work, like always.

I am running late but trying to get out of here.

I text back: Sounds good.

"He better get home soon because I cannot handle this party on my own," I say to no one.

"Louisa," I call across the house. She comes down to the kitchen with a book in hand. "Could you please watch some Julia Child with Charles while Henrietta naps so I can decorate for the party? Dad is running a bit late."

Louisa rolls her eyes teasingly but agrees.

Charles found an entire box of Julia Child VHS tapes at a rummage sale that he just had to have, and he has been obsessed with her ever since. Louisa is as bored with the videos as we all are, but she indulges Charles for his love of all things cooking and Julia.

I start in the basement, digging extension cords and Christmas lights from boxes to string through the yard. I set aside plastic eggs left over from Easter to fill with some bags of chocolate coins the kids forgot about.

After I finish in the yard, I check my phone for replies for the party.

Charles's school lets out two weeks later than Browning for summer break, so he was able to hand out invitations to his whole class, but we still haven't gotten any RSVPs. I send a mass text to every parent on the "call a friend" list, hoping someone will decide to come.

Hi. This is Jane, Charles's mom. This is a last-minute reminder that his birthday party is from five to seven tonight. I hope you can make it. Let me know? I'd appreciate it. Thanks.

The handful of replies that come in are all solid noes. I frown at the texts, worrying my kid may not have anyone at his birthday party but us.

The kids excitedly beg to help me finish making the dessert. They go to wash their hands while I grab what we need to finish the cupcakes before any of the guests arrive.

"Why didn't we pick a cake from the store this year?" Louisa asks as she frosts almost as fast as I do and with more care, even at ten years old. Charles is standing beside her, wearing the most flowery apron I own. He never wants his curly brown hair cut, so it's all shaggy on his face, and his frosting attempts match his overall disheveled self, but he is thrilled to be together in the kitchen. The baby sits in her high chair, watching us, joining in our conversations with her babbling between eating dry cereal.

I glance at the stack of overdue bills tucked into the mail file and try to fake a smile. "Oh, you know, making cupcakes is fun, right? Plus, Charles is the best chef, so he needs to be involved." Charles is in his element and beaming.

"I'm going to be the best chef when I get big, just like Julia Child," he says with a grin.

"You sure can be," I say, placing the last cupcakes on the stand and kissing Charles on the head.

"How about we go get dressed for your party? Maybe Louisa could help you find something to wear while I do a few things?" I wink at

Louisa, and she nods. Louisa gathers Charles while I take the baby with me to clean up before the party.

Matt finally arrives home from school. He doubled up teaching accelerated summer classes for the money, and he had his interview today, so he has been on edge. When he walks in the door, he looks pissed. He joins me in the kitchen.

"It would be nice if the Browning School could pay me what I'm worth. Or at least enough to cover the bills," he says as he hands me a stack of new bills that came in the mail. I place them in the organizers on the desk.

"What happened at the interview? You don't look okay." He walks past without stopping to hug or kiss me, and I start picking at my cuticles as I wait. "What's wrong?"

Matt's angry, but I don't know why or at whom. He is one of the calmest and most collected people, so if he is this upset, it's something terrible. He grabs a beer from the fridge and paces the room with it in his hand. His lack of composure rattles me.

"Not only didn't I get the job, but I'm pretty sure she told me to look for a new job because Browning frowns upon families like ours."

My jaw drops, and I can hear myself breathing out loud. "What?" I can't even wrap my brain around it.

"Despite how hard I've worked to win her over and prove myself these past five years, Dr. Hawthorne doesn't feel we are the right material to represent Browning."

No shit, I think, but I don't say it. He doesn't seem to be paying attention to me anyway.

"The thing is," I say cautiously, "we don't fit in here. I see it. Even six-year-old Charles can see it. Maybe this isn't the place for us."

He turns to me, his eyes narrowed. "What other options do we have, Jane? This is the job *I have*. If I try another school, I'll have to spend years doing the same thing I did here. But I'll be the new guy with no connections. Not to mention that we are broke, so how are we supposed to move anywhere?"

"What did she mean that we aren't 'the right material' for Browning?" My voice falters as I ask. Matt looks at me without saying a word.

"Ugh. You mean the messy van and Charles wearing the dress?" I ask as I put my hand to my forehead.

He stares at me, then shrugs it off as if maybe it wasn't all my fault.

"So my son likes bright colors and sparkly clothes. Whatever. He'll grow out of it. I'm not worried about that, and it's weird if that's some red flag to her about our family. All she told me was that I'm not management material and should look for more suitable options, perhaps in the public sector, where people are more comfortable with a wide variety of lifestyles."

He sighs, shaking his head and going back to pacing. I can't tell if he is mad at me, the school, or both, so I don't ask. My breathing is fast, and my heart won't stop racing. I want to comfort him, but I have no idea what to say.

Matt has worked many extra hours for years and rarely takes a day off. I feel awful for him. The time he spends away from our family working has affected all of us.

When he goes to shower, I stand in the kitchen alone, trying to calm myself and get ready for this party. I take deep breaths until my heart rate slows.

When Matt comes down, his mood is better too.

"What can I do to help?" he asks with a small smile, and I look at him.

"Matt, don't you want to talk about this?"

He takes a deep breath and shakes his head. "No. It's all a shitty situation, but right now, I want to concentrate on my only son's birthday party."

I smile, moving toward him, and he takes me into his arms, where I can almost forget how screwed we are.

"I'm glad you're home to help," I say when he lets me go. "I got a bunch of solid noes on the RSVPs, but since we invited the whole class, I'm still hoping some kids are coming. They should be arriving soon."

Matt nods. "I'm at your disposal," he says with a smile.

"You are my favorite," I whisper into his ear, and he kisses me.

Louisa pops into the kitchen with us. "Henrietta is poopy, and Charles won't wear his own clothes. He wants to wear my purple dress with the cats on it, but it's so long it goes to the floor."

Charles arrives in said dress behind his sister. "It's evening wear for an evening party," he says.

Louisa rolls her eyes, and Matt laughs out loud.

"Okay, I will deal with the poopy baby and the colorful kid. Thanks, Louisa." Matt kisses her forehead before taking Henrietta off her bony hip. "You've got such a good big sister, Henrietta. Now let's get this diaper changed."

While I bring all the food outside, Matt talks Charles into his khaki shorts and a light-blue princess shirt because it's all about princesses with that kid.

Charles comes out to the backyard, wide-eyed and so excited. He hugs me, then runs around the yard, twirling and looking up at the lights. A smile creeps across my face, and I hope he enjoys the evening.

But after an hour of waiting, with Charles peering through the fence with his bottom lip sticking out, we resign ourselves to the reality that this party will be attended by only Matt, our kids, and me.

"Why didn't any of my friends come to my party, Mama?" Charles asks, looking so small and sad as he curls up on my lap like a cat.

"Oh, sweetie. I think it's because it's sports season, and everyone has big games and practices. I heard your friend Annabelle had a gymnastics class to go to. And the end of the school year means everyone is busy. But we can have a great family party with just us."

I try to sound excited, and we move on to finding eggs and opening presents. Louisa made him a card and gave him one of her old dolls with the matching princess nightgowns he loves. Baby Henrietta claps while Charles blows out his six birthday candles. After we all have cupcakes, Matt builds Charles's new purple bike, and the kids race around the backyard.

Matt and I sit down as the daylight fades, and I lean back against his chest. “I can’t believe not even one of those kids from his class came. Even the kindergartners are snobs here. I just . . . don’t think this place is good for any of us.”

Matt nods with a sigh. “We are screwed here anyway. We need more money to live. And I don’t see Hawthorne making idle threats. We need to assume that I might not have a job in the fall, so I need to update my résumé and start searching online for jobs.”

I sit up to look at him. “Really?” I ask, trying to contain my excitement.

Matt sighs and then smiles. “I know this isn’t your scene, and it appears it isn’t mine either. We need a better option, like yesterday.”

I take a sip of my iced tea with a smile, trying not to be hopeful, but I am.

The kids run the yard, making happy noises as the light of day fades. Matt snuggles his face into my neck the way I like. “Thank you for making such a great party for him with so little money. You are amazing, and I know how hard you work at being the best mom.”

Matt is the only person who ever makes me feel like I’m good enough.

Chapter Three

"Are you okay?" Matt's voice is soothing and gentle as I crawl back into our bed at four a.m. I spent half the night in the bathroom with the familiar pains and bloating of a gluten reaction.

I roll over to face him.

"'Okay' is a matter of perspective."

"I'm taking today off, watching the kids, and caring for you." He reaches out and brushes my hair off my face gently.

"No, Matt, don't. After what Hawthorne said in your interview, you're hanging by a thread with the job. Now isn't the time to take days off. Can you get the kids breakfast when they get up and ask Louisa to be my helper today? Hopefully, they will let me lay around on the couch."

"I have a lot of vacation days to take. Henrietta is into everything these days. Charles still has school this week, and you are too sick to go out. Those children will eat you alive today."

"Honestly, I'm more worried about you. Your stomach has been bothering you for months, Matt. I think your ulcer is back. You should take the time to get on some meds again," I tell him. "You've lost weight."

"I'm fine, Jane. It's just the stress of this job and our money situation. You need help today, so I'm taking the day off to care for you and the kids. Stay in bed and sleep as long as you can."

I'm too sick to fight him, though I feel bad about him calling in. He so rarely does, and the timing couldn't be worse.

The sounds of the kids running through the house rouses me after a few hours. Matt gets the kids out the door to take Charles to his last week of kindergarten. I'm still too weak to contemplate returning to my regular duties, so I stay in bed, scrolling through my phone. Matt comes in with some Gatorade and dry cereal for me.

"How are you feeling?" he asks, kissing my forehead and sitting beside me. "You look a bit better than when I got up."

"I'm better. Just weak now." Matt nods. He knows the drill after all this time dealing with my celiac.

"What do you think it was from?" he asks.

"The cupcakes," I answer without having to think about it. "The ingredients said 'possibly processed in a facility with gluten.' It's so hard to find gluten-free stuff here."

"Next time, let's buy the gluten-free-certified stuff from Amazon."

When I bought the ingredients, we had seventy-five dollars to our name, and I barely had the money for a gift or a party, but I don't say that. I appreciate that he took the day off to take care of me.

"I just need to be more careful."

"It's not your fault. Things happen. It's okay. But maybe they won't happen as often if we can make safer choices," he says. I nod at him as I start to cry.

"It's okay. You'll feel better soon," he soothes.

"I hate being sick, and it reminds me so much of being a kid. I just lay there for hours and days, and my family didn't even care. And then . . ." I let my voice trail off, and the tears come. Matt leans in and hugs me.

"Are you thinking about when you got taken away?" he asks as he pulls back.

My bottom lip sticks out involuntarily as I try to speak, and I pull the blanket around me. When I was about nine years old, I got very sick, and my mom forgot to call the school to let them know I would be absent for a few days. She was drinking and never answered the school's calls, so they sent social services to check and found me home, sick and alone.

"It was only five days of my life, a few in a hospital and two in some care facility. It happened so long ago, but it made me feel so vulnerable, like anyone could get taken away at any moment. And now I'm afraid that'll happen to us with our kids."

Matt thinks I'm being unreasonable, but being sick always brings it back.

"Jane, no one is going to take our kids. We are great parents and have no reason for social services to be in our lives. Your mom showed terrible judgment and wasn't the best parent, but you got sent back so fast, and the case was closed. Ultimately, it is just a scary thing that happened to you long ago." I don't argue with him by pointing out that my family didn't exactly get attentive after that. He wants me to let go of the past and be thankful for my family as they are. And I want to make Matt happy because he saved me from that world, and I'm finally safe.

"That's over now. You have me, and I will listen to you. And I believe you. Get some rest or pick up a book. But don't lie there thinking about how crappy they were to you. It will only make you feel worse."

He kisses me and heads out of the room. When he leaves, I head to my sister's social media page, scrolling through pics of her boys on dirt bikes and dark, grainy photos of her smiling face in random bars. We don't see her much, and sometimes, looking at her pictures makes me think we are strangers. When I think of her being my sister, I think of my childhood, not here and now. Now, we are just the occasional tense phone call.

My mom and sister have always moved around a lot. I went to nine different schools growing up. We lived all over the country, but Mickey and my mom have settled out West in the general area of the Dakotas in the past ten years. We haven't been there since they lived in Sturgis after Charles's birth.

Matt is right about not needing to think about them right now, but they always seem so tied up in my feelings when I'm sick, as if I will always want them to comfort me and be there for me, even though they never have.

❦

In the end, Matt takes two days off because I'm too weak to do much.

"I appreciate you doing this, Matt. For real," I say. "But I'm worried about your job. We need it until you can find something else. We can't afford . . ."

But he quiets me with his fingers on my lips. "We can't afford to have you feeling this way, and if we get you the rest you need, you will feel better faster. I've known you for almost fifteen years, Jane. I know what you need. And I'm here. Hawthorne can take a hike, not a nice one, if she wants to be mad at me for taking my sick days. Besides, it allowed me to update my résumé and put myself out there for some admin jobs."

I lean into Matt, so thankful to have such a person to care for me.

"What would I do without you? I can't imagine."

"I don't want to imagine," he says, kissing my forehead and leaving me to rest.

Chapter Four

"Charles is so polite and kind to all his friends. He has a heart of gold, and I hope he keeps it," one of the teacher's helpers tells me at pickup on his last day of kindergarten. I get almost choked up since Charles doesn't say much about school.

He attended kindergarten at a small Methodist school. Matt won't say it, but he doesn't want our kids to attend a public school, even for kindergarten. Despite the expense, he knows more about kids and school than I do, so I see no reason to disagree. Browning doesn't start school until fourth grade, and most teachers' kids don't attend regardless. Louisa tested very high in their placement exams and thrived in their fourth grade. I worry if Browning will be the right fit for Charles, but who knows if we will even be here. The uncertainty of Matt's job looms over us like a dark cloud.

"Mom," says Charles's primary teacher, Mrs. Lambert, as Charles goes to his cubby to collect his bag and art projects. She calls all the moms "Mom" as if it's our actual name. "I'm glad I caught you. Charles has been asking for a playdate with Annabelle this summer. They play together every day and"—she leans closer—"between you and me, I think Charles may have a little crush on her. He follows her everywhere, doing what she does. They are quite the pair. It's very sweet." Mrs. Lambert's smile is genuine, but the whole thing irks me.

"Can six-year-olds have crushes?" I ask with a forced smile because she seems so charmed by it. Even if I'm a self-proclaimed misfit, I want the kids to have friends, so I promise we will contact Annabelle's mom.

"While I have you, I was wondering . . ." I say to Mrs. Lambert. "Did anyone say anything . . ." Charles's teacher looks at me, waiting for me to get the words out.

"It's just, well—no one came to Charles's birthday party last week, and he was so sad. I was wondering if he has friends here."

She smiles at me, but the smile suggests she isn't going to say what I want to hear. "Charles is a sweet, sensitive, shy little guy. He has found Annabelle to be a safe friend, and they enjoy playing. Many of our boys are very rough-and-tumble. *All boy.* They play wrestling at recess and even war if we don't catch them to make them stop. They are *boy's boys.* And Charles . . . isn't." Her comment feels too big to wrap my brain around, so I thank her, and we leave.

Walking out, I ask Charles, "Your teacher said you play a lot with Annabelle. How about a playdate with her sometime?"

"Yes," he answers quickly, then solemnly tells me she isn't his girlfriend. I almost snicker, but he seems so serious that I think better of it.

"Good. You're not quite ready for girlfriends," I say, but Charles stays silent, staring at his feet.

"Or boyfriends," I add, "because that's fine too." Charles looks at me for a second but returns to watching the ground as we near the van. I change subjects.

"It's nice that you and Annabelle are friends. What do you two do together?"

"We play in the kitchen. She lets me wear the apron and be Julia Child *and* the mommy and doesn't say I can't. She can do good cartwheels and has the prettiest hair I ever saw." Charles lets out a big dramatic sigh and says, "I wish I could be Annabelle."

I stop walking right in the middle of the parking lot. It's such a powerful statement. He wishes he could *be* Annabelle?

"Hmmm. She does sound pretty great." In his defense, I have seen Annabelle, and Charles is right: Annabelle is a beauty with long, thick blond hair, huge blue eyes, and perfect little pink lips. "But you get to be you. Being you is fun, too, right?"

Charles doesn't answer. He shrugs a bit and looks down at the ground again.

"Do you have any friends that are boys?" I ask, trying to sound nonchalant.

Charles shakes his head. "Nah. They all like trucks, stupid dinosaurs, and *guns*." He throws his hands in the air at the word "guns" and shakes his head. "All the time. It's so boring."

I let out a small laugh, but he looks up at me with serious eyes. He's struggling, and I should be able to find the words to help him, but I don't know them. We join hands and walk toward the van.

"Hey. How about we stop and pick up some frozen pizzas? Would you like to have a pizza night and watch a movie in the living room? Maybe you could help me make some cookies?" Charles seems to smile a bit there, but I can tell I haven't solved the problem, whatever it is. I always wish it came with a manual, but somehow I feel like I am failing Charles in particular.

After Charles and I make the cookies and pop the gluten-free pizzas in the oven, Matt takes the big kids outside to play ball. Charles and Louisa have little interest in sports, but Matt seems determined to convince one of our kids to be a ball player. He still talks about how much he loved playing baseball in high school, and when we lived out East, before we moved to Texas, Matt even played in a recreational men's league. He hasn't had the time in Texas, with all his extracurricular expectations as a Browning teacher.

I wait inside to watch the pizza and cookies in the oven, listening to the crack of the bat in the backyard. Louisa is batting while Matt tosses slow and easy pitches to her. It isn't the sport she likes, but the time with her daddy. Charles stands off to the side, cheering her on and kicking his leg high, copying the cheerleaders he adores from the football games Matt watches. Matt offers to pitch to Charles, but he tells Matt that he is the cheerleader. Watching them out the window warms my heart. Growing up without a dad makes me appreciate Matt so much. No matter how tired or stressed he is, he always takes the time to play with the kids.

When the pizzas are done, I call them all in for dinner. Matt comes to kiss me, all sweaty from the blazing Texas summer, with Charles in tow.

"Louisa is hitting really well. We need to sign her up for travel ball next summer," he tells me. I can't imagine how we could afford it, but I don't say anything.

"How did it go playing ball, Charles?" I ask.

Charles gives me a shrug, taking off the old ball cap of Matt's that he must have tightened to fit Charles and put on his head for their backyard game.

"Charles seems more interested in cheerleading than playing ball at this point," Matt says with a shrug. "I'm sure you'll get into playing ball with your friends when you get a bit older, right, buddy?" Charles doesn't say anything back, and Matt turns to me. "But in the meantime, his high kicks are really coming along."

Charles hands Matt's hat back to him, and Matt puts a large hand on Charles's shoulder.

"Your hair is getting so long, Charles. We don't want anyone to think you're a *girl*, right? What do you think about us having a dad-and-son day this weekend and going to get that long hair of yours cut?"

Charles freezes mid-step and looks at me with wide eyes. He reaches up and starts twirling his long brown curls in his fingers. His bottom lip sticks out, and I can see he is setting up for a major meltdown.

"Charles?" I ask, waiting till he looks at me. He looks at Matt and then me again, pleading with big tear-filled eyes.

"I don't want my hair cut," he whines, the tears spilling out as he rubs chubby little fists against his eyes. His breathing gets fast, and he hiccups as he gets more worked up.

"Matt," I say gently, trying to calm the waters. "The last few haircuts were pretty rough. Charles cried hard through every one, and was upset for over a week each time."

Matt looks at me with a frown, then glances at crying Charles, before letting out a long, loud sigh.

"Okay," he relents. "But eventually, you are going to have to get that hair cut, kiddo. Before it's long enough for someone to use it to climb up to your window to rescue you."

Charles relaxes visibly, his shoulders dropping back down from his ears, and I feel the release in my own body. I don't know why Charles is so attached to his long hair, but I do know that for him, haircuts are literally traumatic.

I smile as Matt tousles Charles's long, curly locks, then kisses my forehead and heads for a quick shower before dinner. Louisa comes in too, and I send the kids to wash their hands. Despite the money problems and job stress, I feel thankful for my little family, especially Matt. I'll admit that I don't know much about having a dad, but I don't think I could ask for a better one for our kids.

Chapter Five

It's late July, and other than a handful of playdates with Tracy and her kids, we've spent the summer at home in the air-conditioning. Matt and I grow more nervous by the day as the summer slips away because he has still not been offered a new contract from Hawthorne. None of his online job searches have panned out so far. I don't know how many mortgage payments we can miss before we lose the house.

Matt comes in the front door one night, his hair disheveled but a crooked half smile on his face. I stare at him from the kitchen, trying to figure out what happened. He answers me before I ask. "I got this unbelievable phone call on the way home from my cousin Jason in Wisconsin."

I look at him with raised eyebrows. "Your cousin?" Matt doesn't have much family, at least any he sees or talks to.

"Jason and I were pretty close growing up. He was a senior when I was a freshman. We never played school ball together, but he's a good guy. He's running Atwood Prep, and he hates it. The headmaster got sick and left, and Jason has been filling in. But he's a football coach—not a headmaster. And I guess Jason's wife just left him after some torrid affair. He's struggling, and the school needs someone yesterday. He noticed that I was actively looking, and he offered me the job as headmaster right then and there. He said he's got the board in his pocket, and it's a done deal if I want it."

Matt looks thrilled, but I'm frowning at him anyway. It all sounds too good to be true.

"I thought you said you'd never go back to Atwood," I say nervously.

Matt shrugs. "I did. I know." He shakes his head and runs his hand through his hair. "We're drowning here in debt. We can't afford this house! The Browning School will never see me as anything except a teacher—if they even want me at all. I think I'm done here next week when the last summer session ends—like it or not."

I nod. I'm well aware of how screwed we are.

"This feels like our only option." His voice lowers to a whisper because of the kids.

As if I don't know. Our student loans gain interest daily while we struggle to pay our bills.

"Daddy! Come see the cookies we made," Charles yells from the kitchen. The kids are too excited to let us talk until they've been fed.

Matt holds his hand up in the air in his teacher's way. They all pause the melee briefly to let him talk. "Jason sent an email with the whole offer. He wants me to look at it right away, because if we're interested, he wants us there immediately." The kids are rowdy and too loud to talk over.

"We can look at it when these little goofballs give us five minutes' peace." He says the second half of the sentence in a silly monster voice, lowering his hand to show the kids they can return to their habit of speaking over everyone.

When we are all done with dinner, complete with sticky mouths and sleepy smiles, Matt chimes in from his position at the head of the table, where he's been staring at his phone.

"It comes with a house!" He laughs. I stare at him blankly. Even the kids perk up from the food coma.

"Like a place to rent?"

"No, a house. To own. It's a famous old home in Atwood." I can hear the excitement rising in his voice. "The school offers discounted staff housing or covers the down payment as part of a new headmaster's salary, and we can buy it. We would need to sign to take on the payments. Our house here should sell fast. It's a seller's market in Texas right now."

"Louisa," I say. She's getting up before I even finish my question.

"Help me get everyone ready for baths," she says with a smile, looking at me sideways, thinking she's funny.

"Thank you for always being so willing to help out," I tell her, squeezing her shoulder as she moves past me to gather up Charles, who is all sticky fingers beneath his princess nightgown.

"How much is the house?" I ask, ready to cringe. Everything seems so expensive. I can't fathom how we will pay for any of it.

"It's a hundred and fifty thousand dollars."

"What? Why? Is it falling apart?"

"No. I know the house. It's big, beautiful, and stately. It's old, but the widow Wellington had money to keep it up. It sits atop the hill just down the block from the school grounds." I must look doubtful, because he keeps going.

"It's a cheaper housing market there. We can get out of here and not be drowning. This is a good thing. The house is amazing." He turns his phone to show me a picture.

It seems big and old, but my attention is elsewhere. "I think too many years of being shuffled around as a kid made me skeptical about moving," I admit. Honestly, moving in my adult years hasn't changed my mind.

Matt looks at me, sets down his phone before reaching out to take my hands. "This is the real deal. I think this is the break we've been waiting for."

"I can't help thinking about how often you've said you never wanted to return to Atwood. You told me you didn't fit in."

Matt shrugs slowly, like he's trying to get something off his back.

"I don't know. I left there when I was eighteen. I had lots of friends. I played sports and enjoyed it but had a bad attitude, thinking I was being left out unfairly. I wasn't one of the cool kids with a big house or who played the starting lineup like my second cousins. But I look back now and see that maybe I wasn't the best player. I had a pretty nice life there, and maybe it was just teenage angst that got in my way of seeing it."

"You told me you were the wrong type of Zander. You said because your dad worked second shift in a factory and your mom worked at the Gas&Gulp, they'd never see you any differently."

"But it *would* be different now. I'll be running Atwood Prep. I'm finally starting the lineup, not riding the bench. I worked hard, got a PhD, and made something of myself."

It's been literally years since I've seen him this excited. Matt goes to the bathroom to help the kids with their baths. I pull my phone out of my pocket and search "Wisconsin," sighing as photos of cheese, cows, and farms appear on the screen.

"Whatever," I say to myself. "At least it's not Texas."

Matt comes out of the bathroom looking at me, thinking I might say no and smash his dream. As if I could tell him no. And anywhere is better than here.

"I've followed you everywhere. Why would I stop now?" He picks me up, swinging me in a circle like he did the night I said yes to marrying him. I bury my face into his neck, taking in his smell and body. No matter what we encounter in Atwood, Matt is my home.

Chapter Six

Once the house sells, I text Tracy and ask to get together for a playdate with the girls. She's my only friend here, and we aren't exactly close. But we hang out sometimes, so I don't want to ghost her.

Tracy came from Pasadena, California, and wants to go back there, but her husband got a job at a factory nearby, and the cost of living is cheaper here, especially since they live out of town and commute in for school and work. Matt bought us a house in one of the fancy subdivisions near Browning, an unwritten rule for the school faculty. We are expected to show a particular lifestyle since we are representing the school. It's hard to do when they don't pay Matt enough to afford it. But I don't tell Tracy that. We chat and let our kids play but don't usually talk about anything profound.

Tracy and I are at the park with the kids, and like me, she doesn't mind spending much of our time together in silence. When we do talk, it's always Tracy who asks the questions. Some call her nosy, but I think she's naturally curious.

"So, it looks like we are leaving Browning. Matt is giving his notice today," I tell her as the kids play on the monkey bars.

Tracy turns to me slowly, and her eyes widen.

"He didn't get that promotion?" she asks.

My shoulders sag, wondering what to tell her and what to keep quiet about. Social etiquette rules are not my strong suit.

"Hawthorne mentioned that he might not even have a job next year," I admit in a whisper.

She makes a face like she's thinking about it.

"Was it because of Charles?" she asks me, and I startle before giving her a look.

"Why would it be about Charles?" I ask her.

"You know how it is, Jane. People want normal. Anything that isn't considered 'normal' is going to have consequences."

"I mean, he's just a little kid. He likes purple and princess stuff. It's just a phase."

She stays silent for so long that I start to feel queasy. Why does everyone suddenly think Charles wearing pink sparkles is such a big deal? Thankfully, Tracy changes the subject.

"Did Matt find a new job?"

"At a school in his hometown, of all places."

"Oh, that's good. Does he have much family there?"

I shake my head. "No. His cousin got him the job, though, so maybe?" When I laugh, Tracy gives me a look of confusion.

"I'm not sure," I explain. "Matt hasn't seen much of his family since his parents moved to Florida when he went to college. His sister's husband died, so his parents went to help her with her kids. But Matt never wanted to go back to Atwood, anyway. He said he never fit in there. I don't see my family much either, so we have that in common. Us against the world and all that."

"I hope things are better for you there, Jane. I know no one has welcomed you here either."

"I have to believe that Matt knows best," I say, and Tracy gives me a quizzical look.

"Why do you always think Matt knows best?" she asks, and I look at her in surprise. "Look, I don't mean it offensively. You believe in him and seem to put your wants or needs behind his. I wonder why you do whatever Matt wants."

"I don't always . . ." I start to say, but my voice trails off. I feel my hands begin to shake as I try to answer her.

I don't always do what Matt wants, do I?

"I never really had anyone growing up. Once, in high school, I did, but he went to college, and I was too scared to . . . well, I just couldn't be brave enough to trust him. And then I got sick, and Matt was there, and he's always been here, choosing me—every day. I can't be alone like that anymore. Matt and the kids are my everything. And besides, Matt has way more education and expertise on everything than I do. He's got a PhD, for crap's sake."

Tracy nods, and we spend the rest of the time in silence, watching the kids play. She tells me to keep in touch as we leave, but I know it's something people say. I doubt we will speak again after the move, and I don't feel sad. Maybe in Atwood, things will be different for me too.

❦

We settle into bed on our last night in Texas. We start the long drive to Wisconsin tomorrow, and we're both quiet, thinking about what is to come.

"This is the right move for us, going to Atwood," Matt says as he puts his arm around me and rests his head against mine.

"I hope so." I sigh and relax into him.

"I'm super relieved to be out of Texas. Maybe Wisconsin will be different." I stay silent, afraid to get too hopeful. "What are you hopeful for? In Wisconsin?" Matt asks me.

"A friend. I wish I had a best friend." My voice cracks, and Matt hugs me closer.

"I know it's been hard for you, moving around your whole life. But I think now you can settle in and make friends. Atwood will be so good for all of us. We will all bring our A game and catch this break because we deserve it."

I want to believe him. I don't have some terrible track record of gossiping or having big dramatic fights with women—quite the opposite. My relationships with women have always been more like how smoke appears and disappears like it was never there.

Coffee dates happen once or twice. Women who seem great but cancel often. Women who don't have the time, including myself. It's left me with a lifelong feeling that something is wrong with me.

"I wish I didn't remember how fun it was whispering secrets in blanket forts with my sister before she decided I'm a pain in the ass," I say, snuggling into him. He holds me tight.

But now I can hope. Whatever I'm looking for isn't in Texas. Maybe it's in Atwood.

Chapter Seven

Matt leads the way in the moving van, and I follow behind him in our minivan with the kids. We are somewhere in Arkansas when my sister, Mickey, requests a video chat with me. The ringtone for my sister is the sound of a Mack truck backing up because calls from her require much caution. I almost don't answer, but we are stuck in the van with hours to drive. Matt's been bugging me to call my family and tell them we are moving, so now is as good a time as any.

"Hey there, sis," Mickey says as her face appears on the screen. Her voice is deep from years of smoking Marlboro Reds, which she tells me she will never quit and that the doctors will have to pry from her cold, dead hands. I can see it happening that way. Mickey is a force.

"Hey, you. How are things in South Dakota? I've been trying to call Mom but couldn't catch her."

Technically, I tried once. Calling my mom is more exhausting than talking to Mickey. Mom brings shame and guilt, mixed with redneck beliefs and stories of how "the queers" are ruining this Christian nation. It's ironic since all my mother has ever worshipped is whiskey and random men in bars.

Mickey goes off on a long rant about her boys being involved in a car-building contest at a local bar. Her boys are in their late teens and have been enormous and rough-and-tumble since birth. We all couldn't be more different if we tried.

I know what she'll say about her life before she starts. Motorbikes. Fixing cars. Fishing. Mom's flavor-of-the-month boyfriend. Listening to it would be boring as hell if it weren't for how happy I am to no longer have to live it.

"Oh, Mom's camping."

"Camping? Where? With Bob?"

"Bob? No, Mom ain't seeing Bob no more. She's with Frank now. He owns the bowling alley and gets us all free taps and lanes all the time. It's Frank's camper. They go up to Mirror Lake most weekends. Frank has a permanent spot up there in Shady Acres Campground. So Mom is semi-retired."

I almost laugh out loud at the description and can interpret the situation well. Frank is my mom's newest guy, and he has enough money to allow my mom to sponge off him. My mom will never quit bartending, though. It appeals too much to her social and alcoholic nature.

"Well, that's nice for Mom," I tell her. I haven't seen my mom or sister in years, which, of course, is always my fault, even though we always have to travel to them.

"It sure is nice. We go up a lot on weekends. Swim in the lake and the pool, sit on their deck, and grill out burgers and hot dogs. It's been real nice to have a second home in the family."

"Is Frank family now?" I ask without thinking, then wince at myself, knowing it will cause an issue.

"Well, I don't know. But when my boy Buddy had to be laid up on account of his hernia, he was balls deep in bills, and Frank gave him some money. And he lets us all go up there to his second home all the time. But we don't even see you, little sis, my own flesh and blood. So maybe the question is, are *you* family?"

No matter how hard I try, Mickey always finds a way to get under my skin. And then I feel compelled to prove my worth to her.

"Of course I'm family! Jeez. Money has been tight for a while, so we haven't done any traveling. And I'm not saying Frank isn't great. I wanted to make sure I didn't miss a marriage or something. I'm so far out of the loop—"

"And whose fault is that, Jane? You removed yourself from our family when you went off to college and met Matt because you think you're better than us. You don't come to our bowling tournaments, the boys' tractor pulls, or even Mom's semi-retirement party at Johnny's Bar. You're the one who isn't here."

"I know I'm not there. I mean, I didn't even know about the party." She says nothing, so I go on. "I do wish we could see you. And I don't think I'm better than you. It's hard right now." I decide to change the subject.

"You were actually on my list to call. I wanted to let you both know we are moving. We are on the road right now, heading to Matt's hometown in Wisconsin. He got a job running a school." I realize that I am excited. Telling Mickey makes it seem real.

"We are hopeful, you know? This is what we've been working toward." It feels good to let it all tumble out and share my happiness.

But there is nothing but silence from Mickey. I look at her face on the screen and see her rubbing her temples.

"Hang on a sec. You are moving *right now* and didn't get around to telling us? But you're trying to tell me about family?"

"Everything *just* happened. Matt got offered a job running a school in his hometown at the last minute. Our old house sold in two days. And Texas just sucked. You know how much I hated it there."

"Places are what you make it, kid. This new place won't be any different unless you try to be more sociable. Making a little effort to fit in wouldn't hurt, Jane."

"Yep, I know." And I do. She's told me this my whole life. "I should probably get going, though—" I try to get off the call, but she's not done.

"Sure. But I was gonna ask. Why on God's green earth would you make your son wear a girl's swimsuit? Don't you have enough girls? You can't just leave your one boy alone?" She's laughing as she says this, completely cracking herself up until she triggers a smoker's coughing fit. When she recovers, she changes her tone to serious.

"I saw the photos on social media, and my mouth dropped. Speaking of Mom, she said she wishes she had some decent pictures of *that boy* she could show her friends, but the pictures you share would confuse them. The same way you are confusing Charles. It ain't normal."

She always says "that boy" like he's so different. But who the hell is normal, anyway? Either way, I don't see any reason to be so damn hateful about it.

"He was in my backyard running through the sprinklers. No one even saw him."

"I saw it. Everyone online saw it."

"Well, I have maybe a hundred friends on social media, so it's not like a viral photo."

"Look, it ain't my fault you aren't very popular, Jane. But I see no reason to publicly flaunt your boy in girls' clothes. Don't you know that's how you turn kids into one of them transgenders? It ain't right, and it will get you into a mess of trouble."

My jaw and fists are clenched, and I want to be off the phone.

"I've told you before we are letting Charles figure this out because it's *just a phase*. He has two sisters. I'm sure that's why he likes all the pink and purple stuff. I don't know why you always make a big deal out of this. Why can't you drop it and agree to disagree?"

Taking a stand with Mickey is not a good idea, and I realize I've gone too far. She makes me so mad, though. I take breaths through my mouth to calm down.

"There ain't no reason for getting all worked up, kid. It don't work on me," she says in her tough-as-nails Mickey way, as if I'm such a damn burden over here letting my kid choose his swimsuit. As if my having feelings is so inconvenient to my sister.

I wish she could be a safe place to talk about Charles—or anything at all—but Mickey and my mom aren't those people. They always look for what's wrong with me, my parenting, and my kids.

"You know there is a super-easy answer to all of this, right?" asks Mickey.

I snort a laugh out. Fantastic, and just what I need. Words of wisdom from Mickey, who thinks Google is part of some worldwide conspiracy.

"Oh yeah?" I ask, wishing I sounded less on the verge of tears.

She leans into the screen farther like it's a secret, and I get a close-up of her ruddy face.

"Stop putting girl clothes on your boy. Easy-peasy." Her big, dirty finger fills the screen as she ends the call. Mickey is gone as quickly as she arrived, like a rogue tornado that leaves havoc in her wake.

I glance back at Charles to ensure he didn't pick up on anything we said, but he's just staring out the window. His innocent face in the rearview mirror crushes me. I would protect him from the whole world, but I have no idea how.

Chapter Eight

I toss and turn in the hotel bed in St. Louis, worrying about Charles while Matt and the kids sleep. I can't stop thinking about what Mickey said about making Charles transgender. And how she always makes a big deal out of a pink shirt every time we talk. Why does everyone care what he wears? Besides, Charles can't be trans. I mean, what are the odds? Seriously.

Eventually, I start arguing aloud.

"You aren't even using that word right . . . Do better."

It's Matt who notices the arguments in my head have turned verbal. "Jane, you're talking out loud. Go to sleep."

"Okay. Sorry," I say, but I wait for him to fall back asleep and then climb out of bed, trying to stay quiet as I grab my phone and slip into Matt's sandals. He doesn't even wake up to the sound of me heading out onto the little patio. I quietly shut the big glass door behind me to keep the air-conditioning in and the humid night out.

Even at three a.m., it's still hot and sticky. Lonesome cars and semis fly by on the interstate beside our hotel; otherwise, the world is silent. I plop into the plastic chair, move the other to act as a footrest, and pull out my phone. The still night air smells new and strange, as if there could be hope and possibility there.

I stare at my phone, pondering, and whisper, "Researching something doesn't make it real." I look around as if I may get caught and notice I'm entirely alone. The quiet cover of the night feels safe while the whole world is asleep.

I hear Mickey's voice saying, "Don't you know that's how you turn kids into one of them transgenders?" over and over, even from across the country. It irritates me, like a song I can't get out of my mind. In my head, I argue with her, coming up with better comebacks than I could ever manage in person.

It's the middle of the night, and we still have a long way to drive tomorrow. I glance through the glass doors at Matt and the kids, sound asleep, and don't want to keep them up with my tossing and turning. As I settle into the hard plastic chair, I feel a world away from our old life and just as far from our new one. Before I have time to question it, I'm opening up a search engine.

Shaking, I type, "How do you know if your child is transgender?" holding my finger above the screen. As I hit search, I gasp at my bravery. I look around as if someone might catch me. Until now, we've operated on the ignore-the-behavior-at-all-costs method. But what are we ignoring?

My screen fills with more pages than I could imagine, in number and authority. The American Academy of Pediatrics, the ACLU, the American Psychological Association, many children's hospitals, clinics, therapists, and doctors. I find websites whose focus is helping train teachers and schools about kids on the LGBT spectrum, and I even see a bunch of groups to join on social media for trans kids and their parents. There are personal blogs by parents with stories of children that sound so much like Charles. There are tales of kids thriving, many stories of depression, and awful stories about teenagers hurting themselves and dying by suicide. Words I don't understand, like "dysphoria," "intersex," "nonbinary," and "gender-neutral," fill pages as I try to take it all in.

I always believed that we are either female or male, not having a clue that someone could be both or neither. It could almost feel as if someone made up all these terms and words since I haven't heard so many of them, except for the validity of the sources.

A video I stumble across shows the transition of a child everyone thought was a girl but is really a boy. I watch the video with tears streaming down my face, nodding because I can see Charles in every early step of their journey.

I'm still outside in the hot, humid air as the day's first light stretches across the sky. I take deep breaths with my arms wrapped around my knees.

I am certain that my child is somewhere in these pages and definitions. After wiping away the tears, I head back inside, exhausted, hoping for some sleep before the day begins.

Charles is asleep in bed, his brown curls all over his face, so sweet and innocent: no little scowl or look of sadness. I crawl into bed and spoon behind him, laying my head against his and falling into a deep sleep.

Matt wakes me a few hours later to tell me he's taking Louisa and the baby with him to get breakfast for all of us. I snuggle back into Charles, who is already awake, watching a family sitcom and playing with my hair.

"Emma is so beautiful," he says about the main character. "I wish I was beautiful."

I move to look at him. "You are beautiful."

Charles shakes his little head, his brown hair falling in his eyes. "Not like a girl."

I nod, unsure of what to say. "Do you . . . do you want to be a girl?"

I wonder if I'm putting ideas in his head. Matt would probably say I am, but I need to know what Charles thinks.

Charles shakes his head and puts his little fingers to his eyes like he does when he's frustrated and trying not to cry. I sit up and hug him.

"It's okay. You can talk to me."

Finally, Charles pulls his head off my chest and says, "But *I am* a girl. *I am*. But no one believes me because of my penis. That's what Dad said. I'm not a girl because of my penis."

I am unaware of Matt's conversation with Charles, and it irks me that Matt didn't tell me about it. He has always said that Charles is "dressing up" and it's "no big deal."

I hug Charles again because I don't know what to say or do. And I don't know who to ask. He goes back to watching his show, and by the time Matt and the kids return, it's like nothing has changed. I want to talk to Matt, but a small hotel room with three kids isn't the place.

Everything feels different now, and I don't want to feel alone with this. When we get to Wisconsin, there will be more time to talk.

Chapter Nine

We pull into Atwood just as the sun sets in the summer haze, and everything glows orange.

"Mom," Louisa says from the back seat. "This town is so cute! Look at all the little shops and restaurants," she exclaims as we drive through the charming downtown.

"It is so cute," I answer her, realizing I am smiling and already hoping this place will treat us better than Texas.

Matt drives ahead in the moving van, and I follow him through tree-lined streets full of lovely homes and tidy lawns. When he slows and stops, I park behind the truck, looking for a house number or something I recognize from the photos they sent.

"Want to get out, Louisa?" I ask her since she's the only one awake. She nods at me, happy to get out of the van. "Okay, I'll wake up Charles and get the baby."

Be patient. Let them be excited, I say to myself, trying to memorize a mantra to use in three minutes, when I'll be tempted to lose my patience with them again.

I was not taught to be a mother, so I'm winging it and hoping for the best all the damn time. I second-guess myself almost constantly. Matt is the calm, steady beat that keeps us all on the right track.

I stretch my arms over my head before pulling a half-asleep Henrietta out of her seat. I kiss her, noticing her sweaty hair smells sweet from graham crackers.

Matt nods at the diaper bag and my purse, and I sigh with relief as I hand them over. Charles takes my hand, attaching himself to me, his usual position. He gives me a little smile, his shaggy brown hair in his eyes, content in his big sister's hand-me-down pink tutu and T-shirt, which says "Big Sister" in pink sparkles. Matt is grinning from ear to ear. I cock my eyebrow at him.

"Did you see it?"

My eyes follow his pointing finger upward to the biggest purple Queen Anne Victorian I have ever seen.

"Are you kidding me right now? That's ours?" The joy in my voice almost doesn't sound like my own. How long has it been since I've been anything except worried?

Matt is downright grinning. "No, not kidding at all, babe. All ours. Six bedrooms, five baths, and a quarter-acre lot. We signed the papers, remember?"

I stare up at the house as I wander closer, silenced by its sheer mass and height. We stop on the front walk, where I look up with my mouth still hanging open, taking in the detailed etched wood and the intricate but chipping paint job. My eyes travel up to the castle-looking spire at the top of the house.

"Holy shit, Matt."

"I told you this house is one of the grandest in town. It's kind of famous around here." He's grinning at me like a kid. It all feels pretty fairy-tale-ish.

"Purple is my favorite color. It's like my own castle," chimes Charles, wide-eyed with his hands folded in front of his face as if we've arrived at a theme park, not a house.

"Oh, Charles," says Louisa, shaking her head but smirking at him.

We head up the front steps and onto a long, covered wraparound porch as Matt searches through the ring of keys the school mailed us. The porch is full of long-forgotten newspapers and leaves from who knows how many autumns ago. The kids dive for the porch swing while we wait.

I hear a solid metal clunk when Matt figures out the front door, and I turn to see it swing open. Charles runs in first, Louisa following, both taking five steps before stopping. I catch up, anxious to set the heavy baby down.

"This place is filthy," says Louisa.

I can't disagree. The room we're standing in is a haze of the dust we've kicked up.

"Okay," Matt says, always the self-starter and optimist of the group. "We need the porta crib to set Henrietta down. The tablet with the movies. And food from someone who delivers."

"Can't we see the house first? I wanna see the house!" The chorus of excited voices even includes my quiet little Charles.

"As soon as I order dinner, guys," Matt says as he pulls out his phone. I sit down on the ancient couch.

"Matt? Why is all this stuff here?" There is a gorgeous velvet fainting couch and matching settee. I can't believe anyone would leave them. The furniture is primarily antiques, in almost perfect shape.

"Oh, they said it was partially furnished. The widow Wellington didn't have any heirs."

I run my hands along the smooth, old, carved wood and beautiful fading pink satiny material. I worry about Charles's sticky hands as he climbs off my lap in search of adventure.

"This house has been empty and neglected for years, Jane."

"No shit. Years?"

He looks up at me. I've startled him out of his task, and he smiles at me in the hazy light.

"Yes, obviously, it's been vacant for a while. You know what? You should hire someone to clean this place." I raise my eyebrows, looking at him sideways in surprise. "Or hire someone to watch the kids for you so you can clean. We have a little money, and the place could use a good scrub. It will take a while if you clean it on your own. And I have a brand-new job to tackle." Matt is grinning. I haven't seen him this happy in a long time.

"If I knew anyone to clean or watch the kids, I might take you up on it," I say with a smile, getting up off the couch and yelling to the kids to come see the house with us. They come running from opposite directions, telling us what they found.

We make our way to the entryway, where numerous doorways converge in opposite directions, plus a long hallway leads to a closed door under the stairs. I glance up at the vast staircase and touch the etched-wood banisters. I'm not even sure where to go. I already feel lost.

Matt leads us left to the dining room, where a long table sits in the middle of the room with a chandelier hanging above it. We turn on the light switches as we move through the house.

A doorway leads to a butler's pantry, big enough for all five of us to stand in like an elevator. We open the door and find the kitchen with the last light of day streaming in through the windows. The appliances are from sometime in the previous century. I test the burners, and they get hot one by one. The fridge is an old energy sucker but cold and empty.

There is a layer of dust over everything. Below that layer are tiny knickknacks and beautiful glass sculptures on end tables, counters, and shelves. I start collecting choking hazards, but it's a never-ending battle. Everything in this house needs cleaning.

I peek out the windows to the backyard, tree-filled and overgrown. There is an open area for the kids to play that runs back to a fence line covered in a bramble of bushes.

A smile creeps across my face as I think of the kids growing up in this house. "I was nervous about coming here. But this feels right," I tell Matt.

He slips his arms around me and hugs me tightly, and I melt in. If Matt were in charge of ensuring I get hugged every hour, maybe I'd never get anxious again.

"I think this is going to be good for us," he whispers in my ear as if saying it aloud might be bad luck.

"Is the pizza here?" the kids chime in.

"No, not yet. Come on. Let's go see the rest of the house."

There are five bedrooms on the second floor, with ample open space between them. The kids scramble for which room they want as we head up to the attic, where it's over a hundred degrees, even at sundown. We walk down the dark third-floor hallway leading to a bedroom and bath that were initially servants' quarters.

"Matt? Doesn't it seem like the attic is half the size of the other floors? Is there more to it?"

He shakes his head at me. "It could be that they only finished part of the attic or maybe closed it off from damage. I think a tree fell into the house once. Either way, we certainly don't need any more space," he says with a laugh as we wander our nearly four-thousand-square-foot house.

We head back downstairs, where it's a balmy eighty-three degrees in the house, according to the thermostat.

"We don't have air-conditioning, huh?" I ask, and Matt answers me with a laugh.

"I love you." He says this right out loud, which still feels like a miracle to me, even after being with him for many years. I can hear the smile in his voice without looking at him. "You're not mad? I mean, you're okay. Being here?"

It is what it is, but I do appreciate that he asks.

"Yes, I'm okay being here. It's filthy and huge. But I think we're finally home."

Matt pulls more of our things out of the van while I settle the kids in with the tablet. When I hear the doorbell, I walk through the large house, the kids in a zone with their movie. A young man stands smiling at me, holding our dinner.

"Hey. I've got your two large salads. Plus, I've got a gluten-free with no cheese and veggies, a medium with light cheese, and a pepperoni with pineapple."

"Perfect. Thank you," I say, reaching for the boxes.

"You bet," he answers, looking over at Matt as he carries a load of bags into the house. "Moving in?"

"Yep, trying to, anyway."

"I grew up three blocks over, and I love this house. I always wondered about the inside. It's been closed up forever. Ever since the widow Wellington shot herself."

I startle a little at the words. *Shot herself? Jesus.*

"Thanks. We . . ." I mumble, not sure of what to say. What the hell? Who says such a thing when handing you your dinner? "Um, thanks" is what I settle on. I'd tell him I love the house too, but I don't even remember where a bathroom is yet. Now I need to go in search of bloodstains.

I give him money plus a healthy tip because I want him to leave.

After eating, I tell the kids they have thirty more minutes to watch their movie while Matt and I set up beds and check out the upstairs bathroom. The big kids moan in agreement about bedtime, then go back to their movie.

The entire second-floor bathroom is covered in white and pink tiles. The old, moldy shower curtain hides a scum-encrusted tub. I sigh, ready to cry. I lean my hand down on the porcelain pedestal sink and find myself laughing instead. Matt lets out a small, nervous laugh.

"Jane?"

"I'm tempted to go see if there is a hose out back, and we can all use the bottle of dish soap I found to hose everyone off." I can't stop giggling. "I'm so overtired."

He kisses me midsentence. He's hard and excited beneath his shorts. Despite having felt my husband aroused thousands of times, I still gasp.

"You know what else we could do?"

"Are you kidding me, Matt? Where in this house could we even have sex right now? Without picking up some antique form of flesh-eating bacteria?"

He frowns. Like always, I'm doing it all wrong. I worry too much. I would tell him *Later, sweetie*, but I know we'll be done for the day when we hit the pillows tonight.

"I would seriously have sex with you in this dirty bathroom, but my diaphragm is God knows where. What scares me more than flesh-eating bacteria is pregnancy. We have to get these kids in bed. But I love you."

He kisses me again as a compromise.

I've heard many couples lose their desire or interest in each other. Matt and I both seem to crave the same level of affection. I've always felt lucky for it.

The kids are tucked into this big dark house as if they've slept here their whole lives. Even the baby. Although maybe after three days in hotel rooms on the road, even this creaky old place feels like home.

Matt made up a bed in the main bedroom, and he's fast asleep on top of the blankets. I dig in my bag, find a towel, clean shorts, and a T-shirt, and leave Matt to sleep while I head down the hall to shower.

The shower feels magical, washing off the road and the mess, washing off Texas, money problems, and being "the wrong kind of Zander," hopefully.

I pad around the house in my socks despite the heat since the floors need mopping. The house is quiet, except for the sound of crickets through the open windows.

There is a window seat on the landing between floors, so I settle into it. I search "trans kids in Wisconsin" and find a website for the Midwest Pediatric Transgender Clinic, or MPTC. I peruse their website and feel hopeful about the help and resources they can offer trans kids. It's part of a children's hospital.

I save the web page to my bookmarks, determined to talk to Matt about it and make an appointment. These are the experts on all this stuff I read about on the deck in St. Louis. They are the people who can tell us what's going on. I climb back into bed, feeling like I did something important.

Matt made his way under the covers in my absence, so I slip under the sheet beside him. He moves enough to let me curl up into the crook of his arm and lay my head on his chest. He kisses my forehead and whispers, "Welcome home, my love."

❧

I wake up to find the kids in various styles of disarray. Louisa is the only one dressed. Charles is in the tutu from last night and has a shirt on inside out, with a piece of dry cereal stuck to his dark curls. The baby is in the T-shirt Charles had on yesterday with a face full of what I'm guessing are peas.

Matt comes toward me and holds out a piece of paper with a smile. "Our real estate agent stopped to ensure we got in all right. And he gave me this."

I take the paper, which contains the name Mrs. Hillary Driscoll and a phone number.

"Abe's aunt does some childcare. She used to be my history teacher. She's safe, reliable, and free this summer. So if you want some help, call her."

"Thank you," I almost shout as I hug him tight. He picks me up, and my feet leave the floor for a second. He couldn't have handed me anything better if he tried.

"You bet. Abe also said to call the local thrift shop, and they will send a truck to pick up all this junk." I nod, looking around at all the furniture and wondering where we will put ours.

"Also, the movers texted. They should be here by noon. I thought I'd clean these kids up and take them to the store and the park to let you try to get organized in peace before the movers arrive. Deal?"

I kiss him hard. "I don't know how I got so lucky," I tell him.

"We're both lucky."

"We're all lucky," yells Louisa from the bathroom.

"Yes, sweetie. Yes, we are."

Chapter Ten

We've only been in town a few weeks, and almost everyone I meet in Atwood seems to know who I am and who I'm married to. They also know which house I live in. Between buying a famous old house and Matt running the school, I feel like I'm wearing a neon sign. Matt used to tell me that Atwood was just small enough for everyone to know everything. It is not good for my anxiety. I've used getting the house in order as an excuse to stay home as much as possible.

Matt has been "networking," which he never could make happen before we moved to Atwood. He plays tennis and goes to lunch with old friends. If he isn't working or meeting up with someone, he's at the school or in our dining room, which he's claimed as his office. Through years of school and even his PhD, I'm not sure I've ever seen him as dedicated to anything as he is to succeeding here at Atwood Prep. While I wish he had more time with us, Atwood looks good on Matt. He told me his ulcer is better, and he's put a few pounds back on. I'm happy for him, but we all miss him since he's gone so much.

"With a vengeance," I whisper to myself as I watch him submerge in his work each night. The school got left in the lurch in numerous ways, and Matt has less than a month to pull off preparing for a new school year and the end-of-summer carnival, which seems equally important to the parents and people of Atwood.

The highlight of my life here is when Mrs. Driscoll comes over and saves me twice a week. That's honest to God how it feels. An afternoon of no kids can make a mom's whole week.

Mrs. Driscoll, which is what she told me she likes to be called, is a retired teacher with enough stamina and patience to take the kids out for hours, all three of them, to the library, playgroups, and the movies. I could hug her for the peace she gives me, but I can tell she is not a hugger.

Most days, I use the time to unpack or clean. Today, as I'm rummaging through boxes for my kitchen utensils, I find a box of our family photos. I love the idea of hanging some pictures on the walls to start making this place our own, and the project feels exciting.

I start laying them out on the steps. Henrietta's newborn photo. Louisa with her trophy for winning the regional spelling bee. Family photos. The images span the years, and I sit on the steps, lost in our history. As I stack up Charles's photos, I notice he is holding dolls and wearing skirts and dresses in almost all of them.

Has it really been going on that long? I pick up a photo of Charles as a toddler, grinning from ear to ear in a pink princess nightgown he'd found and put on over his clothes in the store.

"It's a phase," Matt always tells me about Charles's affinity for everything girl.

But phases end. This has been going on for *four years*.

"That's not a phase," I mutter.

The pictures irk me. I can't believe it's been so long that Charles has been like this. It's unsettling, so I pack the photos back in a box on the first landing.

A less thought-provoking task is to take some of the most valuable stuff I've found in the house to the attic. It's too beautiful to give away, but it is not conducive to having kids around. And I have a bunch of seasonal decorations that can also be tucked away. I lug the boxes up the back stairs and make a pile near the attic door.

I wiggle the skeleton key in the keyhole to the attic until the lock catches and then slip the key into my pocket. I'm afraid of locking myself in, which may be impossible.

It's hot going up the steps but not stifling. All six of the old cedar steps groan under my feet, as does the first landing, but they feel sturdy enough. There is a turn and another six steps, then another landing, which leads to a hallway. It's dark, with the only light shining from a long window at the top of the steps. I set the boxes down and try to open the window. It obliges, but the sill is full of dead bugs an inch thick. I wipe my hands on my shorts, moving down the hallway, letting the breeze from the window follow me.

The hallway opens to a larger space with a lone door off to the left, which leads to a miraculous bedroom and bathroom amid the plain attic. The steps up to the attic and hallway where I set the box are simple cedar and ancient wallpaper. The bedroom is painted a faded pink.

There is an old chenille bedspread with thin sheets underneath made with neat hospital corners. It sits on top of an old brass bed frame, waiting for a guest who never arrived.

Off to one side is a bathroom almost completely covered in pink tiles, with the most enormous clawfoot tub in the house. The room feels like it was kept in a time capsule for sixty years. The suite on the third floor may be my favorite room.

The first thing I do is open the three windows, which makes it easier to breathe. Even though the hottest part of the summer is over, it's still hot in the attic. I stand at the window panting, hoping I don't pass out or die up here.

I head to the tub, turning on the water to see if it works. After a few loud clanks, cold water rushes out of the tap. The hot water too. My laugh echoes in the old attic.

If I clean the big old tub fast, I can bathe in it before the kids get home from the movies with Mrs. Driscoll. I deserve a nice bath. I never do it anymore because they aren't peaceful at all with kids around.

I race downstairs for a towel and some cleaning supplies. When I return, I find an old fan in the closet with deadly-looking blades, but it runs. I'm thankful for the breeze as I clean, turning on my '80s love songs playlist.

The water is sweet smelling as I undress and slip in, the cool water washing over me. I relax into it like it's a summer lake, feeling very thankful it's mine now. Maybe Atwood won't be so bad.

My phone is on the table beside the tub, so I grab it and return to my current obsession, reading about trans kids online. I even joined a private online page for parents of gender-creative kids. Of course, I'm not going to post anything there. I'm just perusing it to try to understand. A post catches my eye from a mom who says they thought their son was trans, but he's actually intersex.

I've seen the word "intersex" in my reading, but I'm unsure I understand what it means.

I look up "intersex" on my phone, scrolling websites and definitions as I learn. Intersex people can be born with atypical anatomy or chromosomes that may not fit what is commonly considered female or male. They don't fit the XX/XY binary. From what I read, there are infinite ways to be a boy, a girl, a man, or a woman. I'm also shocked to learn that almost 2 percent of the world's population is intersex, as many people as the population of Japan.

I feel hope for the first time in all this. There may be some medical condition that explains this stuff about Charles. Matt would have to understand that and be supportive if Charles was born with it. It would just make it all so much easier.

I get out of the tub and wrap myself in my towel. After I head downstairs and get dressed, I realize I still have a little more time before the kids get home.

I locate the Midwest Pediatric Transgender Clinic website and their phone number and hit Call before I can chicken out. I'm excited that there may be a medical component to all this. The clinic answers on the second ring, and I realize I have no idea what to say.

"Umm, hi. I'm Jane . . . Umm. Jane."

"How can we help you today, Jane?" She must think I'm lying about my name because it's so dull.

"I'm calling about my six-year-old son. I don't know because I'm not a doctor, psychiatrist, or whatever. But maybe he's intersex? Or maybe transgender. I guess I'm asking how I would know. I'm calling because I don't know what to do. And I'm wondering, I guess, what you do there to help kids like mine."

She doesn't seem ruffled at all by what I tell her.

"We are a clinic of pediatricians and endocrinologists specializing in treating gender-expansive youth. We offer suggestions for therapists, provide info about parent and kids groups, and provide medical interventions such as hormone blockers and hormones for kids who are past the second stage of puberty. We have a wide spectrum of gender identities that we care for here. We also help you find the resources you need for your family."

I sigh, understanding some of what she said but not all. "Okay, that sounds good."

"I will tell you that we have an extensive waiting list. We'd need to do an intake over the phone to get you onto the list. We also require a referral from your pediatrician before we can schedule your child. Because of our limited availability, we give preferential treatment to kids beginning puberty, as they have urgent medical components. The wait for prepuberty kids is longer, as there is no medical component. Would you like me to send you an educational packet full of resources? You could ask your pediatrician for a referral in the meantime."

"We just moved here from out of state. I haven't even picked out a pediatrician yet."

I frown, realizing there isn't a quick answer to my questions.

Why am I doing this now? As if I don't have enough going on. Maybe I'm causing problems. But whatever is happening is real to Charles. My voice cracks as I say, "Yes, I'd like the packet. But"—I pause to take a breath—"what am I supposed to do in the meantime?"

Silence is followed by a gentle voice saying, "I know this feels big and confusing right now, and you don't know what to do. The only job you need to worry about is supporting your child exactly as they are. Trans kids who aren't supported by their family and/or community have rates of self-harm and suicidal ideation of up to forty-two percent, with some studies where those numbers almost double."

It feels as if I've been hit in the stomach. I lean onto the kitchen counter to recover.

Forty-two percent of trans kids try to hurt themselves? That can't be right.

"Loving your child for who they are and listening when they consistently and persistently tell you who they are is your best protection to keep them safe. Most important right now is to build a solid support system around them, beginning with you."

She tells me that she will be sending out a packet to fill out as well as some resources we might find helpful. I thank her but feel defeated that there is no easy answer.

Chapter Eleven

Matt has been so busy with school, so it hasn't made it easier to broach difficult subjects like talking to him about how I think Charles might be intersex or transgender. Any energy he does have goes to playing with the kids before passing out in bed. It feels like we haven't talked in forever.

I observe his loose tie, untucked shirt, and tousled hair, but I try anyway. Because when will there be a better time? There hasn't been a good moment in the few weeks we've been here.

"I'm not sure it's a good time, but I think we should talk about Charles." I try my best to sound calm and reasonable, but I've wanted to talk to him about this since that night in St. Louis. I'm already wringing my hands together.

The receptionist I talked to was informative and concise, but I can't remember any of it to repeat to Matt. I feel flustered already. Matt sits down and looks at me, allowing me to say what I need. But when given a chance, I find absolute transparency too much.

"Mickey said something about us turning Charles transgender, so I started to do all this research," I blurt out, not realizing how much it felt like a secret until I said it aloud. I called the clinic back to start the intake process for Charles and talked with a nurse, who was very helpful. But I don't tell Matt that the nurse at the clinic said our child has all the signs they look for in transgender kids. Or that ignoring this will only last so long and we will have to deal with this at some point.

Of course, I don't bother to tell him *I think* Charles might be trans or intersex, because I'm no expert.

"What? We haven't seen Mickey in years. When did you talk to her?" Matt asks with an uncharacteristic edge to his voice.

"She called me when we were driving out here, complaining about Charles wearing a girl's swimsuit, and she said something not even grammatically or politically correct about him being trans."

Matt frowns at me as if I am making no sense. I wait, not sure what to say.

"I would hardly call Mickey the authority on raising kids, Jane. Why are you bringing this up now?" he asks, and I struggle to get the words out.

"I want to get him checked by a doctor at this Midwest Pediatric Transgender Clinic in Madison. It's for kids exactly like Charles. We could get on the wait list for an appointment . . ." I try to explain, but Matt is already shaking his head.

"Kids 'like Charles'? What does that mean?" He waits for me to answer, but I can't. The words don't come out. Matt answers for me. "You mean transgender? You seriously think he's transgender?"

"No—" I say, not even sure myself. "Maybe," I add as he cocks his head at me.

"He isn't. He isn't transgender." He says this with his characteristic confidence. "There isn't anything wrong with him, medically or otherwise. He's just—"

"A kid playing dress-up because he has sisters." Matt and I speak this line in tandem because Matt says it so often that it's become a catchphrase. And I always believed it. I can't bring myself to tell Matt I no longer think it's true.

"The chances of a child being transgender are, what? Probably like one percent."

"I don't know what percent it is. But somebody has to be the one percent or whatever."

He reaches out and takes my hand, and I sit beside him. "Jane, I can see you are worried, and I get that. But I think that you're worrying about nothing. Making a bunch of expensive appointments and turning this into a big deal will add fuel to the fire. The last thing we need is to get someone involved who gives him a diagnosis he will inevitably regret. Then it's too late, and he'll be forever scarred by it following him around. And why? If we both know he isn't trans?"

As usual, I find myself caving to his logic. "Okay. But I wonder . . ." I stare at the floor, not wanting to say the words aloud. I'm deviating from our usual script.

"Jane, what?" Matt prompts.

"I wonder if he's ever going to be normal." This is the closest I can get to sharing how I feel. "I don't think this is common. Most kids aren't confused about being a boy or a girl."

Matt looks at me for a long time, like he's thinking about it. "Who is normal anyway? None of us. Normal doesn't exist. It's a made-up idea meant to keep us all in line. Charles likes purple. Liking a color is not a big deal. He will find his way once he's in real school with boys to hang out with."

"What if maybe he's intersex?" I ask.

"What?" His voice shifts as if I've suggested Charles is from Mars.

"Listen to me, Matt. It's not that uncommon to be intersex. I read all about it online."

"Okay, sure. If you read it online, then Charles *must* be intersex." He says it like a joke, but I don't laugh.

I scowl at him for not even taking this, or me, seriously.

"I think it's possible that Charles is different in some way, and I want him seen by some professionals. This clinic—"

But he cuts me off. "What sparked this?"

I fold my arms across my chest before I answer. "I was unpacking photos to hang the other day and found consistent behavior of Charles wearing dresses. And I realized that his affection for all things girl has been going on for years. *Years*, Matt. He loves dolls and pink and wants to grow up to be Julia Child."

"That's because we've allowed it. If we stop treating him like a baby, he might grow into a little man."

For once, I stand my ground. "I want him checked out by a doctor. We don't have one in town yet, and I want a doctor to look at him."

I stare him down, not letting up. Matt eventually puts both of his hands up.

"If you want to take him to a local doctor, that's fine. We need a new pediatrician anyway. I'll ask around and see who's good in town and even make an appointment for Charles. Fair enough?"

I nod, not feeling like he heard me at all, but at least I got him to agree to have a pediatrician look at Charles.

Matt leans over and hugs me, and I relax in the safety of his arms.

"I think he's got a vivid imagination," Matt says in my ear, always so sure of himself. He pulls away to look me in the eye. "If we ignore it, he will outgrow it. If we make a big deal out of it, confusing him with doctors and therapists picking away at him, he will make it an even bigger deal because of all the attention. We may need to nip it in the bud at some point. For his own good, so he doesn't get picked on. But I think you're giving this whole subject too much of your time."

I don't have the ammunition to argue with him, so I nod in agreement. At least I know that Charles will see a doctor. Hopefully, they will see what I do.

Chapter Twelve

The packet from the clinic arrives the same day as the long-awaited summer carnival, which is all the kids have talked about the whole week. The thought of meeting everyone at the school at once sets off my social anxiety, but I will give this my all because, as Matt reminds me, it's never mattered more.

According to Matt, this is *the* event of the summer. They block off the streets behind our house leading to the school and fill them with rides, food vendors, and games from Friday night to Sunday afternoon.

Our street and this part of town are quiet. There isn't much in Atwood except for a huge car dealership out by the highway with a superstore on the other side. There are strip malls and fast food; otherwise, this place is a small town. I can't imagine our streets being filled with such excitement. It's our first big adventure since moving here, short of a few trips to the library.

Matt stops home after work to change for the carnival and offers to get the kids ready for me. I thank him for the help and use the time to sneak off to my room to look at the folder from the clinic, which is chock-full of resources. There are lists of therapists and pediatricians, a sixteen-page packet from the American Academy of Pediatrics, and resources for playgroups and get-togethers for families with trans kids. There is a letter asking us to get a referral so we can be put on the wait list and encouraging us to "continue supporting your child in how they identify and express themselves."

Matt comes into the room to kiss me. I shut the folder, but he doesn't even look at what is in my hands.

"The kids are all dressed and ready and have clean faces and hands. I'm off to the carnival. Meet you there soon?" he asks.

"Yes. I'm almost ready. Can't wait." I dress fast after Matt leaves and come down the stairs to find the kids ready and waiting. The first thing I notice is a miserable Charles. He's wearing khaki shorts and a navy-blue polo shirt, and his silent tears tell me how he feels about the outfit Matt picked out. How long has it been since we made him wear boy clothes? Months, at least. We spent so much time at home this summer that there hasn't been a reason to pick the battle about what he wears. Charles seems way more upset than the last time I tried to choose his clothes.

"It's going to be fun." I try to sound convincing. "Daddy says we can ride on rides, eat good food, and stay up late. Aren't you excited?"

His big brown eyes are still begging me.

I take his little hand, leading him to the fainting couch near the coat closet. Charles half gets on my lap, stuffing his thumb in his mouth as he lays his head on my chest. He stopped sucking his thumb when he was three years old, and I'm surprised to see it back in his mouth.

"Talk to me, please." I smooth his hair and whisper into his little ear, even though I know why he's upset.

He starts to cry, little puffs of air coming out as his words break up. "I don't want to wear this because it isn't me. It isn't me." He's all-out crying now, and my heart is breaking for him.

"Daddy said . . . I'm a boy. But I'm a girl! *I'm a girl.* I don't know why I have a penis." He looks down at his lap, then up at me. His bottom lip juts out and stays there, making me worry I might cry with him. He buries himself into me, and I hold him, breathing in and out, trying to think what to say. Burning anger starts to build in my stomach, and I realize that making him wear what he hates is not supporting him.

I think of the conversation with Matt—how adamant he is that Charles isn't trans. And then I remember the statistics of self-harm.

"You know what?" I ask. "You can wear what you want. Go pick a dress, princess shirt, or whatever you'd like." It's all I can do to keep my voice from cracking.

Charles doesn't even move. He sits on my lap looking at me as if I've lost my mind, still breathing hard with the occasional little hiccup.

"Really. You can wear what you want. I'm not going to tell you what to wear. I love how you dress." Charles breaks into his crooked smile, wipes the tears off his face, jumps off my lap, and runs up the stairs to change clothes. He has the polo shirt off before he hits the landing on the stairs and lets out a loud whoop of victory. I can't help but laugh out loud.

Louisa stares at me like I've grown another head.

"Do you think Daddy will be mad about the clothes?" she asks.

"Sometimes, moms and dads don't agree. It's okay, though. We're all trying to do what's best for Charles."

Louisa still looks surprised, so I give her a quick squeeze, and Charles comes racing back down the stairs in a pink "I Am the Princess" shirt and a rainbow tutu over his shorts. He pulls on Louisa's old purple princess Crocs like he's in a race and stands there grinning at me, out of breath. I consider getting him to match, but I don't. His pure joy strikes me hard. All I need to do is let him be himself. We head out the door on time, walking the block over to the school grounds to meet Matt at the festival.

Louisa and Charles run ahead laughing, and I realize Charles mostly clings to me when we force him into boy clothes. When we let him wear what he wants, he stops being my shy, serious Charles. I want to share it with Matt. I know that he's going to come around and understand. Matt has always supported us completely as we are.

The festival is quite the event, and I can see why Matt has been held up preparing for it. There are dozens of food trucks, rides, and games. There is a stage with a band, a tent for bingo, and another for beer. The whole place is strung with lights and gives such a hometown-welcoming feel. The kids run ahead, Louisa holding Charles's hand in her sweet, protective way . . . Even the baby is pointing at all the things to do.

Matt texted me from somewhere near the library building, by the "Fried Cheese Curd" stand, whatever that is. When he sees us, his face breaks into the grin I love. And then he looks down at Charles, and his face falls.

My heart starts to race, and I suddenly do not feel good about my decision to bring Charles dressed the way he wants. *What was I thinking?* I ask myself as Matt walks over to us frowning. The words from the receptionist at MPTC repeat in my head—that 42 percent of unsupported trans teens will attempt suicide—and I remember why I let him choose his clothes.

Matt leans in and kisses my cheek but whispers, "Why did you change his clothes when I got him ready for you?" He tries to sound easygoing, but the tone of his voice suggests otherwise.

"I don't think you understand what's best for Charles. You don't have all the information." I try to sound confident, but my voice shakes.

He cocks his head at me and says, "I understand that you're getting your information from sites on the internet, but I have a PhD in education. I have a lot of information about what's best for kids too."

Just then, a woman appears beside Matt, breaking up the moment.

"Matt. This must be the amazing family you are always talking about. Hello." She shoves her way between us and shakes my hand excitedly. "I'm Jillie. I'm responsible for this festival and running the PTA since our predecessor left us high and dry. I think we're going to be such good friends. You should join the PTA!" As if it was all planned, she leads me away with the kids, telling me we will find her little ones so our kids can meet and asking if they want a funnel cake. Jillie is chatty and insistent and a welcome relief from Matt's comment. As she leads me to meet her kids, I glance back at Matt, who is already walking away.

Jillie drags us around to dozens of people as if I am a new toy she wants to show off. I meet so many people that I can barely remember who is who. After a while, Jillie leads us to picnic tables in a well-lit grove of trees near the rides. She has a son who is Charles's age and a daughter Louisa's age. Within minutes, Louisa and Jillie's daughter scamper off with big smiles to ride the rides. Charles and Jillie's son are settled onto a blanket with some toys.

"Should we go with the girls?" I ask, but Jillie waves me off.

"They'll be fine. This school is more family than anything. We all know everyone and everything about everyone, eventually, anyway. The stories I could tell you about why I ended up running this carnival . . . Let me say that some people can't be trusted. My ex-BFF, for example." Jillie kind of laughs at this, but I don't get the joke. Am I supposed to pry for more information?

"So, Jane. Spill it on the widow Wellington's house. I have to know what it's like in there. Did you find any bullet holes? I heard some party got wild back in the day and two people were shot there."

I can't help but laugh. It's all so ridiculous, the rumors about Virginia Wellington. I'd be shocked to hear a sane and simple memory of her.

I look down at Charles, who is not interested in playing with the dinosaurs Jillie's son keeps trying to give him.

"I don't like boy stuff," Charles says.

"Well, of course not, sweetie. You're a girl," Jillie announces, and Charles beams. It takes me a moment to stop looking at him because he seems so . . . proud.

"Umm . . ." Jesus, I didn't think this through. How the hell am I supposed to explain this?

"He's actually a boy. He likes to dress bright and cheery." I feel myself shrinking because the words taste like a lie. But I don't even know what the truth is.

"Oh—" Jillie says, trying to recover. "I'm sorry. I thought . . . Well, that's okay. I love your tutu," she leans down close and says to Charles, who is still smiling because she called him a girl.

"It's okay. I know it's confusing. I'm just trying to make sure he is safe and happy." Jillie nods, now quiet instead of chatty. Not long after, she announces she must keep the carnival running, and we part ways.

I take the kids on some rides and get them food before settling in at the school playground, where a few dozen kids race around. Charles plays with two little girls who look close to his age. His hair is almost shoulder length, so he could just be another girl running around.

Matt finds us when we are ready to head home. We didn't spend any time with him, although Louisa informs us that she rode two rides with Daddy. Charles starts to cry because he didn't get to, and Matt tells him it's too late now and everyone is too tired, so we head out into the night. We walk the block home, listening to Louisa talk about her new friends and ask if she can play at someone's house tomorrow. It fills me with such relief to see her making friends already, but it takes forever to give the kids baths and wind them down. I'm thankful for it because I don't know what will happen after it's quiet.

When I come back down from settling the last kid in bed, Matt is in the dining room, pacing with a beer.

"Are you mad at me?" I ask when we finally have the chance to talk.

Matt takes a deep breath and sighs.

"I'm not mad," he answers, "but how do you think I felt tonight? I kept getting people asking me about my three 'girls.' I don't think anyone knew that Charles is actually a boy, and it was . . . awkward to have to tell them that. I didn't know how to explain it to people. It's why I got him dressed and put him in boys' clothes. Because it confuses people when Charles dresses like a girl."

"This has never been an issue before. Why are you having an issue now?"

Matt is quiet, like he's thinking, and I wait him out.

"Because it matters now. It was never a big deal before, but we have so much riding on this job. We've allowed Charles to play dress-up games because he likes them, but now it's a risk to my job."

"What? Did someone threaten to fire you because your son wore a princess shirt?"

Matt takes a breath.

"No, but it very well could've played into why I lost my last job."

"Hey. No. You don't get to blame Charles because snobby-ass Browning didn't pan out. And you don't get to blame me for supporting Charles." Matt goes back to pacing. I watch him with a mix of panic and anger.

"What has gotten into you, Jane? Is this because you're jealous that I've been spending so much time with other people? Seriously, Jane. I don't think dressing our son in boy clothes should be such a big deal." We rarely argue, and the words hurt and fill me with an old familiar panic that if I'm not good enough, people will leave me. I start to cry, sitting on one of the big old dining room chairs.

"I don't want to fight with you, and I'm glad you have so many friends. This is about Charles; he isn't the same as us, and I know it. And he's trying to tell you, but you won't listen. Did you see him tonight? Did you see him running with the girls, playing? Not attached to my hip, hiding from the world. Did you even notice him at all?"

Matt looks at me for a long time, then shakes his head. "No, I didn't. I was too busy telling everyone that the cute little curly-haired girl in the tutu was actually my son. People talk, Jane. This is a small town. And tonight was not exactly the best start to my dream job."

I rub my temples in frustration, then wipe the tears off my face.

"Matt, I don't get it. I know you've had inclusivity training before you worked for Browning. I mean, we went to Jeff and Andrew's wedding, for cripes' sake. I don't understand why it's so hard for you to grasp that maybe our kid is different. That maybe he is transgender."

He's always been so accepting of others. Why can't he be like that for Charles? Matt stares me down, but I don't avert my eyes from his.

Matt runs his hands over his hair before he answers me.

"It's not that I don't believe people could be transgender, but I do think there is no reason to encourage children to change their bodies with drugs and surgery when they clearly know nothing about life yet. I can understand if an adult comes to that conclusion and needs to change their body. That's fine, and they are grown, consenting adults, so it's their decision. But kids don't understand anything yet. They need protection from this kind of thing, not encouragement."

"First off, no one is talking about altering Charles. That isn't something that happens to young trans kids at all. A social transition is about clothing and hair and pronouns, not surgery. You're misinformed."

Matt sighs long and hard and finally says, "I do know that Charles has never even heard of being transgender, so how could he be that? Kids don't know about this unless someone shows them this alternative lifestyle. Unless someone is 'grooming' them to think so."

My mouth drops open, and I stare at Matt, feeling my sadness and frustration turn to anger.

"Oh, so you think *I'm* doing this? It's my fault?"

"All I'm saying is that you are the one who gets him dressed every morning," he answers. "Think about it."

He drinks the last of his beer in one slug before setting the bottle down.

"I'm tired, Jane," he says, sounding defeated. "I'm going to bed." And he heads up the stairs.

I pace the room for a bit, arguing with Matt in my head, and then I head onto the front porch to sit with the cool breeze to try to calm down. There is a long wicker couch around the west corner, so I lie down there and listen to the merriment of the festival behind me. The vines grow around the porch, filling in the open spots enough to make it dreamy and forbidden. I tuck a pillow under my head, realizing I could fall asleep.

When I open my phone, I find ninety-nine-plus notifications on social media. This has never happened to me. I giggle, sitting up a little on the wicker sofa. "What?" I say right out loud. "Maybe I will make friends in Atwood."

Many of the notifications are friend requests. There are also offers for playdates and requests to tag me in photos. I flip through them, one by one, pictures of Louisa on the giant slide, arm in arm, with a group of girls. You'd never know she's the new kid. I hit "Accept" over and over. There are even pictures of me meeting people and Henrietta with Mrs. Driscoll and her grandchildren. Everyone in this town is connected somehow, including us. My social media went from no-man's-land to a flurry of activity never seen in a dozen years.

A few nice notes on my wall say it was nice to meet me. I get a message from someone named Rebecca Darling saying she admires how I let my children wear what makes them most comfortable. It is undoubtedly the first time anyone has praised me for allowing Charles to be himself. I scope out her profile, where she talks about her messy house, her kids choosing to go to school in clothes too small, or how sometimes kids end up with dirty faces. I'm guessing Rebecca isn't the most popular of moms, and maybe it's because she's overweight and doesn't have the nicest skin, but I'd guess it's because of her brutal honesty. I try to remember her name because I like her.

I lean back into the wicker and listen to the teenagers cruise Elm Street, wondering if Charles is the source of rumors like Matt says. It seems as if whatever we do or however we live, gossip will still follow us around, true or not. Even poor old widow Wellington still has rumors told about her, and she's been dead for over a decade.

For lack of a better plan, I leave the packet from MPTC on the dining room table where Matt eats breakfast, with a note saying, *I'm sorry about last night. Please read these and try to understand where I'm coming from.*

But when I get up in the morning with the baby, I find the packet undisturbed exactly where I left it, with the sole word "Thanks" written on my note and Matt already gone for the day.

Chapter Thirteen

The packet of info from MPTC that Matt didn't even open talks about parent support, the importance of community, and having people around who support you and your child. So I need to make friends here who will support Charles and our family. I mean, this isn't Texas. There must be some affirming people if I go looking, right?

Jillie seemed so nonchalant about how Charles dressed at the carnival, and since she invited me to join the PTA, I'm attending a meeting and hoping to make some friends. Matt promised to come home early so I can get there on time. He keeps telling me I need to make an effort here, although he is cool and to the point with me. He has been since the carnival. I tell myself he will settle down once school starts.

The school is dark when I arrive for the meeting, and the hallway is eerie, like all schools are when they are closed. I make it to the cafeteria at 6:30 exactly. I'm the only one here, which seems odd. You'd think the Atwood Prep moms would have some stance about timeliness.

The big cafeteria is filled with long plastic tables and garbage cans. It smells the same as every cafeteria I've ever been in. Milk and doughy foods. Not a choking hazard for miles.

I start picking at my cuticles. Where is everyone? They will all breeze in here with their long blond hair flowing behind them like rock stars in a back-to-school commercial. I always feel like plain Jane, except for how I have no friends, and my life is a mess for everyone to see.

Being forced to wait makes me nervous. A PTA meeting is most likely a colossal mistake, which is what I think when I hear some noise in the hallway.

A tall, beautiful woman comes through the doors. She does have long blond hair, but she's not breezing in. She's pushing a stroller overflowing with stuff in the cart section; she has a purse over one arm and a big diaper bag over the other. Her hair looks messy, but not in a cool way. She looks sick or tired, despite lots of makeup trying to cover it. She's wearing one oversize hoop earring. Not two, but one. She also has a dried substance that may be spit-up on the shoulder of her shirt. Back-to-school-commercial-gone-wrong is the only look she's sporting.

"Oh," she says, surprised as she looks up. She stops dead in her tracks, and the stroller bounces back in response. The diaper bag slides down her arm and swings heavily from her wrist.

"Hi. I'm waiting for the PTA meeting. Am I in the right place?"

She looks at me with a scowl like I might be some trap, then glances at the clock on the north wall, which reads 6:37.

"Yep, I think you are," she says, sounding pissed and defeated. She lets the diaper bag drop to the floor with a thud. I feel like I'm missing something. I'm always on the outside of all the information and jokes, but something else is happening. My first instinct is to get out of here because I probably don't want to know.

As I pick up my bag and prepare to leave, she scans the room as if expecting to find something. She lasers in on a table in the far corner and bolts toward it fast, leaving the stroller. I watch her cross the room, half-done hair flying behind her. She stops at the table, picking up a plastic bottle and a piece of paper. Her body sinks as she stands there for so long that I consider going over to her, and then she walks toward me carrying an empty bottle of grape soda and a piece of paper.

"The meeting is already over. It must have been rescheduled. The two of us conveniently didn't get the memo."

I half smile out of awkwardness and relief that I don't have to sit through the meeting.

"What? I don't understand."

She sighs, big and long. She straightens herself like she's about to make a speech.

"I'm Libby Zander. My husband, Jason, is second cousins with your husband. He got him the job."

My eyes get wide, and my mouth flies open.

"So, I guess you know I cheated on my husband with my daughter's T-ball coach, and now I have his 'dark-skinned love child.' Or at least that's what my mother so affectionately calls my baby. I also have a not-so-nice, new-to-me half of a house on the crappy part of Spring Street because my husband kicked us out. Pretty much everyone, including my besties"—she holds up the note in her hand—"has disowned me."

My mouth drops open again without meaning to. "I . . . no. I didn't know all that."

She shrugs as if it doesn't matter anyway.

She sighs again as she holds up the empty bottle of grape soda.

"Soda isn't even allowed in this school. My best friend Jillie—correction, my *ex*–best friend Jillie—is the only person on God's green earth, or at least in this town, who even drinks grape soda. She and the whole PTA board used to be my friends. They aren't anymore, or they wouldn't hold secret PTA meetings to avoid seeing me." I watch in awe as she tosses the soda bottle into the recycling bin with perfect precision from twenty feet away and then hands me the piece of paper.

August PTA Meeting notes

Christmas Fair–Jillie and Tanner

Halloween–Libby's problem

Funds and treasury–Kelsey

"They had the meeting early to avoid you?"

In an instant, Libby goes from looking mean and tough to her bottom lip quivering. Like someone flipped a switch, the baby starts to cry too.

"I'm so goddamn terrible they need to go through all this to avoid me? I thought they would have to face me and listen to me. I thought they'd see Mila and me in person, and they'd remember we have been friends forever." I have no clue what to say, so I listen.

"I don't even know if I want to work it out. With any of them. Which means I have no friends. My parents took Jason's side. The baby's dad is . . . gone. I have *no one*."

She looks down at her shirt and cries harder. "And now my boobs are leaking because I forgot goddamn nursing pads."

I laugh out loud without meaning to, and so does Libby. Before I know it, we're both laughing way too hard.

Despite her current state of mess, I like her. She's raw and real. And who am I to judge anyone's mess?

"I have no friends," I say to her with a shrug. "I'll be your friend."

She half laughs, half sobs. "You don't want to be associated with me. It will be bad for your prospects here."

"I'm not going to be one of the cool kids. That's not who I am. Clearly." I gesture around the empty room. "I shook hands and met every mother from this school at the carnival. None of them as interesting as you."

She looks at me sideways, studying me, then laughs. "Thank you for being nice. I needed some nice."

The baby starts to wind up more, and I look toward the stroller. "May I?" I ask, nodding toward the baby. Libby waves me over without looking up, sitting all defeated at one of the lunch tables.

Peering into the car seat reveals an unhappy but beautiful baby. I reach down and unbuckle her to pick her up. She's still little enough to need cradling. She snuggles into me, looking at my face.

"Hi, little one. Aren't you the sweetest thing I've ever seen? Yes, you are." The baby smiles at me, happy to be in my arms. I'm in love with her little dimpled face. I get lost talking to her and look up to see Libby watching us.

"We missed the meeting, and I no longer have anyone to impress." She says this with a laugh as she looks down at her shirt. "Want to go get some dinner?" I nod, excited for the first time in a long time.

I follow Libby to a little Italian restaurant downtown, where the food smells amazing. Libby arrives wearing a new shirt she must've magically changed into in her SUV. Even with her life such a mess, she's still cooler than anyone I've ever hung out with.

We tuck into a booth in the back where no one will see us. The restaurant is the place for clandestine affairs. I wonder if this is on purpose. It seems Libby is hiding.

"I'm freaking starving from nursing. I never nursed any of my other kids. Jason thought it was gross. He flat out told me boobs were for husbands, not babies. But Jason isn't here, and this baby isn't his, so I'm nursing my baby and eating whatever my fat ass wants."

I laugh, realizing I've calmed down. At least for now, I've forgotten about my problems with Matt about Charles. I feel lighter than I have since moving here and for months before.

Libby tries to hand me a breadstick, but I don't take it.

"I can't have gluten. I have celiac."

"Oh, wow. I tried not to eat gluten for a while for weight loss. It was so hard. How did you find out? How old were you?"

"When I was in college. I was sick with it my whole childhood, but my family . . . well, they thought it was in my head," I say, looking up at her. "But then I got sick in college and found out when I was hospitalized." I stop myself, realizing I always say too much or nothing at all. She's watching me, listening.

"Your family didn't believe you were sick?" she asks, shocked.

"I think it was more about me being an inconvenience to their drinking schedule."

Libby frowns but then nods. "I hear that. Wisconsin has its share of drinkers."

"So, tell me about your kids," I say, changing the subject to something less dramatic.

"I have four. Jordan, my oldest, is in high school. She's a sports nut and so talented. She's always the MVP of something and considers herself to be better than everyone else. She's got the same surly attitude toward me as my husband. Or, soon-to-be ex-husband." She pauses, and I realize how completely her life has been upended. "My son, Jenner, is a sweet guy. He's ten and a cuddly, gentle-souled video game kid, much to my ex's dismay. And my daughter Vonn is five and a little social butterfly. She loves dance class and gymnastics and all things girly girl. And then you met my little Mila. She will be three months old this month," she says, smiling at the sleeping baby in her car seat beside us.

"I'm fighting my ex for custody of the big kids because it's all such a hot mess. But I'm figuring it out." Libby is putting on a brave face. I get the feeling it's the only one she has. "How about your kiddos?"

"My oldest is Louisa, who is ten. She's a total bookworm and acts like a tiny little grown-up. I'm unsure where her presence or maturity comes from, but she's always had it. My son, Charles, is six, and he's my sensitive guy. He passed out last week when he saw a little blood on his baby sister's scraped knee. He loves to bake, and he's obsessed with Julia Child." Libby doesn't so much as raise an eyebrow at my descriptions of Charles. "And my youngest, Henrietta, just turned a year. She's as fast as the others and keeps me on my toes in that big old house. They keep me busy."

"Did you ever have a job other than being a mom?" she asks as she picks up another breadstick and dunks it in the marinara sauce.

"No. Matt and I met in college, but I ended up dropping out. Once I got pregnant with Louisa, there wasn't the money for both of us to pursue careers. It just made more sense that I stay home. I always thought I'd go back, but with three kids . . ." I look down at my plate.

"What were you going to school for?"

I look up at her, trying to remember when anyone was so genuinely curious about me.

"I wanted to be a therapist. My childhood sucked, and I always felt like something was wrong with me, or the people around me. Maybe both. I thought perhaps I could figure that out and help myself and other people to not feel so . . . alone." I let out a sigh as I say it, feeling brave and vulnerable all at once.

"It's not too late, you know. You'd be a really good therapist," Libby says, and I warm to her even more. "In the meantime, according to the PTA meeting, I'm on my own with the Halloween Dance this year. I know you're busy, but would you consider being my sidekick and planning the dance with me? It's a lot of work, but I promise it will be worth it."

I break out into a grin. "I'd love to help you."

"Great. We can find a time to let the babies hang out while we work. I'm so glad we met, Jane."

"Me too."

Chapter Fourteen

I get up early and head to Darling's Market for supplies to make a big breakfast for the first day of school. I want to make it memorable for Matt and the kids.

While I wait to pay, the cashier scans my items and keeps looking at me. I start digging in my purse to avoid her since she's creeping me out a little, and then she says, "You live in the Wellington house, right?"

I smile and nod, getting used to the question. When I got the oil changed the other day, the mechanic I'd never met knew where I lived. Even he had a story about Virginia Wellington.

"Yes," I tell her. "We live in the illustrious Wellington home."

She looks enchanted. "I would love to see your house. I've dreamed about what it's like in there my whole life."

I smile, feeling proud to live in one of the beautiful old historic homes in town.

"I heard there was a ballroom up there, on the third floor."

She looks at me, hopeful, and the word conjures up ideas of huge ballrooms in fancy hotels. I'd have noticed that, I'm pretty sure.

"I'm sorry to tell you, but all that was left was a lot of old furniture and stuff. But no ballroom."

She looks deflated as I gather my groceries and head home.

I start preparing our huge celebratory breakfast before anyone is up, and I enjoy making the pancakes and bacon without interruption. I put the doughnuts on a pretty plate I pulled out of the widow Wellington's china cabinet.

I want to make Matt feel special on his first day. The kids and I even made a banner above his "desk" at the edge of the long dining room table.

"You have worked so hard, and I'm so proud of you," I say, wrapping my arms around Matt when he comes downstairs dressed in a suit and tie, ready for his big day. He leans into me for a moment, and then he sees Charles walk into the room in khaki shorts and his favorite princess shirt, and Matt lets go of me.

As we all sit down to eat, the kids chatter about who their teachers will be and what the school is like. Even Charles seems excited about school this year.

"Time to load up and hit the road. Can't be late on our first day," Matt says, not looking at me as we head out.

Parents join the kids in their classrooms for the first hour of the day, listening to their teachers introduce their class plans before we leave them to get acquainted.

Charles's teacher, Ms. Keaton, informs us that she believes in a gentle-parenting teaching model and a gender-free environment. She tells us that the single-stall bathrooms in the first-grade room are gender-neutral, meaning anyone can use either one. She tells us the kids will line up by various themes such as shirt color, the month of birth, or even our feelings for the day. And there won't be any "boys" and "girls" talk, because those words don't always include everyone.

I am about ready to jump out of my chair and hug this woman. This is my dream teacher for Charles, and we wouldn't have found her in Texas, at least not at Browning.

I remember Jillie telling me at the carnival how Ms. Keaton is so well liked and how Charles would be lucky to have her. As I sit there, I agree. Ms. Keaton is a young female Mr. Rogers. The weight of worry over Charles's school year lifts off me as I listen to her.

Louisa's new friends from the carnival are in her class, and she is so excited to start school. Her teacher tells me she will be substituting some advanced courses for Louisa based on her scores from Browning and that they will move her up to the sixth-grade class for some of her work. Everything seems to be falling into place as we'd hoped.

The halls are full of parents, and many recognize us from the festival and stop to say hello. We bump into Jillie, who is dropping off her youngest. She's got another mom with her.

"Hello, Jane. And, Charles," she says, "don't you look fabulous?" Charles pushes out his belly to better show off his pink shirt, and Jillie smiles at his beaming. "This is Joann," she says, "another Atwood Prep PTA mom."

I can't help but feel wary of Jillie for inviting me to the PTA meeting and then not telling me she'd changed the time. I also get the vibe that I should not mention going to dinner with Libby.

Joann and I shake hands, and she asks how old my kids are.

"I have a fifth grader, Louisa. This is my first grader, Charles, and this is baby Henrietta," I answer.

"Very cool," she says, sounding sincere. "I love how Charles has such style, and you're cool enough to let him be who he is."

The compliment hits me off guard, but I thank her sincerely.

Atwood Prep feels much friendlier already. The bell rings, notifying the kids to head to their classrooms. Jillie and Joann promise to catch up soon as we all send our kids off to start their day. Charles walks away with his new teacher without incident or tears, and I sigh with relief.

We walk toward the door, and I try to take Matt's hand, half out of habit and half because I'm happy.

"I think you were right about us fitting in here. I think we found our place," I say, leaning my head against Matt's shoulder.

He steps away stiffly. "Have a nice day," he says cordially, without looking at me before he walks away.

What I don't love so far about Atwood is how Matt is acting here.

Chapter Fifteen

Jillie told me all about how Libby Zander is a lying, adulterous person and how she is to be avoided at all costs. Then she assigned me to be co-chair with Libby for the school's Halloween Dance. What kind of fuckery is that?

"No one else will work with her," Jillie told me, "but it has to be done. Too many of us rely on the party for the school, and Lord knows Libby can't even keep her life together right now. She needs help, so please make this happen. And besides, you don't have all the *feelings* we all have with her cheating on poor Jason and lying to all of us. You don't feel betrayed." It pisses me off. Why is it her business who Libby was sleeping with?

Jillie doesn't know that I had dinner with Libby, how we've become texting friends, or that she already asked me to help with Halloween. I also haven't told Matt I'm talking with Libby. I'm already making waves by letting Charles wear what he wants to school. Matt got stuck between a rock and a hard place with the super-loved first-grade teacher being so supportive of gender creativity, and I think he's feeling ganged up on, so he's retreated into silence about it.

Libby sometimes comes over during the day to work on the Halloween Dance with me, but we end up sitting in the little table nook in my kitchen, talking not just about the PTA but also sports for the kids or life in general. The big kids are in school, so it's only the babies and us. We jump from subject to subject. I usually feel sweaty and anxious with new people, but hanging out with Libby is the simplest thing in the world.

"Why haven't you asked me a million questions about Jason and me or Mila's dad? Everyone else in this town is dying to know."

"I figured you'd talk to me if you want to, but you don't have to."

She nods her head down a little. She chokes out a thank-you, and I wonder if she is teary-eyed, but she straightens up.

"I thought I was losing my mind. My soon-to-be ex-husband's main interest in life is memorizing every sports statistic from every game. He is passionate about coaching kids but nothing else. We had no sex life. We didn't talk, not really. He did his thing, and I ran our lives. It's my job to chase kids, and somewhere along the way, I forgot there was even me in here. And none of my friends felt so alone and bored out of their damn skulls with a life they didn't pick. I felt like I copied my mom's whole suburban housewife life and pasted it onto myself like a sticker. I couldn't breathe there, and then I met someone who understood me, or that's how it felt. Like he really saw me, you know? And it was so hot." Libby lets out a real laugh, but then a sad shadow falls over her face as she talks about Mila's dad. I can see this affair was not only about sex. She loved him.

"Anyway, he chose his family because they were there first. And once the baby was born and clearly not Jason's, my family chose Jason, and so did the whole town. That's how it feels, anyway. Kelsey and Jillie won't talk to me. I mean, I knew they were not very nice, but I never thought they'd do it to me. I tried to make myself feel something and ruined my whole life."

"You didn't ruin your whole life. Things will settle down, and the people who deserve you will show up."

"I'm starting to believe popularity and status are made up, like Monopoly money. It can make you feel rich, but it isn't real."

Libby runs her hand along my china cabinet, peering into the glass at all the old dishes.

"So, what's it like living in the Wellington house?" she asks, changing the subject.

"Everywhere I go, someone tells me some bizarre random rumor about the lady who lived here. One told me she shot her husband. One said she shot herself. Another said she was a model in Europe." I shake my head. "I never seem to hear the same one twice. It's wild to me since she's been dead so long. This town loves to gossip."

"The rumor mill in this town is brutal and not at all forgiving," she states, speaking from personal experience.

"What did you know about her?" I ask.

"Well, no one *knew* Virginia Wellington. She was a hermit in this house for many years. She had everything delivered, so it was rare to see her out."

I stare her down. "I *know* you have a Virginia story."

She laughs. "Okay, yes, I do. My grandmother played bridge with her and said she went nuts, like institutionalized and everything. Either way, it seems like she had a rough life and that she let the talk around town draw her into her own little world and she didn't let anyone in. But to be honest, now I don't know what to believe about her. I look at all the rumors flying around town about me, and almost none are true. So maybe we don't know other people at all."

"Hell," I chime in, "I think it's hard enough just to know ourselves."

I want to talk to someone about Charles and all I've been learning about gender diversity. I take a deep breath because talking to someone about it feels big, especially since Matt is so adamant that it can't be true.

"Do you want to see something I've been working on?" I ask, sort of petrified to show her.

"Sure," she says, as if it's something exciting, making me even more nervous. But there is no turning back now. I lead her into the room we call the office because the printer lives by the door, but it's a room full of boxes needing to be unpacked, so, of course, no one goes in there but me.

On the wall is a corkboard and a little desk with articles, websites, and information about being transgender, nonbinary, and intersex.

Libby peruses the wall, but her expression doesn't change at all. There's no hint of prejudice or excitement. She looks it over like she's taking it in.

"Have you ever heard of someone being intersex?" I ask her, trying to keep my voice as normal as possible.

"I have. I . . . It's like being both a boy and a girl, right? I don't know much more than that."

I nod fast. "Yes, it's being born with female and male anatomy and/or chromosomes that aren't XX or XY. And it's way more common than we think. Nearly two percent of the population is intersex. Japan has two percent of the world's population. So does Russia. Or it's how many people naturally have red hair."

"Wow. I didn't know that. I thought it was super rare."

She picks up a printed article and peruses it.

"But why are you studying all this stuff?" she asks. I still have no idea how she feels about all this. "Is it because of Charles and his girl clothes?" She's never said a word about Charles, though I know she's seen his outfits at pickup and drop-off for school.

"I guess it got me thinking that maybe there is a medical component to this stuff with Charles. If he's intersex, it would explain why he's so adamant that he is someone else. I'm still learning and researching all this stuff because until recently I didn't know any of this. But I feel like . . ." I pause and look at Libby. "Like somewhere in here is my child," I say, waving my hand at the articles and information I've gathered.

"Do you think maybe he's transgender?" she asks me, just flat out, like it's no big deal to say out loud. Unlike how Matt whispers the word like it's a secret to keep.

"I don't know. Maybe? I'm not sure he's old enough to know that. Is he? But if he's intersex, then it's a medical issue."

"I mean, if you're old enough to know you are cisgender, you'd be old enough to know you are transgender," she says, and it lands like an epiphany.

"But no matter what label may get pasted onto your kid, Jane, it's still your kid. It won't change who he is. But maybe it can help you understand it better." I nod, thinking it over. She stares me down briefly before asking, "What does Matt say about all this?"

"Not much, since he's never here, but mostly, he thinks Charles is too young to be trans. When I bring it up, his crabby ass doesn't want to talk about it," I blurt out. Libby gives me a side glance, and we both burst out laughing. When we stop, I rub my temples for a few moments.

"It isn't funny, but I needed that laugh. But he did find us a new pediatrician, and we have an appointment to take Charles to be examined. We couldn't get in as a new patient until October, but it's better than nothing. I hope they will recommend a referral to a clinic for trans kids. I'm not having any luck convincing Matt on my own."

"I hope you find your answers, Jane. And I hope Matt comes around."

I can't turn my brain off. I lie awake in bed, trying not to toss and turn while I think about Charles. Eventually, it's too heavy to wrestle with, and I start thinking about Virginia Wellington and the rumors I hear everywhere.

"Go to sleep, Jane," Matt says quietly.

"You're still awake?" I ask as I roll over to look at him.

"Barely."

I pause, feeling guilty for keeping him awake.

"What do you know about Virginia Wellington?"

"What do you mean?" he grumbles. He rolls over a little as if I have his attention.

"Everyone has a Virginia story. Everyone I've met in this town. What's yours?"

Now he does wake up, at least enough to roll over and look at me. The moonlight behind him lights up his whole head. It's bright enough to make out the tiny pink roses on the faded sheets.

"I gave her a bag of Halloween candy when I was a kid. Rumor was she was unstable or delusional. I found her smart as a whip. When I told her I wanted to be a teacher, she said, 'Aim high. Always aim higher than you want. In all things. Chances are you'll land below your target.'"

"You marched up to her, gave her some candy, and discussed your career goals?"

"No." He laughs, and I feel myself relax. It's been a while since we were so at ease with each other.

"We were trick-or-treating. Me, my cousins, our friends. The widow Wellington always sat on her porch on Halloween or in her window if the weather was bad. She watched to make sure no one egged her house. I heard that some nasty pranks happened to her over the years. Anyway, I saw her out there and had an extra bag for my sister because she was sick. I took some of my candy out, put it in the extra bag, and marched it up to her porch. We'd been standing there waiting to cross the street, and I was thinking how no one ever did anything nice for her. They only talked shit about her, you know?" I nod, feeling warmth for my husband for being kind to Virginia. I grow increasingly protective of her by the day.

"She was a spitfire. She told me she didn't give out candy, and I'd wasted the twenty-seven steps up her front walk for nothing. I handed her a bag of candy, but she asked me if it would blow black powder in her face or if a dead rat was inside. It gave me the feeling she wasn't used to anyone going out of their way to be nice. But she trusted me enough to look inside and then smiled a real smile. She took out three pieces of chocolate and a sucker, then returned the bag to me. She told me it was better to rot my teeth than hers."

I laugh out loud, smiling at the thought of such a feisty woman owning this house.

"Then she asked me what I would do with my life. I told her I wanted to teach because I wanted to help people. She said I should be in administration because I was smart and the person with the most power can do the most good."

"How old were you? Is this why you wanted to be an admin?"

"I doubt it. I was only eleven or twelve. I forgot about all of it, to be honest with you. I haven't thought of it in years. I guess it could have planted a seed."

"You didn't talk to her again?"

"Well, she wasn't one to be seen outside a lot. Coming out on Halloween created its own spectacle because she was such a recluse. I thanked her, and she said, 'Be well, young man.'

"It was all sweet until Jason yelled, 'Hey, crazy widow Wellington? How does your garden grow? With the bones of your dead husband, don't you know?' Then this loud, terrible cackling from him and his friends."

Matt winces at his own story. "I forgot that part. What a dick Jason was. How I wanted to hit someone for the first time. The big kids all laughed, already running away, having had their fun. I had no power over Jason, with his money, status, and popularity. Not back then, anyway. I looked back at the widow Wellington, who was flipping Jason off. She never looked at me again."

I kiss his cheek, holding my lips there, then lay my head on Matt's chest, settling in for the night.

"That's the nicest Virginia story I've heard."

"That's really sad, Jane."

Chapter Sixteen

Jane! I'm so sorry I forgot to tell you that the PTA meeting got switched. I feel awful and would like you and your kids to come swimming at my house on Friday! It's been a warm September, and the pool is heated. Let me know if you can make it so we can hang out!

I reread the text from Jillie, contemplating.

I didn't intend to get "the Plastics," the new name Libby has for Jillie and Kelsey, in trouble. But I told Matt that they rescheduled the first PTA meeting without telling me, and apparently, he mentioned it to Jillie.

I chose to believe the rescheduled PTA meeting was an innocent mistake and accept the invitation. If I want to build a community here for all of us, I must keep stepping out of my comfort zone.

I didn't think the whole thing through, because swimming means swimsuits. And what the hell am I going to put on Charles?

Or rather, which Charles will I choose to bring?

The Charles whom I force into a boy swimsuit, who will hide beside me with a towel wrapped around him the whole time? Or the Charles I let wear an old girl suit of Louisa's, who runs around jumping in the pool, swimming like a fish, and doing his favorite thing?

"Fuck it," I say to myself. "I'm bringing happy Charles." And I yell to the kids to grab their swimsuits. I am letting my child choose their clothing. Why should it be a big deal?

After I get the baby ready, I put her in her playpen while I check on the kids. Charles is still changing in the bathroom, so I head to Louisa's room and find her sitting on her bed, quietly playing with a fidget toy.

"Hey. Are you okay?" I ask, and she looks up at me with a sad face, then looks down at the floor.

"Yeah, I'm fine," she answers softly.

"Well, you don't look fine. What's going on?"

Finally, she turns to me with tears on her face. "I'm just worried. What if someone picks on Charles for wearing a bikini? Kids are mean, Mom." She wipes her eyes as I reach out for her hand. "And Daddy is going to be mad about it. You guys never used to fight, but now you do, and it's always about Charles. I don't care what Charles likes to wear, but I hate how it's screwing everything up . . ."

I lean in and wrap my arm around Louisa, feeling guilt that all this is heavy on her little shoulders. I take a few deep breaths, trying to think of what to say and knowing that I can't fix any of it in this moment. Not for any of us.

"I know this is hard," I admit. "It's hard for me too. I really don't know what's right, Louisa. But I do think that it's okay to let Charles wear what he likes while we figure it out. And I don't want you to worry about me and Daddy. Sometimes parents fight, just like sometimes you and Charles fight. It doesn't mean that we don't love each other. We are going to figure things out, okay? But we are both here for you, and we always will be. I want you to remember that."

"Okay, Mom. I'll try," she says, and gets up to collect her towel as if the conversation is over. I stay on her bed for a moment, questioning my choices and wondering if there is a good solution to any of this.

Jillie handles our arrival with class, even Charles's sparkly swimsuit top with a pink swim skirt. Jillie is either nicer than I assumed or good at faking it. Considering Libby calls her "plastic," I'm guessing it's the latter, but I'm trying to have an open mind.

"Hello, Zanders. You all look marvelous and ready to swim. Let me help you with your bag," she says as she welcomes us into her house. It's a big, sprawling home in the suburbs outside town, with an open-concept layout that reminds me of hotel conference centers. It is very minimalist, and all the colors are done in varieties of grays and off-whites. I realize how very much I appreciate our old home, which is so colorful and full of character.

When we enter her backyard, I notice fellow PTA mom and school secretary Kelsey is here too, with her kids. After we apply sunscreen to the kids and go over the rules, we let them head to the enormous in-ground pool.

"I hire a lifeguard when we have pool parties to be safe," Jillie says, "and it gives us a chance to unwind and have a cocktail."

"Oh, stop, Jillie. She's your niece, and you pay her ten bucks an hour," Kelsey says with a loud laugh.

"That's how much she gets paid at the community pool," Jillie fires back, sounding hurt. Kelsey waves her off, and I wonder how they are faring without their popular mom leader. It's weird to be having a playdate with Libby's ex–best friends.

We sit in big, comfy chairs with enormous umbrellas over them. I'm not much of a drinker, but I find myself saying yes to a margarita when Kelsey does, and Jillie arrives fast with a full tray and a pitcher. Maybe it's the drink, but I feel relaxed. We watch the kids play, and I listen to them talk, occasionally chiming in.

"Jane. We are so excited to see your house. The widow Wellington is famous in this town. Some people say the house is haunted, and you can still see her in the windows at night. Have you seen her ghost?" Kelsey asks, completely serious.

"Did you hear anything about her? I heard she was batshit crazy," Jillie chimes in. The fact that they are on the edge of their seats is hilarious. It sounds like a ghost story somebody tells to scare a kid.

"The only thing Virginia left was a bunch of clutter and breakable items I've been sending to the thrift store. But no, we haven't seen her ghost."

They seem disappointed. Jillie switches gears.

"Well, Jane, if you're going to be part of the group, we need to catch you up on Libby, our ex-BFF, and the current town scandal."

I open my mouth to say I'm friends with Libby, then shut it again.

Kelsey reaches across the table to fill her margarita glass and chimes in. "And no worries, Jane. What we say here stays here. But we all need a safe place to put all this, because it's been hard. Like, *traumatic*, on Jillie and me. The whole school, if we're being honest. I mean, the person who ran this school from the mom/PTA side committed an ungodly sin and disappointed everyone. But on top of that, she flaunted the affair with a baby? It's too much for our little school. She's made all of us look bad." Kelsey is very good at looking hurt by Libby's affair.

"Exactly," Jillie chimes in. "I thought that the other day. How we"—she spins her finger around our whole group, and then the kids—"all get a dark mark on us from our association with her. People may think we knew. Can you imagine? It's important to show that I do *not* support her and am one hundred percent on Jason's side. I don't want any confusion now."

Jillie looks at me as if she's just remembered I'm here. "And now we have Jane. So who needs Libby and her childish behavior?"

I'm supposed to say something. "So, she had an affair?" I ask.

Jillie sets down her drink and puts a hand in the air, super excited. "Not just an affair. Oh my gosh. With another dad. A married dad! And he was"—she looks around to ensure no one is listening, even though we're the only ones here—"Black." She whispers this word as if no one should hear it.

I scowl without meaning to, and Kelsey notices.

"Not that we are racist, because we *aren't*. This isn't about skin color. It's more about how there are the right kind of people and the wrong kind of people. We are good friends with the Smiths, and we go to dinner with them and play golf at the country club. He manages a bank in town, and she is a clothing buyer."

Jillie nods in agreement, then chimes in, "Yes, they are great people. But Adam, that's the 'baby daddy.' He worked in a factory. Their family only got into Atwood Prep on scholarship because they came from, well, 'the projects,' I guess. No matter his skin color, Adam was not the right kind of guy. I mean, no affair is right. But Libby, she lost her marbles. It was inappropriate in so many ways."

I'm stuck for a single thing to say that won't be considered rude when all the kids come up for a snack. Kelsey's youngest asks Charles why he's wearing a girl's swimming suit.

"Because I'm a girl," Charles answers as he performs a little dance, twirls in a circle before curtsying, then scampers off, leaving Kelsey's son open-mouthed and all of us moms breaking out into laughter.

"Your kid is a hoot. He's going to keep your hands full," Jillie says, sounding sincere.

"That is for sure," I say, uncertain how to talk to them about this.

"Are you raising your kids gender-neutral? Or is this . . . ?" She doesn't finish her thought.

I sigh, hoping the words all come out right. It all feels personal and hard and scary. But isn't that what friends are for? To be there through your hard stuff?

"I don't know," I answer, rubbing my hands together. "We're trying to figure it all out. If I make him wear a boy's suit, he will sit in a towel on a chair the whole time because he doesn't want his chest exposed. If I let him wear the girl suit, he runs around happy as a clam."

"Do you think maybe he's just, like, gay? Because that would be a relief." Kelsey says this with a laugh as she takes another drink, and I can't think of how to respond.

"No, gay is not the same thing as gender. I saw this documentary that explained sexuality as who you go to bed *with*. Gender is who you go to bed *as*."

They say nothing. They sit there, silent, staring at me with faces full of pity.

"For goodness' sake, he isn't dying of some awful disease. Being trans or gender fluid isn't the worst thing in the world, right? I mean, *if* he is." I realize as I talk to them how much I mean it. I've been so worried, but this isn't the worst thing in the world. It's mostly about letting him wear what he wants.

"What does Matt say?" Kelsey asks, and something in her tone makes me think she already knows what Matt says.

"Matt thinks it's a phase. For years, he's said if we ignore it, it'll stop. But it hasn't."

I feel myself getting teary-eyed. What the hell? I've already said too much.

"I want to make sure Charles knows he's loved as he is, whoever he is."

"Well, we all want that for our kids. But I also think, at this age, they don't even know how to do anything. Kids can't even care for their teeth or make food. Don't you worry he'll resent you someday for letting him do this?"

I sigh and nod. "Every day. No matter what I do, I will worry about that."

❧

The kids and I swing through a drive-thru on the way home because we stayed later than planned, with all the kids getting along so well. I tried to do a good job fitting in and talking with the moms. I tried to be authentic, hoping it would pay off this time.

When I get home, Matt greets us at the door, helping to take the bags of hot food. He kisses me and then looks down at Charles in his sparkly suit and swim skirt, and his body stiffens. He pulls away from me and asks, "Were you drinking?"

I cock my head at him in surprise.

"Jillie had margaritas for the moms. I had half of one hours ago, with a ton of snacks. You know I don't drink much at all." I'm not even in the door yet, and it feels like he's picking a fight with me.

"That's why it's so concerning you'd choose to do it while driving your kids around and while they play in a pool." He's scowling at me, but I'm mad too.

"We all had a drink, and we all watched the kids. And since you asked about safety, Jillie also had *a lifeguard* there. But either way, no one is trashed here."

I'm tired and hungry.

"And you know what? You keep harping at me to fit in here and how it's never been as important as it is now. So I try. I show up and do all I can to fit in here, and here you are, mad at me because I'm doing it wrong."

"Okay, Jane," Matt says as he heads to the dining room with the food, and somehow the conversation is over.

Chapter Seventeen

The kids and Matt are in bed, and I'm folding laundry in the basement. I head up the stairs and hear the rain, and I remember leaving the attic windows open. The loveliest breeze blew through the treetops this afternoon, so I took a bath up there because it's the most calming thing to do in Atwood. But I got caught up and had to rush to relieve Mrs. Driscoll, who is a stickler for time. I figured I'd come up later, but everything got too hectic. Now it's eleven p.m., thirty minutes after the torrential thunderstorm started.

I hike up the back stairs to the third floor with a big beach towel and my phone as a flashlight.

A sole light hangs by the ceiling of the attic stairs, illuminating a part of the hallway. The rest of the walls remain dark and daunting. The slant of the ceiling and the dark wood creep me out. The pounding of the rain on the roof doesn't help. The house is beginning to feel familiar, though it's cavernous enough to spook me at night.

There could be anything up in this attic. Mice. Bats. Possums. Who knows? I'm afraid I left the fan plugged in, or I wouldn't be up here.

The flashlight guides me as I scan the hallway up and down, looking for anything scary. Everything is soaked in the bedroom, so I close the windows, wring out the curtains, wipe down the sills, and then lay the towel on the floor to soak up the water.

I notice something on the wall as I come out of the room and let out an involuntary gasp. My first instinct is to freeze, then shine the light back, trying to find whatever startled me. Whatever it is blends into the darkness halfway up the wall. It doesn't move, so I edge closer.

It's a bulge inside several layers of wallpaper over a large bump. I shine the light around, finding smaller, thinner lumps beneath the paper.

Standing back, I notice the outline. "It's a freaking door!"

As I say this, the lightning flashes bright enough to illuminate the hallway, and thunder booms on top of it.

I hurry back into the storage room to the table where I've left my cleaning supplies, grabbing a pair of scissors and struggling to shine the light while I cut at the fragile old paper.

"I want to see if it's a door . . ." I mutter, curious and scared. What the hell is behind it if it is a door? Do I want to know why it got wallpapered shut? Every Virginia rumor floats in my head as I dig and discover it's an old door handle. Tarnished metal, a long twelve-inch handle with a thumbpiece. I push it, hearing the lock open. The whole door is still papered in tight, so I dig with the scissors until I find the seam. It could feel like I'm desecrating private property, but this is my house. I'm allowed to remove wallpaper and find secret doors if I want to.

I imagine Matt searching frantically only to find me dead up here because of the horror behind the door, but that's too far-fetched to happen to someone named Jane. I find the seam and rip straight up to a curved top, but the door is taller than me, so I can't reach the top two feet. I cut as high as I can toward the top of the doorway arch. Who knows if the door will even open?

"Never know until you try . . ." I say as I clasp the handle, push the thumbpiece down, and give a good pull. The door swings open without a problem, and my phone lights up a cloud of dust. I shrink back with my arms up out of instinct and cover my face with my T-shirt, waving my hands to clear it, though it's useless. The light does nothing to help me see until the dust settles.

It's an entrance to another room—an ample open space with light from some windows on its far end. The rain slows to dull tapping on the roof as the air clears. I inch myself into the space.

The flashlight reveals old but perfect plank hardwoods in some intricate design. As the dust clears, I see big wooden posts, chandeliers, and a long wooden table full of crystal glasses. One corner of the room seems set up for a party that never came. I step inside, drop my shirt from my face, and walk toward the curved window seats, thick velvet curtains, and matching footstools in the big castle-looking corner of the house.

There is a full bed in the far corner and a nightstand to go with it. I'd guess the space to be maybe a thousand square feet as I scout the room and find a desk with filing drawers and a lamp. There are also boxes and belongings up here, like an antique kid's bike and Christmas decorations. And in the far corner is a small kitchenette with an ancient mini-stove, a kitchen sink, and plenty of counter space.

I've lived here for almost three months and had no idea this was here.

The cashier at the grocery store said there was a ballroom up here. It makes me wonder how many of Virginia's rumors are true.

Chapter Eighteen

Finding the ballroom has left me dreaming of the widow Wellington, and I can't help but think of her during the day, wondering what is true and what isn't. It's a welcome distraction from thinking about Charles or fighting with Matt.

I asked for information about the widow at the library the last time I brought the kids there. Someone wrote a book with some local history, but the only copy had been checked out and not returned. They suggested I go to the Atwood Historical Society and Museum, which I didn't even know existed.

While the kids are in school, I ask Mrs. Driscoll to come over and watch the baby so I can go to the museum. It's tucked away in an old building downtown, and it's only open on Mondays and Wednesdays from noon to three p.m. The whole thing feels secretive and bizarre, not unlike what I've learned about Virginia Wellington already.

The inside of the building is covered in old photos and maps on the walls, stacks of old books, antique bicycles, and pieces of rusty old farm equipment. It looks more secondhand store mixed with antique mall to me, but I approach the desk and stand there while a frizzy-haired gentleman behind it studies a photo under a magnifying glass with a handle. He finally says, "May I help you?" without looking up.

"Yes. Please. I'm looking for some information about Virginia Wellington. And her house. It's on Maple Street—"

"I am aware of the house," he interrupts. "And why would you want to know about her?"

"Because I live there," I say, and he sets down his magnifying glass and looks up as if I've suddenly gotten more interesting.

"Huh," he says, like it's a full sentence. While I wait for him to say more, I think of what Libby told me the other day, that small-town people are their own brand of weird.

"Anyway, I was told at the library that there was a book about local history and there might be some information about her in there. And they directed me here, thinking you might be able to help me."

Without a word, he gets up from behind the desk and starts slowly moving around from table to shelf, pulling out books. After a few minutes, he comes over to me holding a stack of books and hands them all to me.

"That should be about everything. But we aren't a library. All the books have to stay here," he tells me, and he goes back to his desk, ending the conversation.

I look around until I spot a half-empty table, where I set it all down, pulling up a nearby stool to start reading.

Numerous books contain nothing but old newspaper clippings, and I flip through the dusty old pages, but all I find are a handful of mentions of Virginia Wellington's name as an attendee to a party or event in the early 1940s. Nothing is indexed, so I'm searching for a needle in a haystack. I sort the pile of books the man handed me and find the one about local Atwood history that the librarian had mentioned. I find her name in the back, Virginia Wellington, page forty-eight. When I flip to the page, right there on the top is a photo of my house. It's in black and white, so I can't tell what color it is, but even in the grainy old photo, it's evident the home is stately and well kept. The trees are much smaller, but the house is surrounded by garden beds of flowers and roses. It makes me realize how neglected it has been. I begin to read.

The Wellington house on Maple Street stands as one of Atwood's most historied homes. Built in 1906 by John and Margaret Hansen, the home was considered one of the grandest in town. The Hansens, owners of the local sawmill and numerous other small businesses, were well known for their extravagant parties, always attended by the most influential members of Atwood society. Though the Hansens had four children, only Virginia survived past childhood, and she inherited the stately home after the sudden death of her parents in an automobile accident in the late 1930s.

In 1936, at the age of eighteen, Virginia married Thomas Wellington, a businessman whose fortune was rumored to have been made in oil fields somewhere out West. Thomas and Virginia had two children, Mary and Thomas Jr. Virginia kept her parents' legacy going by hosting grand parties and social gatherings. Virginia's reputation was shadowed by the mysterious death of Thomas Wellington in 1946, which occurred during one of their parties.

The Wellington children left Atwood upon reaching adulthood, and Virginia remained in the home she was born in until her death in 2010. Though remembered for her affluence, style, and reclusive nature, rumors of her misfortune and unanswered questions surrounding her husband's untimely demise still linger in local memory, ensuring the Wellington house on Maple holds its air of mystery within Atwood's community.

I turn the page and find a photo of my ballroom, full of tables with elegant place settings and crystal glasses on them. Standing prim and proper with her hands folded neatly in front of her is a woman with a sad face. Beneath the photo is a caption: *Virginia Wellington, 1945.*

Maybe it's because I live in her house, but I feel connected to Virginia. I pull out my phone and take a picture of the text and then one of the photo of her. I flip the page and find a photo of a young Virginia in 1925, still wearing the same sad expression, and I wonder if she truly was sad, or if it merely appears that way since smiling was not encouraged in photos back then. There is also a photo of our backyard, which is now an overgrown forest of trees, bushes, and weeds. But in the early 1900s, it was an immaculate garden with paths and a tiny pond. The last page in the chapter contains a photo of a group of well-dressed partygoers in front of the house. They are standing beside an old horse and carriage. The photo reads *1907*, just after the house was built. Beneath the photo is a list of the partygoers. I scan the names and stop short when I see my own last name.

Theodor Zander.

I pick up the page and bring it closer to my face. I glance over at the guy at the desk, but he's still using his magnifying glass, and I wouldn't exactly say he's friendly. I pick up my phone again and take a picture of the photo, and then I zoom in on my phone, trying to see if the man looks anything like Matt. It's hard to tell given the age of the photo, so I sit staring at it. It can't be a coincidence, right?

I flip to the back of the book again, looking up the name "Zander," and find it listed with a page number. When I locate the page, I find a chapter dedicated to the Zander family.

> The Zander family played a key role in the early development of the town of Atwood. After emigrating from Germany in the late 1800s with their five sons, the family established themselves very quickly as important figures in the area. By 1910, the Zanders were responsible for the construction of buildings that now define Atwood's downtown. As the sons grew

> older, their industrious spirit further developed the town by starting the well-known Atwood Foundry, the German bank, and even the town's first hospital. The Zander family also designed and allocated funds to provide the community with several parks.
>
> Though most of the family's descendants eventually chose to leave the area for larger cities during the mid- to late-twentieth century, the Zander legacy remains in Atwood as a symbol of hard work and success.

I flip through the pages, looking at old pictures of the Zander family, searching for faces that look like Matt or my kids, and wondering how closely related we are to the people in the old black-and-white photos. I snap a few photos of the pages to show Matt and the kids and take my pile back to the guy at the desk, thanking him for his help. I head outside because I need to get back to relieve Mrs. Driscoll, but I'm excited to share this with Matt, so when I get to the car, I call him at work. He answers on the second ring.

"Hey. What's up? Everything okay?"

"Yeah, I'm good. Do you have a minute?"

"Sure," he says, but he sounds distracted. "You caught me between meetings."

"Well, I spent a couple hours at the Atwood Historical Society today, and I found this book that has a whole chapter about the Zander family," I exclaim. I'm met with silence. "Matt? Are you still there?"

"I'm here" is all he says.

"There was all this info about the Zanders and how they basically started the town. There were old pictures and—" I say, but Matt cuts me off.

"Why were you going around town researching my family?" he asks.

"Well, I wasn't. I actually came to do some research about the widow Wellington, and when I found a chapter about her, there was a photo of a man with the last name 'Zander' in a photo in front of our house in the early 1900s. So I looked up Zander and found all this history about your family."

"I wouldn't exactly call them my family. That was over a hundred years ago, and there have been lots of Zanders through the years," Matt tells me, and I frown, wondering why he isn't as excited as I am. "And why are you so interested in Virginia Wellington?"

"I'm not. I mean, I don't know. We live in her house, and everywhere I go, someone tells me yet another wild story about her. I was just curious . . ." My excitement has faded into something close to embarrassment. I wanted to share the news with Matt, but now it feels like another thing I'm doing wrong.

"How is Henrietta?" Matt asks, changing the subject completely.

"She's with Mrs. Driscoll," I tell him, glancing down at my watch. "I'm heading back home to her now."

"Okay, I'll let you do that. I need to get to my next meeting anyway. But I'll see you at home tonight. Thanks for the call," he says before hanging up.

If I found out my family had basically started a whole town, I'd be excited about it. But Matt almost seemed like it was something he didn't want me to know or didn't want to be reminded of.

I drive home thinking about the Zanders, and Virginia Wellington and her ballroom, and all the secrets that get buried in the past that eventually make their way back into the light.

Chapter Nineteen

The playground at Atwood Prep is the place to be after school. Kids clamber on the slides and equipment, swing on swings, and cross monkey bars. They zoom by, leaving the parents to chat.

I gather the courage to stand at the playground and talk with the other moms a few days a week. They seem nice enough, and we need to create a supportive environment around Charles, especially at school.

No one asks why Charles wears pink shirts or rainbow leggings to school. The kids seem to take it in stride, and if the parents wonder, they don't ask me.

Today, while I'm wandering the playground chasing after Henrietta, who just learned to walk, Rebecca Darling comes over to me. I only know her from online. She lives on a farm outside town and is on the school board. Jillie calls her "farm girl" because Rebecca has always lived on a farm and is rumored to smell like it. As far as the eye can see, we're in the middle of farmland, but it's obvious farming is not regarded as cool by the Plastics.

Rebecca smells fine to me and is easy to talk to.

"How are you liking Atwood Prep? Do you miss your old school?" she asks.

"Oh, no, I don't miss our old school. Browning had quite the hierarchy, and we couldn't seem to . . . well . . . but Atwood Prep seems more accessible. We fit in somewhere here. At Browning, we didn't fit at all."

"Atwood definitely has its own hierarchy. All schools do, I'd guess. But I'm glad you're finding your way here." I smile at her, enjoying her company. "Also, I wanted to tell you about a group for families with young gender-fluid kids. It's in Madison but has dozens of families with kids all under ten. It may be a nice fit for your Charles. My nephew is nonbinary, and my sister loves the group. They meet up once a month."

No one has approached me and just started talking to me about how to support Charles's gender fluidity before. It kind of floors me.

"Thank you. I appreciate it. I'm not sure . . ." I stop myself, remembering her position on the school board and how Matt said people like to talk. "But maybe send me the info for when or if we need it?"

"You bet. No pressure, of course. It's a safe place for kids to figure out who they are. They meet in person and have a group online. I'll send you the info, and you can do with it as you wish." She sounds sincere, and I appreciate it.

"Hey. Any interest in a playdate with us sometime?" I ask before I can chicken out.

She turns to me with a big smile. "We'd love to. We have a farm outside of town. The kids can come explore."

❧

One week later, instead of playing at the playground after school, we head west of town toward the Darling Farm. A winding gravel road leads up to a pretty white farmhouse set apart by two large barns and a big glass greenhouse.

The kids take off as soon as I open the van doors. The Darling kids are waiting and have much to show them.

"Anywhere but the pond, you hear?" Rebecca calls out, and the oldest Darling, a boy who looks about twelve years old, puts a hand up as a reply while they run off.

"Come on up to the house. I have some toys and a cookie for this sweet baby." Rebecca has a welcoming way about her that makes me feel at home, even with my kids running off to who knows where.

"How long have you lived here?" I ask her.

"My whole life, almost. I was born here, along with my four brothers and sisters. My grandparents and aunts and uncles were born here too. Our family has owned this land and house since 1887. It runs in my veins," she says. "I tried to leave for a while, went off to school, and had a couple of kids—gasp, without getting married." She looks at me with a smile and a twinkle in her eye like it's no big thing. "And now I'm back here. My parents and siblings help with the kids, and it feels like home."

"It must be amazing to come from a place with such history."

"It is. Places can get into our souls, I think. Do you miss Texas?" she asks as we sip iced tea on her front porch and watch the kids play on a tire swing on a big tree nearby.

"God no," I say without meaning to. She laughs, and I say, "It wasn't a good fit for me. We were in this very cliquey community, and we were not the right material. I was a self-imposed hermit because I couldn't find my people."

"I've never been to Texas, but I can understand cliquey. This town and Atwood Prep are still run by the same varsity players from high school."

"Matt always talked about how he was the wrong kind of Zander. He said it would never change. But he changed."

"Then Matt seems to be an exception to the rule. Don't get me wrong. Everyone is happy to have him here because we were so screwed with Jason in charge. But people don't seem to change how they feel about someone around here."

I look at her, hoping she will tell me more.

"I went to the museum the other day to look up Virginia Wellington. But I stumbled across all this history on the Zander family and how they were pivotal in starting the town. I was excited to tell Matt about it, but honestly, it's like he didn't want to be reminded."

She shrugs. "Yeah, I can see that. Especially with Matt's background. Sure, he's a Zander. But growing up here, there were basically two kinds: the ones with power and influence and the ones who lived on the wrong side of the tracks. There were the Zanders who owned the factory and then ones like Matt's dad who worked on the factory floor and barely scraped by. I'd imagine it's hard to have your paycheck signed by some distant or not-so-distant relative of the same name who lives in a big house with a swimming pool in the fancy new subdivision while you live in a crappy rental and your wife works at the gas station. And Matt's dad had a lot of expectations on Matt to prove his name. I can see how he'd feel . . . resentful."

"Wow," I say, nodding at her. "I can't believe I've never known all of this. It makes so much sense how . . . invested Matt is in his image here."

Rebecca nods at me. "I went to Atwood Prep with half of them back when it was St. Ignatius Holy Angels. The nuns died off, but the rumor mills here never quit. I mean, look at me. I'm all grown up, and I still run the farm I grew up on. I run it because I love it, but despite my school board seat or my master's degree in agriculture, the popular girls still call me 'farm girl' under their breath like teenagers. I am not cool enough for them. And you know what?"

I look at her, wide-eyed, and shake my head to say, *I don't know.*

"I don't care. People will always talk, and some will never grow up. But none of them really *know* us. So we do what is best for our people and ourselves and let the rest roll downhill. But some people, well, they still care a lot."

I nod, knowing that she means Matt. I am learning that she isn't wrong.

"What did you find out about Virginia Wellington?" she asks, changing the subject.

I sigh. "More questions than answers, honestly. She seemed like such a sad woman. And talk about rumors!"

"Some people take the gossip and misconceptions that people spout about them and they fight tooth and nail against it. But the widow Wellington closed herself into her house and never let anyone in. I don't know her secrets or her truth, but it seemed to me she was more misunderstood and ostracized than crazy or dangerous."

I nod. "I get that feeling too, although I can't even say why. I love her old home so much. I don't suppose you know why it sat empty all this time since she passed?" I ask.

"It didn't sell," she tells me. "It was on the market forever, and eventually whoever was in charge of her estate donated it to the school and took the loss. People usually don't want a house that old because they worry that there must be something wrong with it. Plus, there are all the rumors that it's haunted or it's bad luck. Mostly, though, I think people don't see the true beauty in a rambling old purple house with so much charm and character. They want open concept with clean lines and eggshell-white walls. You know? Ordinary."

It makes me think of Charles, with his bright, sparkly shirts and rainbow leggings, in a world full of little boys with navy-blue shorts and plain white shirts. No one seems to see his beauty or uniqueness as special; instead, they think that there must be something wrong with him.

The kids play until the sun sets and don't want to leave. Rebecca's son Tyler and Louisa sit by a tree together, reading their books and talking. Charles has made friends with two of the youngest girls around his age. Even Henrietta has fun trying to catch the farm cats and the elusive chickens.

"Mom," Charles says to me on the way home, a sweet little grin on his face.

"Yeah, sweetie," I say, smiling at his happiness.

"We need to play with them again. I told them I was a girl, and they said, 'Okay!' Then they called me 'she.' They asked if I have a different name, and now I want one."

I squirm in my seat, unsure how to talk to Charles about what seems possible and what doesn't.

"We've had a wonderful day, and I'm so glad you had fun with your new friends. Let's save name changes for another day, shall we?" Charles is too happy to do anything but agree with me.

Chapter Twenty

"When we met, you said you don't have friends. But you seem to be making them here," Libby comments as we sort through bins of decorations she brought over from Halloween dances of the past.

I shrug. "Maybe I am. I'm trying. Truthfully, I never really had anyone until I found Matt, except . . ." My words fade away, and Libby raises her eyebrows at me as if things just got interesting.

"Except?" she asks with a hint of a smile.

"I moved around a lot growing up. Then, even when I did settle anywhere, I never seemed to fit in with anyone."

Libby waits me out as if she knows there is more to the story.

"Ben," I finally say, and just his name coming out of my mouth makes my heart race. I never talk about Ben.

"It was in high school, and I was . . . so young. We were so young. Eventually, he went off to college. He had a rough life, like me, but different. He was lonely too. We really connected, you know? And he asked me to go with him. To live with him in an apartment near his college. But I didn't go. I can't even tell you why, except that I was scared. And after him, before him, I was so alone. He was my first love, and I let it go. I didn't chase it. I lost him. And after a lifetime of feeling alone, I chose Matt when he came along. I choose him every day because he chooses me too. I don't want to be alone again like that. I can't be alone like that again.

"But other than that, Matt was my first real friend. And for many years, he was my only one—until we got here."

She nods, contemplating this.

"I've always had friends," Libby says, not trying to show off, just letting her thoughts tumble out. "I don't even remember meeting them. Their moms were my mom's friends, so they were inherited. I mean, I knew they were backstabbing bitches. I knew they lied and did things out of spite. I just never thought they'd do it *to me*. I never thought a person could make a mistake because they were lonely and needed some goddamn affection and then be shunned from everything. It never occurred to me it could all be taken away."

I don't say anything. She's talking more to get it off her chest than anything.

I can tell Libby's wary of me still. She thinks I may dump her the second someone says the wrong thing about her. But I won't.

"What about your family? Are they still big drinkers who ignore you?" she asks. I smile, but only because she remembered what I told her.

I shake my head. "It's only my mom and my sister."

I pause, trying to find the words. Or the energy to say them.

"And yes, they are. They are alcoholics whose priority is the bars, campgrounds, and volleyball leagues," I say, nodding. "It's all a reason to drink. Maybe it's watching them be so stupid my whole life, but I have almost no interest in drinking. But it isn't just the alcohol. They don't even believe in college. They think it's a waste of money. They believe too much education makes someone a snob."

Libby raises her eyebrows at me and blinks.

"They act like I'm so terrible." My voice breaks, but I keep talking anyway. "Nothing I do is right. They outright pick on me. They have for years. Even about my health."

"That is awful," Libby says gently. "What about your dad?"

"He left when I was seven." I think about stopping there, but I go on. "Before my dad left, there were hugs. There were smiles. I remember happier times. Once he was gone, we moved a lot. I could never be a single mom because my mother was not up to the task.

"My clearest memories are of my dad kissing my mom, coming up behind her to hug her tight, and making her laugh, you know? From my child's perspective, they seemed happy.

"But my dad obviously wasn't happy, since he left and never came back. I wonder if my dad told my mom he'd never leave her. I wonder if he promised to love her forever.

"I used to need Matt to promise he wouldn't leave me. After Louisa was born, something snapped. I felt . . . vulnerable. Suddenly, I had so much to lose. *Too much* to lose. I'd never cared so much about anything as I cared about her and our family, and I feared it would all disappear. Matt assured me, over and over, he'd never leave me, pulling me back from some dark place.

"I didn't know what 'abandonment issues' meant until I found an article online years later.

"Matt insists that I stay in touch with my mom and sister, and I know they're my only family, but they are *not* easy. It's always drama, and I'm always a problem."

Libby sits up straight when I say this. "You aren't a problem, though. Your family sounds like—excuse my French here—*assholes*. Screw that. They were shitty to you, but now you are a grown-up. You don't have to let them be shitty to you anymore. You can walk away. God, I wish I was taught I could walk away. Why are we always taught we have to stay no matter what?"

Libby's words land hard. I don't have to allow them to treat me like crap. I am a grown-up, and I deserve better. I never realized it until Libby said it.

"Everything changed in my whole life when I met Matt. He said he didn't feel like he fit in either. He never wanted to come back here. The deal was anywhere but Atwood."

"Until Jason called."

"Until Jason called."

I suddenly remember the space I found in the attic and am so excited to share it with someone. I haven't shown Matt or the kids yet, but it's too cool to keep to myself.

"You want to see what I found? It's a secret. No one knows."

Libby sets down her tea with a big grin. "Yes. Whatever it is, it must be good, because you have the biggest grin I've ever seen on you." We check on the babies, who are fast asleep in porta cribs. I grab the baby monitor, and we head up the servant steps. Libby groans. "This isn't going to freak me out, right? I have enough drama."

I laugh, shaking my head at her. "Not at all. This is too cool."

Libby follows me to the entrance to the third floor. We head up the steps, around the corner, and through the long entry room to the bedroom and bathroom.

"I always thought the attic was supposed to be bigger. Matt had me all convinced it was blocked off because of roof damage or maybe not finished," I say as she notices the wallpaper around the door is still all torn up.

"Is there a door under that wallpaper?" she asks with the creep of a smile. I nod.

I open the latch, and the door creaks open. Libby gasps when she sees the vast space. We circle the room, touching light fixtures and crystal glasses still sitting on the tables.

"I heard the rich people who built these homes in the late eighteen hundreds built ballrooms in some of them. I could see this space being used like that."

Now I gasp. "The girl at the grocery store told me there was a ballroom in this house. Isn't that nuts?"

Libby looks at me with a smile. "I guess some rumors are true."

"I'm not exactly sure what this room was used for. But I'm going to make it into a playroom to surprise the kids. For heaven's sake, it's big enough that they can ride their balance bikes. Won't this be the coolest space?"

"It's amazing. You could make this place into an awesome suite. Did you see the butler's pantry in the back and the full kitchen? You could rent this as an apartment! It's too cool."

I don't think of it until she says it, but I realize I want to make this space somewhere safe for Charles to be himself, without anyone telling him who to be. I can't help but think this ballroom stayed hidden behind a sealed-up wall despite the whispers about its existence all these years, waiting for someone who would see its beauty and uniqueness to find it. Just like Charles.

Chapter Twenty-One

I haven't spoken to my sister, Mickey, since the drive to Wisconsin. I saw that she called once, and I'm not avoiding her on purpose, but things are going pretty well here, and I don't want to pop the bubble with a dose of Mickey, much less my mother.

What Libby said about me not owing them my time hit home. It's been so painful for so long. But I decide to call Mom and Mickey, hoping it will at least get me in better graces with Matt.

I request a video chat with Mickey, pacing around while waiting for her to answer. It's bowling night, and she always has dinner at the bar with my mom. They have a few drinks before the league starts, so catching them both is easy.

"Kill two birds with one stone," I say as Mickey answers.

"Talking to yourself there, slugger?" Mickey says. She always uses these ridiculous names for me like I'm still six years old, which might be cute if she was nice to me in any of the years since then. I sigh without meaning to lose my composure, but I don't care.

"Oh, you know, just the usual losing my mind. How are you? How's Mom?"

Mickey swivels the phone from her face and shows Mom sitting behind her on a barstool, beer in hand. She waves at me with a smile, and her cigarette leaves a trail of smoke.

"We're good. About to get our bowling on!" I can tell that they are both half in the bag. They are much more agreeable after a few drinks.

"Bowling sounds fun. How are the boys and Earl and life in general?"

"Good. Boys are up to no good most days, but nothing so bad as to get the law involved, and that's all I hope for."

I nod, thinking it's a low bar to set.

"Not much going on here since it's too late to camp and too early to hunt. Guess we're forced into drinking." Mickey and Mom laugh hard, sending Mom into a coughing fit. Mickey smacks her on the back a few times and hands her another beer.

"How about you, sis? How is Matt's hometown? Is it cute and quaint and perfect?" she says with a slur, and I wonder for a moment if Mickey may be jealous of me. "Did you stop playing dress-up with that boy?" she asks with a sideways grin, and I cringe.

"Why do you always have to be so hurtful about Charles?" I ask.

Mickey looks shocked at my question but fires back, "Why? Because *his* name is *Charles*. Don't you understand?" She turns and murmurs something to Mom I can't hear.

She hands the phone over, and Mom says, "Jane. Listen to me. *You* are the one playing dress-up and confusing that poor child. *You* are the parent, so you choose the clothes." She points her finger at me. "It's simple, Jane. We have every right as his family to worry about him and the long-term effects of this kind of abuse."

At the word "abuse," I see red and cut her off.

"Abuse? You think I abuse my child by letting him wear a princess shirt?"

Mom looks at me with a quiet stare as if I've lost my mind. But I haven't. I know that now.

"You know, even Matt is worried, Jane. That's all I'm saying." I let out a hard laugh because my mom is no fan of Matt and thinks of him as the one who "took me away," which is ridiculous since they never seemed to want me.

"You talked to Matt?" I ask as I rub the tight muscles in my neck.

"Matt answered your phone while you were in the shower last time I called. Matt is a good daddy, and he's worried about his son.

He's worried about you and this cockamamie teacher putting ideas in Charles's head about who he is and confusing him. Matt was hoping we could talk some sense into you and help. He's very upset and said you've never been so unreasonable before. I told him you did the same thing to us before you left."

"That isn't true," I say, but I know I can't get them to see where I'm coming from. "You know what?" I ask. "There is no reason to try to explain any of this to you. You have decided how you feel, and there isn't anything I can do about it."

"Jane. Don't be so unreasonable. Matt is worried about his job. You are playing with fire here. Not to mention eternal damnation for you and Charles. You have to think about the repercussions of your actions."

I nod, so angry that I can't think of what to say. They are so far off base on so many things. I can't even think of where to start with them, so I don't. I am too mad, most of all, at Matt for talking to them and not even telling me.

"If you think our sinful life is so dangerous, you should avoid us altogether. I'm letting you off here." I hang up and look down at my hand. I'm not even shaking or scared. I'm pissed because, for once in my life, I know I deserve better than what I am getting.

After hanging up, I text Libby.

I told my mom and sister off because they are hateful assholes. Thanks for showing me I could.

I hit send with a heart emoji.

Libby texts back: Great job! They don't deserve your time.

I walk away from the whole thing with a smile, which is not something I can ever say about talking to my mom and sister.

Chapter Twenty-Two

Libby and I are finalizing plans for the Halloween Dance and doing our usual flip between work and chatting. I hope we continue to hang out even after the dance is over.

"After much arguing, I got Jason to agree to let me have the kids more. And I got a job offer, part-time, as a receptionist in a chiropractor's office, but it pays okay. I need something until I can get on my feet. Trying to get some reasonable damn day care for the baby is a joke. But once I find a place for Mila, I'm all set. It feels good to walk in with good news for once."

"That is great news. I'm so happy for you. Any leads on day cares?" I ask.

Libby shakes her head, changing the subject. "So, you and Matt? Not so good, huh? He looked chilly with you at the science fair last week."

"For ninety-nine percent of my marriage, Matt has been the sweetest guy: loving, understanding, and supportive. But lately, he's been dismissive with a chip on his shoulder, and it feels like he doesn't listen to me at all. I've recently noticed it happens when I stop saying yes to him every single time." There is something about Libby that makes me pour my truths out, maybe because she does the same with me.

Libby startles and looks up at me from her planning spreadsheet.

"You really used to say yes *every single time*?" she asks, her mouth remaining open.

I hem and haw on how to answer. "Give me a break. I have abandonment issues." I say this with a laugh. "My freshman year of college, about five months after we started dating, Matt planned to visit his parents in Florida for Christmas break. He kept asking about my plans, and I kept skirting the issue until he got me to blurt it all out through my tears. I told him I didn't have a home to go to because my mom had a new boyfriend staying with her for the holidays, and they had plans and wanted privacy. There was no room for me at 'home.'"

Libby looks so sad as she listens to me.

"Matt looked at me like you are now, as if he'd never heard such a sad story in his whole life. He put a ticket to Florida for me on his credit card. He took me home to meet his family for the break when I was seconds from being homeless for a month. He just . . . saved me. I vowed then and there that I would do everything to keep him happy. I don't ever want to be alone like that again." I sigh.

"But now, we just can't get on the same page about Charles. I'm worried about how distant he's been. I feel like I'm letting everyone down."

"You're amazing, and he's lucky to have you. For real, Jane." She looks at me until I nod at her. "Also, you and Matt were good until recently, right?"

"Yeah, we were great. I'm always such a mess, and he's always supported me. We never fought. We were always on the same team."

"Jane, you need to stop this whole 'I'm such a burden' stuff, because it isn't true. You are a wonderful person. And sure, you have flaws, but we all do. Every one of us. Even those of us who cover our mistakes and our flaws in a perfect, made-up life. We all have our shit. Yours is not some terrible burden."

I nod at her, whispering, "Thank you for that. I just worry that I'm ruining everything."

Libby looks me in the eye. "You're not ruining everything. You're trying to stand up for your kid. You're evolving. I think it's what we're supposed to do."

I nod, hoping she's right.

"Jason and I were never on the same side. He always had his self-interest in mind, and I had mine. We weren't close or lovey to each other, at least not since high school. I'm not sure I even cared until I met Adam. But you and Matt, you're different. You two are in love, and you will find your way through this. I believe it."

"Maybe I'm always going to worry about people leaving."

She frowns, then lays a hand on mine. "I'm not leaving," she says, and though this whole friendship is new, I feel the same way. All the people who didn't fit in my life have shown me how well Libby does fit. I look at her and nod, realizing how much we have become real friends in the past few months.

Always good at changing the subject when it gets too heavy, Libby says, "But I didn't get so lucky with the ninety-nine percent great guy. Jason was never the sweetest guy ever to me. That was . . ." Libby's voice trails off.

"That was?" I ask. I can see she's emotional. "It's okay. You don't have to tell me, but you can talk to me. I don't think you are terrible for looking for love and affection."

She stares me down, deciding. "I mean, I never talk about it. At first, it was a big secret, and then it was over, and now there is no one to talk about it with because everyone left me but you."

"I'm always here if you do want to talk," I say, and she nods, then looks away as if the subject is closed, so I switch gears.

"Can I help with the baby while you work? I am happy to help. I understand being broke and in a bind. Plus, I'm here all day with my baby anyway. Having Mila here a few days a week will be nice for our girls."

Libby looks at me as if she isn't sure she can trust me.

"I'm not a vindictive bitch like Jillie and Kelsey. Some people are good, you know?" I say to her to answer the way she's staring me down.

Libby laughs a little, then says, "I never thought of trying to find nice people to be friends with. I was always pretty, so I had pretty friends. We only hung out with popular kids and kept the trend going into adulthood, and I never noticed I still only associated with 'cool kids' until they dropped me. I swear to you, finding a nice friend who wouldn't stab me in the back never occurred to me. I was supposed to match, like a handbag with a pair of shoes. Even Jason, I married him on that whole premise. Because I thought we fit together like we were the same kind."

"And the baby's dad? How did he fit?"

Libby blows the air out of her mouth, all dramatic. "No one in my whole damn life fit so well. Suddenly, I was real and not this illusion I put up.

"I like to think it's Jason's fault because he signed me up without my permission to coach Vonn's freaking T-ball with Adam." She pauses as if his name startled her. "So that's how we started hanging out all the time." I've noticed Libby is almost always collected and in control, so it's easy to see the moments she's rattled, but then she moves on.

"But it all started when I found an old picture of my mom. It reminded me of a picture of me pregnant with Vonn that I have hanging on my wall. I put the pictures side by side, and they are startling. The photos look staged, but they aren't.

"In the photos, my mom was at Lakeview Park, and so am I, with the same playground equipment in the background despite twenty-five years going by. She's pregnant with my brother, her third child. In my photo, I'm pregnant with my third child. Our friends are all around us in both pictures, laughing at our actions. My photo is Jillie and Kelsey on my left and right. My mom's photo from decades ago shows Jillie's and Kelsey's moms flagging her like bookends. We all have perfectly pasted-on matching smiles.

"It strikes me how much I look like her, and it irks me because it seems more that *I am* her. It's like I pasted her entire PTA-president, work-from-home, carpool-driving, dinner-making, smile-through-it-all self onto me. Then I labeled it as my own life.

"And the funny part was I remember being pissed and exhausted the day the picture was taken, despite my pasted-on smile. I was arguing with Jason about getting a vasectomy for the millionth time in our marriage. I didn't want any more kids, and birth control always triggered terrible migraines for me. Since Jason hated condoms, I asked—no, I begged—for him to get a vasectomy. I couldn't handle any more responsibilities, and I thought maybe it would help us to have more of a sex life.

"The whole big smile on my face in my picture was a lie, so I started to wonder if the whole thing was a lie. I mean, my whole life.

"So I showed my mom the pictures. She was also startled at the similarities, but more by my question of, 'Are you happy?'

"My dad sleeps in the recliner, can't cook a meal or make a doctor's appointment if his life depended on it, and refuses to learn to use the computer. So I asked her, 'Are you happy with your life? Happy with Dad? Were these your dreams, or do you remember them?'

"And I meant it. I wanted to know.

"She said, 'Well, no. Not exactly happy. It's not a Ferris wheel; it's life. Who is happy, anyway? Honestly, Libby! The things you ask.'

"As if happiness wasn't a necessity. As if it was ridiculous to even want it. Once I saw that my whole life was something I'd pasted onto myself, nothing in my life looked real, not until Adam. But Adam was mine. He had nothing to do with Jason, school, PTA, Jillie, Kelsey, or my family. He'd send me songs and lyrics. He brought me chocolate. And mind-blowing orgasms." She smiles a genuine smile, and I can't help but feel happy for her for what she found with Adam.

"Jason, despite his stellar reputation as the perfect coach, is not a perfect guy. He was not very warm or loving. Or helpful. I felt lonely. I guess I fell into some weakness when I met Adam." Libby pauses at his name.

"If we're calling out bullshit, I'm calling it on you saying needing love is 'weakness.' Bull. Shit," I say, bringing her back from wherever she went.

"And, Libby." I wait until she looks at me. "I can watch Mila so you can take the job. I know you don't have many options. I can help."

Libby won't look at me; when she does, she has tears in her eyes. She nods and swallows before saying, "Yes. I don't know what else to do. And I know you're risking a lot by doing this. I hope you know how thankful I am for you and not just for this."

"That's what friends are for, right?" I ask, and she leans in and hugs me.

Chapter Twenty-Three

"So, tell me about the doctor," I ask Matt on the short ride to Charles's long-awaited doctor's appointment. A hospital and medical complex are out by the highway, but we don't head in that direction.

"Dr. Fontaine was my doctor as a kid. He still has a little practice out of his original building downtown. He's not in our network, but I love that we have a trustworthy doctor."

Matt sounds excited, but I frown at him, not feeling trusting at all.

"How old is this guy?" I ask.

"He's seventy-three and fit as a fiddle, or so he says. I feel safer with a doctor I've known my whole life. What? We're being ageist against doctors?" Since the appointment is already made, I feel like I don't have a choice. But I have to wonder how much training this guy has had with transgender children.

We are already downtown, so we all get out, heading into the appointment with Charles, who is moping about his bright-orange polo shirt and khaki pants. He begged for the princess clogs, but I knew it would never fly with Matt for the doctor's office.

Dr. Fontaine seems capable enough; I'll admit he's a spry and energetic man for his age. He looks Charles over, talks to him about school and feelings, and checks his eyes, ears, and all his parts. After a short exam, he asks us to talk in his office while Charles waits in the hall with a sucker.

"What makes you think your child is intersex?" the doctor asks me with a smirk and one eyebrow raised.

"He likes girl stuff and dressing in his sister's clothes—" I begin, but he cuts me off there.

"I think that can be attributed to kids playing dress-up. Most of the kids I see these days are on nothing but screens. It's a good sign to have such a creative child. Playing dress-up and pretending to be someone else is key for kids' development."

Matt gestures at the doctor as if to say, *See?*

"It isn't just how he dresses or the toys he likes. He . . ." I look at Matt, knowing I will be in the doghouse for this one, but I say it anyway. "He says he *is* a girl. He believes it as much as he believes anything. I have been reading about transgender kids, and—"

Dr. Fontaine frowns and waves a hand at me as if I'm being ridiculous. "Well, that's just childhood. My granddaughter is this age, and she wants to be a unicorn. Of course, she can't be, but she will understand that soon enough. It's my medical opinion that this transgender business is happening because so much is being made of kids *just being kids*. Kids don't understand our intricate rules about how to dress or even who they are. That's where they need our guidance. He will grow out of his fascination for girl stuff, I promise you that, especially if you don't encourage the behavior. But I assure you that there is nothing physically wrong with him. He's all boy."

I want to ask him how he knows that, but my face burns. If even the doctor says it is impossible, I may be wrong. But how would they even know?

Matt is, of course, tickled pink by this.

"I hope you feel better now that you got an actual medical opinion on Charles," he says as we leave the office. "I don't mean to say 'I told you so,' but he confirmed what I've been saying. That Charles is just a very imaginative boy, and this is just a phase."

More than my disappointment about Matt not learning a damn thing, the doctor saying Charles is "fine" rattled me. I want a way to help Charles, and we seem to be moving in the wrong direction.

Chapter Twenty-Four

"We need to thank Jane Zander for her amazing work creating this Halloween Dance for our kids and families. As many of you know, Jane is the headmaster's wife and took on the huge task of running this event shortly after moving to Atwood since her predecessor was not up to the task. Thank you, Jane, for saving the day! We all appreciate you." Jillie stands in front of everyone with the microphone she took from the DJ, and as the gym erupts in applause, I wave from the back of the room.

They don't mention Libby, as if she didn't put in the brunt of the work behind this dance. They also don't invite me to the microphone, so I can't right the wrong.

They act as if they are nice girls, when those women are anything but nice. And they aren't the only ones. As I wander around, I start to overhear people talking. I eventually realize that everyone is talking about me.

"Did you hear she is watching Libby's baby while Libby hooks back up with the baby daddy?" I hear someone say as I head to the cafeteria to make sure everything is running smoothly. A cold fear spreads across my stomach at the words.

I go looking for Libby through the flurry of kids running everywhere, navigating my way between black lights and smog machines. I notice the parents talk into each other's ears or go silent as I walk by. Maybe some of it is because I'm the headmaster's wife and am not out on display much, but between my rounds to and from all the rooms to keep things running smoothly, I overhear Kelsey and Jillie talking behind the curtain of the common room.

"It just killed me to have to praise her publicly like that. I feel doubly backstabbed. I couldn't believe it when Claire said she'd seen Libby dropping off her baby at Jane's house! We've told Jane how Libby betrayed us in the worst possible ways, and she knows how we feel about her. And she decided to watch our enemy's baby? What the hell is that? We have been so good about allowing her to be our friend without question or anything, especially with how ridiculously she is dressing her son. All we asked her to do was steer clear of Libby. I don't get it."

I can picture Kelsey nodding in solemn agreement.

"We tried to let her be in our group, but she clearly doesn't understand the kind of commitment it takes. There is no way we can hang out with her. She's a liability, just like Libby."

I turn on my heel and walk out of the room, intent on finding Libby. She's in the library near the office, leaning against one of the tables.

"I'm taking a smoke break," she says, half smiling as if it's been a rough night. "I used to smoke years ago. Right now, I'd sneak off for one if I still did." She turns to look at me.

"But what are you doing in here, Jane? We decided you shouldn't be seen with me unless there's a problem. Those women are brutal, and you need to keep your status, girl. Go find the Plastics." She smiles, waving me away.

"Someone saw you leave my house without your baby, and it's all the rumors out there." Libby goes silent and stares at me with big eyes. "Also, they say maybe I've been taken over as a poltergeist because my house is haunted."

Despite the heaviness of all of it, we burst into laughter.

"You know what? Come on. Let's get some food and find a spot to watch our kids enjoy what we created. We can even watch them all gossip about our terrible friendship."

Libby looks at me sideways. "You know you need to keep up appearances. You still need to suck up to Kelsey and Jillie if you hope to fit in around here. I've been kicked off the popularity train, but you can still have it."

I shake my head. "I'll try to be as fake nice to them as they are fake nice to me. But I feel awful pretending we didn't create this magical night for the kids together. Pretending we didn't become friends. I'm not going to hide our friendship anymore."

Libby links arms with me, and we head out into the school together, come what may.

Charles is dressed as Snow White and waltzing with an imaginary friend, while Louisa darts in and out with her friends, all wearing magical fairy wings. Baby Henrietta is asleep in her stroller in her lion costume.

Libby's kids come up, asking for more money to play more games. We follow them as they scamper ahead.

"It's nice that Jason let them come," I say.

She shrugs. "I told Jason that my lawyer said if he keeps holding the kids away from me, he may lose them for good."

"Do you have a lawyer?" I ask.

"Hell no. I can barely afford rent. But he's an idiot, and I knew he'd believe me. And I'm tired of him holding the kids hostage. I had an affair. And a baby. Get over it already." We laugh as we head down the hall to play games with the kids.

Despite the stares and the whispers, Libby and I spend the evening together. We laugh at how bad I am at the basketball game and marvel at how good she is at it. Each room has a new game or theme, and we explore them all.

We don't run into Matt until we enter the first-grade room to do the cakewalk. Matt gives me a small wave as if I am just some parent and not his wife. I try to ignore him and enjoy my night.

Before the night ends and we start the big cleanup, Libby and I go into the photo booth and take pictures together. Despite trying my hardest, I look silly because I'm so happy I'm trying not to cry.

When I get home, I smile and put the photos on the front of the fridge.

I found a best friend in Atwood.

Chapter Twenty-Five

"Why would you watch *her* baby?" Matt asks out of nowhere while we are having his favorite meal the following night.

Hours earlier, I stood on this table, my T-shirt over my mouth to keep the dust away, cleaning the beautiful crystal chandelier. I pulled out some of Virginia's fancy china, and I'm wearing the dress Matt loves, but he hasn't noticed. Or if he has, he's kept it to himself.

Apparently, he heard the same rumors at the dance as I did.

The kids are playing at our feet, having eaten hours ago. I ask them to go play upstairs for a bit. They scurry off without me having to ask twice.

"Because I was being nice. Because she needs a friend."

"She's using you." He says this coldly and as if he has some special authority.

"How do you know? You tell me to make friends, so I do. Then you get all picky and tell me I chose wrong."

"Of all the eight thousand people in this town, why did you have to pick my cousin's soon-to-be ex-wife? Who cheated on him? Who has been half of what turned this school upside down . . . ?"

"Whoa. Wait. Do you hear yourself? How has she turned this school upside down? She had a *baby*. It's her right and not anyone else's business. Except for her husband and their family, which is their business. What happened to 'no one gets left behind'?"

He frowns at me, but I'm mad too. And I will not let him take this friendship from me.

"What you do at work for thirteen hours a day is your business. You've made it clear that you don't have time for us right now. I get it. You have a school to save. You have a career to build. I'm here too, trying to keep my head afloat. Which means if I want a friend, I can have one. I don't need your permission. If I want to help her out and babysit during the day, I can. Seriously. You are being a jerk."

"I just don't know what's gotten into you, Jane," Matt says as he leaves the room. I head into the kitchen to finish the dishes, but I'm shaking so hard I'm afraid I'll drop one. I hear him gather the kids for bedtime and let him because it gives us space away from each other. This rift is widening, and I don't know how to cross it.

Once I calm down, I stand scrubbing dishes in my sink, turning my head from side to side to stretch out my neck. My body soaks up drama like a sponge. Matt used to rub my shoulders and help me settle down. As the daylight fades, I scare myself, wondering if this is how marriages end. We can't seem to find a place to connect.

The kids come down for kisses, and Matt puts them to bed. When he goes to shower, I gather the baby monitor from our room and head to the attic. I want to forget about everything else.

I sit on the bed in the third-floor bedroom, trying to piece together all my research about trans kids. I take out most of the intersex stuff and concentrate on young trans kids. There are so many instances of self-harm, with statistics showing they get more prevalent in the teen years. I push it all aside and text Libby.

I just read that the life expectancy of trans women of color is only thirty-six years old.

OMG. That's terrible. Why?

Violence, self-harm, suicide, lack of support, medical or otherwise

Yikes. That's so frightening. Are you okay, Jane?

I got in a big fight with Matt.

Oh hell. She includes a sad face. Was it because of me???

I hesitate to answer, but I don't want this relationship to be about hiding or half-truths.

Yes.

I get no response for so long that I think she's done until she texts back.

You don't have to do this, Jane. You don't owe me anything. I'll be your friend either way. I can use all the friends I can get, and I don't want to complicate your life.

I shake my head at my phone and reply.

You need my help. There is no reason for me to stop, except for Matt having an attitude.

Libby sends me the symbol of hands together in prayer as a thank-you. I text back: I can use all the friends I can get too.

I know Matt is upset about it, but Libby is the friend I have waited for. I'm not giving her up because Matt is afraid of rumors.

Chapter Twenty-Six

Without planning it, Libby and I find ourselves dropping off our older kids for a birthday party at the same aquatic center in Watertown, a larger city about thirty minutes from Atwood.

"I need to go to the outlet mall across the highway. Do you want to come? The kids have outgrown everything, and Jason won't send any clothes with them from his house. He's such a slimeball."

I giggle at her. "Let's go. I need a few things too."

"Did you say 'shopping'? I love shopping," Charles exclaims as he peeks out the van door.

"Did I mention that Charles here is, like, a professional shopper? He finds all the best stuff," I tell Libby.

"Maybe you can help me? I need to spruce up my image a bit."

Charles nods with a big smile, ready to help her with clothing and accessory needs.

The outlet mall is outdoors, so we put the babies in a rented double stroller, and we let Charles and Vonn run ahead a little. Louisa and Libby's son, Jenner, will be at the birthday party for a few hours, so we have time to kill.

Charles starts rattling off a list of his favorite stores that he'd like to go to, amusing Libby as he talks a mile a minute.

"I'm not sure what stores they have here. But you will find things you love. I promise."

I peruse the girls' department in one of the kids' clothing stores with Henrietta and Mila in the stroller. Libby wanders to the boys' department, and Charles runs back and forth with things he likes: sparkly leggings and a pink hoodie with an iridescent unicorn. I have to repeatedly send him back to get his correct size and tell him we can't buy everything he likes. I'm holding a shirt to Henrietta to determine the size when I hear Charles yelling from nearby.

"I am not. Stop saying that!"

"This is the girls' clothes. You aren't a girl. Go pick out boy clothes."

I turn the corner and see Charles wearing a very sparkly tutu next to one of the girls from his school. Vonn is standing back with wide eyes.

"What's going on?" I ask as I get closer.

They all say nothing, looking at me with matching frowns.

"Charles. What happened?"

His shoulders round in a slouch, and he looks at the floor. Just then, the girl's mom comes over. It's one of the moms from the PTA at Atwood Prep. I don't remember her name.

"Hey. I didn't know you were here." She seems happy to see us until she looks at the kids' faces. "Everything okay?" she asks with a fading smile.

"Eva said I can't wear this tutu because I'm not a girl," Charles blurts out with a pout.

The mom says nothing.

"Clothes are for whoever wears them. There aren't girl clothes or boy clothes because clothes don't have a gender," I tell him, putting my hand on his little shoulder.

At this, the mom laughs right out loud. I shoot her a glare before I can think of stopping myself.

"Okay, I'm all for inclusion and all that. But there are boys' and girls' clothes. There are actual girls' and boys' departments because they are so different," she barks at me, her hand on her hip, ready to argue.

Just then, Libby joins us from out of nowhere.

"Hey, Amber," she says, super confident and smooth. It almost irks me until I realize she's messing with her. Amber seems happy about the distraction.

"Libby! Hello. How are you?" Her voice is forced, like she's trying too hard.

"I'm okay. It's been a rough year. Just lots of assholes who think what I do is their business, you know?" She says this and lets it lie while Amber squirms. I don't know her, but I imagine she is part of what's perpetuating the rumor mill around Libby.

"I think that's why I don't like it when people pick on little kids for things like what they wear and who they are."

"Libby, I wasn't picking on him. But come on. There are girl clothes and boy clothes because that's all there is: boys and girls. I don't know why everyone has to fight about this. It's science and so stupid when people can't understand it."

"Stupid? It's stupid to let someone wear what they feel most comfortable in? If you're upset about what a person is wearing, how about asking yourself why it's any of your business? It isn't hurting you." Amber looks like she's been struck and stands there with her mouth hanging open, staring at Libby.

"You know what's stupid, Amber? Bullying little kids because your 'all lives matter' ass is afraid of someone wearing a tutu."

"Jeez, Libby. I think you misunderstood something here. I'm not a bully. I just said—"

At this, Libby interrupts her as she puts an arm around Charles.

"We know what you said. Now, we want you to go away. My friend and I are shopping, and shamers aren't allowed."

I don't know what kind of power Libby has, but Amber is visibly upset.

"C'mon, Eva. It's bonkers over here," Amber says as she reaches for her daughter's hand and walks away without another word. I look down at Charles.

"Are you okay?" I ask.

He shrugs. "I don't understand why I can't just be a girl."

Libby kneels in front of Charles. "Don't listen to those haters, Charles. They don't know what's right for you. I think you are perfect just the way you are." He crumples into her arms, and I swallow the lump in my throat. No one except me has ever defended Charles before. He looks up at me and smiles; I know he realizes it too.

⁂

Matt came home with flowers and a kombucha tea for me. Not even the fancy five-dollar glass bottle of kombucha from the grocery store that I like. This knockoff comes in a can and smells like fermented feet. I'm pretty sure he bought it at a gas station on his way home from the seventh graders' championship game he attended in the Wisconsin Dells, but he knew I was mad, so he tried. I hope it will lead us back to some semblance of friendship so we can talk.

He puts the kids to bed, comes up, and rubs my shoulders while I finish the dishes. It's been so long since he's touched me that the act of it makes me pause washing.

"Your shoulders are tight," he says with a soft voice I haven't heard in months.

"No shit," I answer without thinking, but I do not regret it. He's been a jerk to me, and I don't think I deserve it.

"I know things have been difficult and that we've had a hard time connecting," he says, kissing the side of my neck the way I like. "But I want to tell you that I see how much you are involved with school and making friends, and I am proud of you. I don't want to fight anymore. I miss you. I miss you so much." He wraps his arms around me tight, and I put the dishes down and grab his arms. He turns me around, and we hug tight.

"I miss you too," I say into his neck.

Matt takes his hand and slides it into my hair, leaning in to kiss me. The part of me wanting to stay angry gets smaller, and I forget why

I'm mad as his hands move across my body, knowing how to touch me and make me hot. And I let him, his hand traveling up my legs, teasing me briefly as he reaches with both hands to pull my pants down. I gasp because it's been a long time since we had any hot sex. He scoops me up onto the counter in one quick motion and starts kissing me again. I forget all about the tension, and it's Matt and me, better than ever.

Afterward, we cuddle up on the couch and have sex again. We lie naked, watching an old sitcom and sharing a pint of ice cream in front of the fire. The November chill makes it cold enough to use the fireplace for the first time, and it is dreamy sitting beside him with a roaring fire.

"This reminds me of our little apartment above the deli when I started teaching."

"Yeah, except the whole place would've fit into this room, plus we had mice in the walls."

Matt laughs. "They never came out of the walls."

"Doesn't matter. I'm still scarred for life."

"I was more talking about how close we were then. We did so much more talking and making each other a priority. We need to do that again. More date nights, or maybe a weekend away?"

Matt and I don't take weekends away from the kids because there has never been enough money or help with the kids. But now, maybe we could swing it. We have a lot more help here in Atwood.

"I would love a weekend away with you. I'm not sure of the logistics to make that happen, but I would love it," I admit.

Matt takes my hands and looks at me, saying, "I want us to go back to a simpler time. It felt so much easier when we'd just had Louisa. We had so much less craziness, and we connected so much better. I miss that, and I want to get back to it."

"You miss poverty and six hundred fifty square feet with mice in the walls?"

"I miss how much less complicated our life was then."

I didn't dare to tell him that we couldn't swing both of us in college, so my college career got sidelined for good, and he raced forward, front and center, into a PhD. Not that I'm bitter, most days. But I do wonder if it ever occurs to Matt that I have made huge sacrifices too.

For two hours, everything fades away except for us. With the kids, school, and all of life tucked away in the dark, I can almost forget how we are on opposite sides in the real world.

When I wake up, it's three a.m., and Matt is still asleep on the couch. For a moment, I forget about it all and feel safe. Then his inability to see what is happening with Charles comes flooding back.

No matter what we're dealing with, I think it's more than hot kitchen sex and gas station kombucha can fix.

I head up the stairs, too awake to sleep and too upset with Matt to curl back up with him. I climb into bed, wishing things could go back to the way they were between us.

Chapter Twenty-Seven

I'm mopping floors when Charles's teacher calls me to say something happened at school and that I need to get there. I panic before I even leave the house.

When I arrive at the school, I head straight to the first-grade hall and can hear yelling immediately.

"She's terrified and traumatized! As she should be. That is not something a child should see."

Charles is sitting on the benches outside the room, looking forlorn. Brianna, a little girl from his class sits on another bench down the hall, cringing at the yelling from inside the classroom.

I hear Ms. Keaton's calm, steady reply before I reach the room.

"Mr. Budde. Please, let's discuss this. No one *saw* anything. I understand some confusion, but I have a lesson plan with resources and guidance for helping the class understand gender. Kids understand quite easily. It's generally older people who have a harder time."

"Are you trying to call me stupid? Because I ain't stupid, and I know the difference between a boy and a girl. And if a girl is standing up peeing, she's got something perverse in her and needs to be out of this classroom and away from my child."

They notice me standing in the doorway, with Charles attached to my leg, his thumb in his mouth, both of us taking it all in.

"Are you shitting me? It's the principal's kid who's the freak? Oh, hell no. I ain't having it." Mr. Budde heads toward the door as we get out of his way. He takes Brianna by the hand as Ms. Keaton follows him, trying to finish the conversation.

"Mr. Budde, we are an inclusive school. Please take the time to read the bylaws before we meet again."

He storms out, dragging an unhappy Brianna, and as he walks by me, he hisses, "This ain't over by a long shot, lady. I won't have my girl growing up with freaks." His words and hate stun me. I've read the awful comments online about how trans kids are an abomination or worse. But to have someone up in my face with such hate is shocking.

Ms. Keaton comes almost running toward Charles and me.

"Mrs. Zander. I am so sorry. Brianna opened the bathroom door and saw only the back of Charles but could tell he was standing and urinating. She yelled about it and gathered half the class before I could get there. I feel awful. And what he said to you . . . We won't allow it. We are an inclusive school, and we love Charles. I promise we will fix this, and things will be fine."

I'm shaking, but I nod, trying to believe her. We both look down at Charles, deflated like a balloon, with all the air released from him.

"Will he be fine?" I ask quietly, knowing she doesn't have the answer. We head to his coat hook to get his backpack.

"Come on, my sweets. Let's head home." Charles takes my hand, not even waving to his beloved Ms. Keaton on the way out.

❧

"Charles, I need to understand why the dress is so important to you," Matt asks when he gets home. He's zeroed in on Charles like a target. I've never seen him so worked up.

"I'm wrong no matter what," Charles says, looking at Matt. "Either my brain is wrong, or my body is wrong." His voice is almost monotone, all cried out.

Matt sighs. He clearly still hasn't read a damn thing about gender. "Charles, boys pee standing up and don't wear dresses. Girls wear dresses and pee sitting down. That's why this whole thing happened. It's simple."

Charles looks at him, silent.

"Buddy, Daddy needs to know exactly what happened," Matt says, trying to force more info out of Charles with a harsh edge to his voice.

"I already said. I was going potty, and Ms. Keaton said we are always supposed to knock on the door before we go into a bathroom. But Brianna didn't knock! And she started screaming that I was peeing standing up in a dress, and then everyone was there, watching me pee." Charles starts to cry again. This time, he curls up into a ball. I reach out and rub his back.

"I know you told us. It's okay. Daddy just wanted to hear what happened." I give Matt a sideways glare in hopes he will change his tone, but he isn't paying attention to me.

"And then Brianna's dad was there, yelling at me and calling me names. And Ms. Keaton was yelling at him, and it was a bad, awful day."

Charles stops talking and sits there, silent.

"I am so sorry that happened to you, sweetie. You didn't deserve it," I say, petting his head. He tries to put his thumb in his mouth, but Matt stops him. He takes Charles's arm and holds it away. Charles looks up at him with big, tear-filled eyes.

"What do you think we can do so this won't happen again?" Matt asks as if he's a teacher doling out punishment.

"Brianna can learn to knock," Charles says, sounding defeated, and I can't help but let out a small laugh.

Matt shakes his head as if he's annoyed. "I also think not wearing a dress would help. You are confusing people, Charles. And you don't want to upset people, do you? It makes it very hard to make friends."

Charles rolls toward me and pops his thumb in his mouth before Matt can stop him.

"I think we've talked enough," I interject. "This isn't solving the problem, and Charles has had a rough day. Can we put a pin in this, please?"

Matt runs his hands through his hair. He looks at Charles and me for a long time, contemplating something.

"Fine," Matt says as he gets off the bed and heads toward the door. "But this kind of scandal is bad for a school, and it's terrible for a new headmaster. This situation could literally make me lose this job, and I won't have it." He stares me down.

"You won't have it?" I ask because his tone and his words are so out of character.

"No, Jane," he says, dead serious. "I won't." He turns the corner and heads down the hall before I can say anything.

Ms. Keaton asked us to come in for a meeting at school a few days later. I know there have been internal meetings at school about what happened, and Matt has decided it isn't appropriate for him to fill me in on what other kids do any more than he should to another parent. He shut me out of the school's side of things, other than our meeting with Charles's teacher. When we arrive, she doesn't mince words.

"First of all, I apologize for what occurred under my watch. I can't go back and change it, and I feel everything was blown way out of proportion, but you have my apologies for the pain this has caused." Matt looks smug, as if he won something. I've watched my child refuse to go to school and wither away since, so I know that no one won here.

"I think the situation escalated because of Mr. Budde's loud presence. If I'd had the time to de-escalate the situation and read one of the books I keep on hand, the kids would've walked off more informed and no worse for the wear. But Brianna happened to be leaving early for a dentist appointment, and her dad came into the room to collect her. She informed him of what she saw, and sadly, Mr. Budde saw red. He felt threatened and afraid, creating a huge scene in front of the class that I could not keep in check. Many factors led up to a breakdown of what should've been a more controlled environment." She looks up at

Matt, and I notice that she's nervous, as if Matt is sitting here as the headmaster and not as a parent.

"I hope that as I work with the school in the coming days and weeks, we will alleviate any more problems." Now she almost sounds scripted. Did Matt say something to her? I want to ask but don't even know how.

I chime in because Lord knows Matt won't.

"From all I know of this school, it doesn't cater to discrimination and haters. And I think it's clear our child demonstrates some gender fluidity." I look at Matt as I say this, but he is looking down at his hands. "But my worry now is not so much what the Mr. Buddes of the world think but about Charles. I'm worried about his emotional and mental state. He is deflated, to say the least."

Ms. Keaton nods at me before she answers. "I agree with you. Our focus needs to be on giving Charles all he needs to figure out who he is. I see some gender fluidity too, and I applaud you for supporting Charles with his own choices in clothes and hair. Please know I'm here to help you in any way I can to help Charles. The school counselor is also a great resource, and she can direct you to a clinic at Children's Hospital, although the wait can be quite long, I've heard."

I feel validated by her words, but Matt is silent with me these days because I don't say what he wants to hear. I can tell he is done with this meeting and wants to cut his losses and get out of there.

"Ms. Keaton, you've given us a lot to think about. Thank you for your time," Matt states before he starts rushing me out the door without talking about solutions. I'm tempted to stay behind, but he shakes her hand and leads me out the door as if we have somewhere to be.

I stop in the hallway and say, "Matt. Stop. Talk to me. Did you hear everything she said? Why did you run out of there like that?"

He waves me off. "Keaton is a quack. She came from freaking Berkeley, for God's sake. Of course, she's all 'gender isn't real, and flowers make you happy.'" He waves his hand in the air around his head. "She deals in first grade, not real life."

"No, Matt. She's saying our child is displaying gender-creative behavior, and we need to do something about it because ignoring it hurts Charles. Now you have two people telling you the same thing."

"And the doctor told us that Charles is fine. Considering your sources, I'm sticking with the doctor's expertise."

He's already heading out of the school and toward the van. I'm so mad as we leave the school that I almost yell at him.

"You keep calling it expertise. Do you know what I call it? Blatant ignorance," I say, then wave him off. I choose to walk home.

Chapter Twenty-Eight

"Jane, I've been thinking," Matt says as he enters our room, where I'm folding laundry.

"Oh boy," I say, half joking and half not.

"I'm sorry for how I acted about that scene at school. I'm just upset. And I'm stuck between a rock and a hard place here as a parent and the head of the school. I hope you understand how I must look out for the well-being of everyone."

I scowl at him. "What are you trying to say?"

He steps back like he's deciding something, and I get worried.

"Spit it out, Matt."

"I think you were right. It wouldn't hurt to schedule an appointment for Charles at that clinic. Maybe by the time he gets an appointment, there's a good chance it'll be unnecessary. But it won't hurt to talk to them."

I stand looking at him in disbelief.

"What made you change your mind?" I ask as I cross my arms. I'm not sure I trust him.

"Just all this stuff with school and how that is causing such a big scandal. I think it will be good to talk to some experts."

I take the win, but it almost feels too easy. It's like something else is going to come along to derail it.

❧

Libby and I are hanging out at my house the following day. The little ones play at our feet while we sort through catalogs for the summer carnival.

"So, what's up with Matt? How's it going with him after the meeting at school?"

I shrug. "Matt must've known what a jerk he's been because he even agreed to let me make an appointment with the clinic at Children's Hospital."

"Well, that's great news, right? You've wanted to get in there since we met. Why did he change his mind?" she asks.

"Maybe he felt bad for being such a jerk at the meeting at school? Maybe he's coming around and going to take this seriously. I don't know, but I'm glad."

I look at Libby, who doesn't seem convinced.

"At least it's a step in the right direction. I got the pediatrician to call in a referral, so I will call the clinic today. I'm glad we will get some real answers. It's a huge win, but I'm leery of Matt."

"Maybe he's acting like this because you're not giving in," Libby suggests.

I shrug.

"I don't want to say the wrong thing because I'm always a little too honest for people," Libby says, studying me.

"Well, go ahead and be honest. I never say enough, so I could use the inspiration."

Libby nods and sits up a little. "You told me that you always gave Matt what he wanted. And now you're taking a stand, and he doesn't know how to handle it. And he suddenly seems very invested in what everyone thinks. He thinks you're trying to ruin his chances here."

I think about it and nod.

"I always felt I should follow his lead because he does have so much education. But he's seriously wrong about this. Ignoring what's going on with Charles or trying to drill it out of him comes with some scary statistics. All I want is Charles safe, and the best way to keep him safe is to support him and get him the help we all need."

"Maybe the clinic can give you all some answers, and hopefully, Matt will listen."

It's what I'm pinning my hopes on. But when I call the clinic after Libby leaves, the receptionist tells me she will have an appointment for us in October, which is ten months away. I take the appointment, but I can't help but feel a sense of dread thinking of almost a year with no answers or help. I hope we have the time to wait.

Chapter Twenty-Nine

Libby calls me a few days later while I'm babysitting Mila.

"Jane, did you see the email from the school?"

"No, I've been putting babies down to nap." I smile. I enjoy watching her baby and talking to Libby during her check-ins.

"You may want to sit down for this," she says, and I can tell from her voice that something is wrong.

"What is it?" I ask, feeling my skin grow cold in fear.

"Ugh. Here, I'll read it to you."

I hear her put me on speaker, and she starts to read:

"The Atwood Preparatory School is holding an informal, impromptu meeting this evening at seven p.m. to discuss a situation regarding bathroom use. Of course, student safety is always our first priority.

"The school board will use this opportunity to revisit our bylaws and discuss the possibility of a gendered dress code or uniforms. Any parent wanting to discuss these topics and how these rules can help create a safer school is encouraged to speak out tonight."

I ask Libby who signed it, and she tells me it merely says *Atwood Prep Staff.*

"I have no sitter, so I can't even go," I say.

"Oh, hell no. You have to go! Those bitches want a witch hunt. You have to be there to protect your child. What if Matt . . ." Libby trails off.

"Despite all the fighting, Matt will have Charles's back. I mean, he *is* his father."

Libby stays silent, and I can tell she disagrees. But I'm pinning my hopes on all the good years, which make me sure Matt will stand up for our child when push comes to shove.

As soon as I get off the phone with Libby, I call Matt.

"It's a shit show around here, Jane. I am about to head into a meeting. We can talk later, okay?" And the phone goes dead.

Great. He couldn't even take five minutes to talk to me about this.

I receive numerous messages on my social media from friends at the school telling me they are here to help if needed. A couple say they will be at the meeting to support us. The support is fantastic, but my stomach is churning about what Libby said and Matt not talking to me. I can't shake the feeling that everything will come crashing down.

Mrs. Driscoll agrees to watch my kids so I can attend the meeting. Libby parks at my house, and we walk over together. Libby has Mila bundled in her arms, and we crunch through the December snow toward Atwood Prep in silence. I'm too nervous to talk.

Many cars are parked in the lot and along the drop-off point, more than I've seen since the carnival. All I want to do is go home. I pick my cuticles until one starts to bleed and then shove my hand into my pocket.

The meeting is in the library, where the school board meetings are held. The space is packed with an impromptu crowd, making it feel rowdy and buzzed with feelings. As soon as we walk in, the room hushes into whispers. Libby keeps walking, dragging me along with her by the arm to a spot where we can stand near the periodicals.

Matt is standing beside one of the tables in the middle of the room with a politician's smile. He's leaning against a desk, talking to a board member like it's just any other day. He looks so confident and casual. His smile is unnerving, and he won't even look at me. He only gave me a very mollifying three-minute phone call, saying, "Everything is fine,

Jane. You're blowing this out of proportion. It's a meeting about bathrooms and clothing—no big deal. If you can't get a sitter, stay home. I'll fill you in."

Brianna's parents come in: her rotund father, with his tall, solid frame, carrying a folder of papers, and his wife following along behind him, looking pissed, or maybe that's just her face. They sit at the table where Matt is standing as if they have been given this prime location while the rest of us gather in the wings and fill the space.

"Ladies and gentlemen, can I have your attention?" Matt says in his best teacher voice to quiet the room.

"I've met most of you, but for those I haven't, I am Matt Zander, the new headmaster at Atwood Prep. It was brought to my attention that we had a situation involving an incident in the bathroom. Due to privacy, we won't be using names." A hush of whispers crosses the room, but it settles when Matt surveys the crowd.

"We are not here for blame but to find the best way forward for all of our kids. I will give the floor to Mrs. Karen Swenson, our school board president."

Matt hands the mic over, and I feel a little calmer. At least we aren't using names.

"So far, so good, right?" I ask Libby. She raises both shoulders in ambiguity.

Mrs. Swenson begins, "I appreciate you all coming out here on this cold night because you care about your children. I know we all want them to be safe at school. That has to be our number-one priority. I will pass the microphone to a concerned parent to address why we are here this evening."

She hands the mic off to Brianna's dad with a kind smile, as if they are old friends. He stands up, shaking her hand warmly. I feel a new cold wash of panic run over me. Are they seriously giving him the mic?

Mr. Budde moves into the middle of the room with the microphone so all eyes are on him. I slink back farther into the periodicals. I am very sure this is not going to go well.

"I'm Erv Budde. I've owned Budde Towing since my dad passed. You all know me. I pay my taxes and do right by my family and this community. When you are stuck on the side of the road, I'm the one you call, and I show up."

There are nods across the room. Clearly, Erv Budde is well known in town.

"But when I send my littlest child, Brianna, to this school, I expect her to be safe here. Safe from pedophiles and other kinds of sexual predators." The room rumbles at his words. I press my fingers to my forehead, wishing I could disappear.

"I came into school last week, and my daughter told me she saw a little boy dressed as a girl peeing in the bathroom. Now, that ain't something anyone should have to see, especially a small girl. She is traumatized, and unless we can find a way to settle this where I feel safe, I will file a lawsuit against the Atwood Prep School for damages to my child to the tune of two million dollars."

The room erupts in angry voices and the occasional shout. Matt starts waving his hands, trying to get everyone's attention, and waits until the room quiets.

"No one is suing anyone, Mr. Budde. We are here to talk this out. We have a special school in many parts because of our ability to work together. So let's talk about this. What changes would you"—Matt motions to Erv, then at the rest of the room—"or any of you like to see at the school? Because safety is our number-one priority too, but so is the happiness of our kids and their parents."

"There ain't no reason for my girl to see a boy pee. They belong in separate bathrooms." When he says this, some parents begin to clap.

"They *belong* in *their own* bathrooms," he adds, and more applause comes. "That little freak"—the room collectively gasps at the word; the applause stops, but Matt says nothing, so Mr. Budde continues—"should not be allowed in bathrooms with my daughter."

Ms. Keaton chimes in, yelling to be heard. All eyes and ears settle on her.

"This situation is presented as if a child was in the 'wrong' bathroom. The incident in question happened in the gender-neutral bathrooms, with one child accidentally walking in on another child without the courtesy of a knock. This is not a rampant problem in the school. This is a one-time *accident*."

"And you can tell me for sure my girl ain't going to walk up and find a boy in a dress peeing in the girls' bathroom? Can you guarantee that? Because that's what I want, and I will take it to court if we can't all see eye to eye here. I ain't allowing my child in bathrooms with perverts."

I am shaking and feeling sick. He keeps calling my child a pervert. And Matt said we're not naming names, so how am I supposed to defend my child? Libby nudges me and leans in to whisper, "Jane, you have to say something."

I look at her and shrug. What could I say to de-escalate this? It isn't a quality I possess even when I'm not in complete panic mode. I look at her and shrug, and she nods at me and squeezes my hand as she stands, raises her hand, and starts yelling, "Excuse me!" It doesn't take long for her to get attention. The murmurs and whispers about her remain as they give her the floor.

"What exactly is being proposed here tonight? Because we should be aware that we are treading a morally reprehensible line here."

"Look who's talking," someone yells as quiet laughter trails around the room. I look at poor Libby, trying to defend Charles and me, only to end up the butt of their jokes.

Rebecca Darling rings a bell she has on the table, and the laughter and talking turn to murmurs.

"I'm with Libby. We are not thinking of the whole picture. Not all kids fit into society's gender roles of boy or girl. Gender is a spectrum, and there is science to back that up."

Erv seems happy to cut Rebecca off. "Yeah, let's cut to the chase. I got a ball game to watch at home. Here's what I want. Boys' bathrooms and girls' bathrooms, like normal. Same as everywhere else in America. None of this shared-bathroom shit. And uniforms so we can all tell who is a boy and who is a girl. My poor girl is traumatized because she doesn't even know what that kid is."

"Erv, what you're suggesting is anti-trans and anti-anyone with any gender diversity. We have always promoted an inclusive stance as a school," Libby says.

Charles's teacher, Ms. Keaton, joins the conversation again. "And aggressive gendering of bathrooms and children is going to cause harm to children. This is a *fact*. The problem isn't your daughter's confusion. The problem is that I wasn't allowed to de-escalate the situation immediately, and you have refused to explain it to her simply so she can understand."

"Wait—now *I'm* being blamed? Me and my innocent girl, when it's the *headmaster's son* who wears a dress and pees standing up in a dress, traumatizing little girls." Gasps echo throughout the room as everyone realizes it's Charles they are talking about. I look at Matt, who has lost his confident air. He looks like he got punched in the gut.

Mr. Budde goes on. "This is another liberal takeover of traditional values, with my impressionable daughter having to see 'sexual variance' at her age. And I ain't going to stand for it. Girls and boys should be separated in bathrooms!" He raises the microphone and half the room cheers for him. I feel sick, so I lean down and put my head between my knees. This is my actual worst nightmare. Libby rubs my back for a moment, which affirms this is bad because Libby isn't super touchy.

The room erupts in voices, both talking and yelling, a hiss of whispers. I contemplate walking out. What good am I doing here?

Matt whistles and quiets the room, except for a roll of murmurs.

"We've gone off track here. Let's return the mic to the board to discuss adjustments to accommodate everyone's needs." His voice makes me know he's siding with Mr. Budde. He isn't going to take a stand, even for our child.

"Thank you, Headmaster Zander. This has been quite the trial for your first year, and we see you," Swenson says as she claps her hands together to get the rest of the room to clap for him.

"Why are they clapping for him? Like, poor guy?" I say to Libby. She looks at me and nods. We both know this is going to be bad.

"Based on the situation and the evolving state of our world, the board is recommending Atwood Preparatory School will now *only* have separate bathrooms for girls or boys. Gender-neutral bathrooms will not be allowed. Anyone seen using a bathroom not matching their gender will be at risk for suspension or expulsion."

The room stays quiet, and I feel like all the air has been pulled out of me. I am shaking my head, thinking of Charles. The board president doesn't even understand the difference between gender and sex at birth but is still in charge of this decision.

"We also think, in the interest of conformity and understanding, it will be best to switch to a uniform dress code of skirts and polos for girls, with khakis and polos for boys. This school has had a long-standing practice of uniforms over the years, and we feel the time is right to return to those traditional values. An email link will be sent to you this week to purchase the uniforms, and we will switch to mandatory uniforms as soon as we return from Christmas break."

This creates a whole new slew of complaints and mutterings.

Libby stands up again and starts yelling over the noise.

"Again," she says once she has everyone's attention, "don't you think these laws are anti-transgender? Don't you worry about those types of lawsuits? I sure would."

Even in my panic mode, I'm in awe of Libby. Here she is, the rumor mill incarnated, yet she put herself in the hot seat to defend my child. I swallow back the lump in my throat.

Mrs. Swenson answers with a broad, fake smile. "We don't have transgender kids, so your concern isn't a problem."

"Matt?" Libby asks. "Are you absolutely sure this would hurt not a single kid in this school?"

But Matt stays silent. And so do I. Libby looks at me.

I whisper, "I don't have proof of anything. It's my word against the whole school." I say it in a shaky voice. She looks at me and nods.

The school board votes, and Rebecca Darling is the sole no vote, so they approve the new "gender bylaws" for the school, effective after Christmas break.

"Please order your uniforms now, ladies and gentlemen. On day one of the new policy, we will post photos of the kids looking sharp in their new duds on our school social media pages," Matt says, his voice all cheery like he's giving away bikes. I stand up and walk out amid the rumors, with Libby following me.

"Are you okay, Jane? You've barely said a word, and you went silent in there. It took everything I had not to scream, and you were so quiet." Libby's voice is soft and without judgment. She takes my hand as she says it and holds it in hers, reminding me of how I take my kids' hands when they are overwrought.

"I have panic attacks," I whisper. I'm still shaking hard. "It's . . . I can't talk. Or move. Every time it has mattered for me to use my voice, I choke."

Libby squeezes my hand. "It's okay. They were determined not to listen to anyone, for what it's worth. Let's stop power walking and take a few deep breaths."

Libby still has my hand, wrapped in mittens to combat the December cold front that has moved in. After a few minutes, I feel myself calming down.

"All Matt said to me before the meeting was that this was a good thing because it would mean some rules in place to help avoid 'upsetting' scenes in the future. How can I ever trust him again? He thinks he can 'fix' Charles. This whole thing might ruin my marriage. And I'm pretty sure I'm right about listening to Charles, but what if I'm not?"

"Jane. You know your child. You know Charles is different, and you're trying your hardest to help him. That's all you can do."

"As you can see, I'm pretty powerless. I'm not brave like you are. You were amazing. I go blank when it counts."

Libby stares me down, so I go on.

"And honestly, am I going to change their minds?"

"Maybe. Maybe you would. But you can only do your best from right here. It's okay."

"No," I say to her, thinking about Charles and how he will react to these new rules. "I don't think it's okay at all."

She slings an arm around me as we walk the last half block home.

Chapter Thirty

After the meeting, I come home and relieve Mrs. Driscoll, who has gotten all three kids to bed and asleep, bless her soul. Matt texts me that he's going out for a few beers with Jason. I don't even text him back because I'm too hurt to say anything nice.

His silence. His refusal to do anything at the meeting. I replay it repeatedly in my head—all the things I could've said and didn't.

I'm pacing the house feeling sick, when Matt comes in the door just after eleven. He probably hoped I'd be asleep by now, but sleep doesn't feel possible again. I'm too keyed up.

Matt doesn't drink much either, but he's clearly past his limit. He's not trashed, but he's tipsy. I watch him wrestle with his tie.

When he notices me, he reaches his hands out and says "Jane," as if he hasn't seen me in years and I'm his favorite person. How long has it been since he's talked to me like I am his favorite person? I don't move.

He frowns and shuffles over to me, reaching out to hug me. "Don't be mad. It's okay. It's going to be okay now. No more problems." He waves his hands in the air, and I scowl at him.

"Even drunk, you're delusional about our child. I'm going to bed. You can sleep down here."

"Don't you miss me? Don't you miss us?" The tone of his voice stops me from leaving the room because I do miss him. "Jane. Let's talk. Let's talk and fix it."

He sits on the love seat and pats the seat beside him. He's drunk enough to believe it's so simple.

"Okay, call the board and tell them you were wrong. Tell them the new rules are anti-trans, and you have a gender-fluid child." I say all this and watch his face change.

"No!" he half yells as he stands up. "This *is* what's best for Charles. Everyone says so, and they agree with me." He points to himself as he glares at me. "Charles needs to learn his place. We let him play at this shit too long, and he is too confused, so I had to step in."

"Step in? Wait, what? You mean, you made this happen?"

He looks at me, blinking, realizing he's been caught. He wobbles and takes a step backward, then sits on the edge of the couch, running his hands through his hair.

"So, you weren't innocently going along with things at the meeting. You were a coconspirator." I shake my head at him. "Is this why you agreed to make the appointment at the gender clinic? Because you knew this was coming. Because you helped create what happened tonight."

"Hey, I'm trying to make it fair here. You give, I give. For the sake of the school, I made the best decision for bathrooms and clothing. But you insist the infamous Midwest Pediatric Transgender Clinic must see Charles, so I'm hoping that appointment can put all this foolishness and ridiculous fighting to an end. This is me compromising."

"I don't think you know what 'compromise' means. I don't even know who you are anymore."

Matt stands up fast. "Same. What happened to the woman who had my back no matter what? It was us, just you and me. And we made it work together. Where is that?"

"You left her at the school board meeting along with your promise that we are your priority," I say, and I walk up the stairs to bed. There is no reason to fight with Matt, drunk or sober.

"How do you expect me to choose between my kid and my job? I can't choose. It shouldn't be my decision, so I left it to the board, and *they decided.* You don't get to be mad at me," he yells at me as I leave the room. I stop and turn to him.

"By allowing this, you already chose your job over your kid. And you left your wife out here on her own to deal with this."

I bring the baby monitor to hear the kids and head to the attic. The idea of pretending to be civil is sickening to me right now. I need space, and I need to feel safe, and Libby makes me feel safe. The attic makes me feel safe. Because, most upsetting, my husband no longer makes me feel this way.

I pull out my phone and text Libby. You up?

I'm guessing you still being up means it didn't go well with Matt? she asks.

You know me well, I type with a smile. And Matt sucks right now.

Chapter Thirty-One

Matt's family showed up one week after "the meeting from hell," as I call it. Matt invited them to celebrate the week of Christmas and New Year's with us. We rearranged rooms so everyone had a place to sleep, and I got booted back to bed with Matt. It bothers me to sleep beside him and have his sister in my attic. It's become my favorite space in the house.

Matt's parents and sister are nice, but I've only spent short vacations with them half a dozen times or so. They enjoy their life in Florida, and Matt's mom hates to travel. We haven't had the money to visit them in recent years. Still, Matt insisted that we all have a merry Wisconsin Christmas together in Atwood since we are back, and his family obliged.

Matt's sister, Andrea, confronts me about Charles the very first day they arrive.

"Matt says you two are on the outs about what Charles wears?"

I purse my lips, thinking of how to answer. "We do not see eye to eye on this."

"Huh," she says. "It's strange, right? You two always seemed to agree on everything. You were two peas in a pod."

"It was more how I gave in to whatever he wanted, which kept things all friendly and warm," I say, watching the shock cross her face. "But this is too important to stay quiet. If you'll excuse me, I need to go check on dinner."

I feel her staring at me as I walk away.

I don't know how to fake being nice to Matt for a week. He has apparently had numerous heart-to-heart chats with his family about Charles and how "out of hand" the whole situation has gotten because of me. Matt doesn't talk much with his parents and wouldn't have spoken to them about me before we got here, but things are different now.

I've never been anything but sweet and compliant around Matt's family. It never mattered. They have never made any real special effort to get to know me. They keep in touch with Matt via text and social media occasionally. I always hoped they could become my family, but like my mom choosing Mickey, Matt's family chose his sister. The truth is that none of us are very close. It feels even more insulting that Matt would talk to them about me.

With his family there, Matt is being so ridiculously sweet to me. I cannot get myself to fake it back. I appear to be the asshole, and Matt looks like he's the one trying. Good times.

I'm trying to keep my distance from all of it. I wish I'd taken the attic room with Henrietta and let them all have the second floor.

Matt insisted that we wait to decorate our tree together with his family. Shortly after they arrive, Matt and his dad pick out a Christmas tree at a farm on the edge of town. They return with a giant Douglas fir that will take up the whole living room corner.

"We went out to Jenning's Farm every year when we lived here," Matt's dad, Fred, informs me as they are stringing the lights. I'm opening bins of ornaments, and the kids are helping me while stealing cookies and fudge from the plates I set out. There is Christmas music and a fire in the fireplace. It feels perfect, even with so much wrong just under the surface.

"You sure do have a pretty life here, little bro," Andrea says to Matt. The two are civil, but there is always a hint of condescension between them, bordering on busting into an argument.

Matt looks at her cautiously and answers, "Yes, I do. I worked hard to get here. It feels . . . poetic and meant to be that it's in Atwood." He smiles at his mom as he says it.

I watch them, realizing Matt had a life here of Christmas tree farms and sibling rivalry, which I know very little about.

"I mean, you always wanted to be the cool kid. You practically disowned us all for not being good enough when we lived here. And now here you are, in the big, fancy Wellington house with a big, impressive job. Good for you." Andrea raises a glass of eggnog that I can only assume is spiked. She's usually more resting bitch face and silent with the occasional two-word insult.

"Now, Andrea . . ." Matt's mom, Barbara, starts as if she's trying to settle an agreement over a toy, but Matt ignores her and turns his attention back to his sister.

"Uh, thanks?" he says, glaring at her.

"What? It's true. You'd have sold your soul to be popular in school. And now you have another chance, if no one blows it." Andrea looks at me at the last part, but Matt still focuses on what she said about him.

"Seriously, Andrea, what's wrong with wanting to be popular? To have more money. To be better?" He turns to his dad, a proud factory worker of thirty-eight years. "I know you did the best you could, and you raised us well. But I want more for my kids and my family. I want them to have the best schools, so the sky is their limit."

"If you ask me, you're doing just fine, Matt. You've made me proud with how you carry the Zander name," Fred chimes in, and Matt visibly swells with pride. "And your kids will follow suit, especially if you take Charles over your knee a few times about all that sissy girl stuff," Fred adds, and I nearly panic at the mere suggestion of spanking Charles.

"We don't spank our kids," I say, but Matt's family looks at me like I've grown an extra head. Matt stays silent and doesn't meet my eyes, despite our promise to each other that we will never spank our children.

"Nothing wrong with a few swats on the behind to keep a kid in line, Jane. Heck, Matt had his share, and look how he turned out. Remember that time you and your friends dyed the holy water at church, and everyone ended up with blue foreheads? I had to buy Susie McNamara a new silk blouse because hers got three blue dots on it when she did the sign of the cross." Matt's dad's laugh booms across the room. "It's funny now, but you needed to learn your place and how to obey. I spanked you because I loved you and needed to raise you right. And look how well it worked! You've got a PhD and you're running a school now, Matt. We did right by you."

Matt shuffles uncomfortably. "I don't really think getting spanked made me into the man I am. I worked hard for many years to get here, in school and jobs. I made this life for us. We did, me and Jane. It's all finally paying off," Matt says, and I breathe a sigh of relief that he spoke out against spanking but also for giving me credit in the life we have.

"And that's why we encouraged you to chase your dreams, Matt. Andrea needed us in Florida when her husband died, and you are busy building your life and career. We love to see you, but we know you're busy. It's okay. You want more." Matt's mom is sweet, like she's licking old wounds. The kids come back into the room with a fresh plate of cookies, and the conversation is dropped, leaving me thinking about all that was said and all I am learning about Matt and his family.

I stay home with the kids so Matt, his sister, and his parents can attend Midnight Mass, making Matt suggest that our family attend church—for the first time ever—after his mother says it could help his standing in the community. It almost feels like some alternate-reality version of Matt was dropped here in Atwood.

By the last couple of days of their visit, we've all found a rhythm, and it turns out not to be such an awful week. The kids love playing with their grandparents and cousins, Matt has bonding time with his sister, and everyone has a pleasant holiday.

On the second-to-last day, Matt's mom enters the kitchen, where I am making gluten-free bread. I've been finding distractions all week to keep away from them as much as possible. Since there are so many people in the house, it's easy to use the job of cooking to stay holed up in the kitchen.

Barbara stands and watches me for a minute until I turn to look at her.

"Can I get you something, Barbara? A glass of water? Or coffee?"

"I'd take a coffee. Thank you," she says, sitting at the kitchen island to be near me. I fear the worst because it's been a rough couple of weeks.

"I wanted to tell you I see what you mean about Charles. Umm, I don't remember what Matt called it. But I see that Charles is different." She seems nervous, and I look at her with wide eyes because I'm afraid of scaring her away.

"I talked to him, Jane. I said, 'Charles, what is this business with you thinking you are a girl?' And he said, 'No, Grandma. I *am* a girl.'" She looks shocked, but I'm not because I've been listening for a long time. "He truly believes that, Jane."

I nod at her, trying not to cry. She is the first person in our family to talk to me about Charles like this. She pats my hand gently.

"But you know what else I see?"

I shake my head at her.

"I see how hard and scary this world will be for a child who is so different." I look at her, wishing she could be the ally I need. But then she says, "Matt wants to do all he can so Charles can have a normal life. He doesn't want him marked forever. Why not show him how to be a boy? And then, if it doesn't work, you can see doctors and therapists. But I think if you show him how to be a boy, he will pick it up, and all this princess business will be the same as how Matt used to be so obsessed with outer space."

"Matt still collects space stuff. He just bought fifty dollars' worth of planet stickers for his work laptop," I tell her, not trying to be combative, but it's true. I don't think they are taking in the whole picture. His mother sighs as if I'm not behaving.

"Please, Jane. You are his mother. Help him learn to fit in."

I shake my head at her.

"Trying to fit in has been my life's work," I say. "I wish I could tell you I had the formula. For Charles or me."

"No one expects perfection, Jane. But for a long time, you and Matt agreed to let Charles try out whatever clothes he wanted. It makes sense to take some time to have him wear what he needs to and be a boy in the same way as all the others, and I think he will figure it out. And if he doesn't, Matt will get him the help he needs."

"Did he say he would get him help?" I ask, and she cocks her head at me.

"Eh. Not in so many words. But you and I both know how influential moms can be in all ways."

I can't help but be happy she is trying to be my friend. She has never had much interest in me over the years. I can't decide if she's trying to turn a corner or if she's trying to help Matt, but her admission of seeing that Charles is different hit home enough to warm me to her.

I decide to choose peace in the spirit of the new year.

Chapter Thirty-Two

I'm still mad at Matt, but I need to keep up appearances for the kids until we figure all this out. For harmony's sake, I will try things Matt's way. In truth, based on the new rules at school, we don't have much choice.

"I ordered uniforms for the kids," Matt tells me as I fold laundry. "Three skirts, five polos for Louisa with two cardigans, and three khaki pants and five polos for Charles. I wasn't sure if you saw the school emails with so much going on, so I made it happen." I nod, thinking he wants me to thank him as if he's being so helpful. I'd appreciate his effort if it wouldn't traumatize my child so much.

All I can muster is to mutter, "Great."

Matt comes over to me and takes my hands. I'm having a hard time even looking at him.

"Jane, please. Let's find some way to come back together."

I frown and look up at him. "I don't know how to compromise here, and you aren't willing anyway. You wanted it this way and forced every hand to make it so. I have no power here, and you ensured I have no say. We aren't friends right now. But I will do my best to fake it for the kids because that seems to be the life you want now. We all fake who we are to keep up with ever-increasing appearances and avoid gossip."

"Jane. That isn't true," he almost yells, and I can't believe he can't see it.

"Are you serious? All you've cared about is appearances since we got here."

"Of course I do. We finally made it. A well-paying job with perks like this house. A school full of people I know who now like and respect me. A safe place to raise our kids. Of course I will do all I can to keep this life I've created."

"The problem is this isn't just about you. Who is getting the shaft here? Me and our marriage, but it's mostly Charles. It will be so hard to tell him about the uniforms and bathrooms . . ." I admit.

"Then let me talk to him. I don't think this is the big deal you are making it out to be. He's a boy, so he'll use the boys' bathroom and wear his uniform. He probably won't even notice, much less care."

I can't decide if he's delusional and out of touch or if he believes his own bullshit.

"I think you're wrong" is all I say.

"It seems like you're trying to—" Matt stops and pauses and runs a hand over his hair, trying to compose himself.

I stare him down until he finishes.

"Sometimes I think you are trying to sabotage this. You've never felt like you fit in, and this place"—he pauses again, looking right at me—"is threatening to you. Maybe you wanted it to be only us?"

I shake my head as I scowl at him, out of shock as much as hurt, and fight the tears in my voice as I attempt to talk. "I am trying here. You don't see me trying? I have a pretty nice life here, minus the fighting with you. The teachers and school are nice. I have friends. I'm involved with the school because you asked. But you accuse me of trying to sabotage us for worrying how Charles will handle this?"

"I will tell Charles, and his teacher will explain it too. All the kids will adjust to new rules, which will be no big deal. This school used to be this way when I went here, when it was St. Ignatius. Uniforms were mandatory then too, so this is nothing new. I need you to be on board and put him in the uniforms every morning." His tone changes, as if he is talking to a child. I glare at him momentarily, considering fighting, but choose peace.

I return to folding laundry but give him a thumbs-up in agreement. "I got it, Matt. No worries."

❧

On the first day of school after Christmas break, Louisa and Charles come down dressed in their new uniforms. Matt stays home long enough to take the kids to school, and I would've thought it sweet, except he only did it to ensure Charles got there in uniform. I know he talked to Charles, who has been quiet and reserved since.

Charles comes home from school the same way, and I can tell even as they climb into the van that the mood is sour. Louisa gives me a look to verify it, so I pick my words carefully before I say them.

"Hello, my loves. I missed you all today. Are we ready to go home, have snacks, and tell me about your day?"

"Sure, Mom," Louisa says, attempting to sound enthusiastic. I have to give the kids points for trying.

"How about you, Charles?"

He shrugs and answers, "It was fine." He buckles into his seat, staring out the window through his long, curly locks.

I made carrot cake cookies for a treat and spaghetti for dinner, which is everyone's favorite. I'm trying so hard to stop fighting things I can't control and do my best with what I can change. Maybe I can make Charles's homelife and friend life outside of school so accepting that it won't matter what happens in school. There must be some way to support him still.

When we get home, I ask the kids to change out of their uniforms, telling them that they can wear what they want. Louisa comes down and turns on a show to watch, but Charles doesn't come down. After a while, I look for him and find him on his bed with a pile of clothes.

"What's up, friend?" I ask him, and he doesn't even look up.

“Nothing” is all he says.

“What’s with all the clothes?” I ask, pulling out his new favorite princess shirt I bought for him for Christmas. I try to hand it to him, but he turns away and cries.

I hug him, not saying anything for a long time.

“I know you’ve had a crappy day. I wish I could fix what you have to wear at school. I wish I could. But I can make sure you are always allowed to wear what you want and be who you are here with me.”

Charles looks up at me with big, sad eyes. “But Dad said no. He said no more girl clothes until I get used to it. He told me to make the pile for him to throw them away.” Charles starts to cry again. “He keeps saying I’m only a boy . . .” I hug him back into me.

“I can talk to Daddy,” I say, but Charles shakes his head and breaks free from the hug.

“No. He’s already mad at me for messing it all up. I’m grounded from watching cooking shows on my tablet because I got upset about my clothes.”

I sigh. Matt certainly never told this to me.

“I don’t know how to fix this, Charles, but I will try. And I’m always here. Okay?”

I don’t know what to say or how to bring his joy back.

Chapter Thirty-Three

"I thought maybe we could go to my old church, St. Michael's. Many of our friends go there, and it would be nice, you know, to make some new friends around town. And it is good values that are being instilled," Matt casually suggests one Sunday morning.

I look at him blankly, though I've half expected it since he went to Midnight Mass with his parents. "We've never been to church or practiced religion at all. But now you want to go to St. Michael's?"

"Why is this a big deal, Jane? No, we haven't gone to church before. Maybe we never needed to. I don't know. But I thought it would be nice for all of us. If you're that against it for the sole reason that we've never been before, I guess I can take the kids and give you free time."

"If it's that big of a deal to you, fine. I'll go. Jesus Christ."

Matt cracks a grin, and I cock my head at him.

"Jesus Christ. See? That's the spirit. Hallelujah!"

I can't help but laugh at his terrible joke. It's the first happy moment we've had with each other in a while.

We all forget to look at Charles's feet in the Sunday-morning shuffle to get out the door and arrive for church on time. We don't realize until we are out in the full light of the parking lot that Charles is wearing his light-up tennis shoes in bright pink with his polo shirt and khakis.

Matt stops dead a few feet from the open church door.

"What the hell, Jane?" he asks me with contempt in his voice.

"Hey. You were there too. Neither of us noticed his shoes." I say this and regret it as soon as the words leave my mouth. He's going to take it out on Charles.

"Why did you wear those shoes? You know better," he hisses, and Charles shrinks into my skirt, latching on to my leg. "Don't do that, Charles. Stop hiding. I'm not going to hurt you."

"Are you coming in?" asks the man at the door. "We're ready to close the doors for the service."

Matt gives me a look like I planned all this, and we head inside before the doors close.

"The kids have their own services and lessons downstairs in the great room. I'll show them the way." The man gestures toward Louisa and Charles, who reluctantly lets go of me in exchange for Louisa.

"Go have fun, you two. I love you." I swing Henrietta to my other hip while Matt and I walk in, looking for seats near the end of a row in case I have to take the baby out.

The church service is long, hot, and dull, which is what I expected. But when I go to the church basement to pick up the kids while Matt is schmoozing with friends, I find Charles sitting in the corner, looking sad. I motion for him to come with me, but he shakes his head and shoots a look at the middle-aged lady who teaches Sunday school.

Louisa joins me and tries to whisper something to me, but the teacher spots me and heads over fast.

"Hello. We're so glad that you could join us today. We did have a little problem with Charles, so he's in the corner communing with the Spirit."

"I'm sorry. He's what?" I shift Henrietta on my hip, and Louisa reaches out to take her from me, which I thank her for.

"Your son"—she enunciates the word "son" hard, as if I may be deaf or not very bright—"was telling everyone that he is a girl. He also suggested that God made him this way for a reason. We tried to explain that God doesn't make mistakes, but he was adamant about not being a boy. We can't have this kind of outright flaunting of our beliefs. And, of course, he did confuse our poor little souls in his class. But no worries. The Spirit moves fast. This church will help him find the righteous path."

"The righteous path? He's six years old. He doesn't have a cruel bone in his body. He collects litter that could harm wildlife. His favorite thing is baking. He is sweet and kind and a good kid."

I sigh. I'm irritated even to be having this conversation.

"Clearly, your child does need this. Because he doesn't even know who he is. I've never seen a more lost soul."

"Charles," I almost yell, my voice high and tight. "Get out of that chair. We're done here." I reach out my hand to him, and he scampers up fast, as far from the teacher as possible.

"Mrs. Zander. We can help you. We've been praying on this since your husband called, and we think that with some meetings with Father O'Brien, you will have a whole child full of the greatness of God."

I grab Charles's hand, take Louisa with the other, and we hightail it out of there. When we get upstairs, everyone is milling around, eating doughnuts. I don't want to be here anymore. And I'm so mad at Matt that I could spit. Charles is hooked to me like glue, and even chatty Louisa is silent. What the fuck happened down there?

Matt is talking with a school board member, but I interrupt anyway.

"Excuse me, Matt. We need to get going. I'll get the kids in the van and meet you there."

"Jane, I thought we'd stay and have fellowship." He raises his powdered-sugar doughnut to me with a smile. I look at him like I did the woman downstairs, with seething rage just below the surface, ready to blow.

"The kids need to get home, and Henrietta needs a nap."

Matt considers this for a moment. "I'll tell you what: How about I stay here, and I'll walk home?"

"I can always give you a ride. I don't mind," says the guy from the school board.

"It's settled, then. See you at home," I mutter, but I'm already heading for the parking lot. Matt never even bothered to ask what was wrong. Maybe he doesn't even notice anymore.

When we get home, Charles goes to his room and curls up in a ball on his bed. I can't get him to talk to me, so I try Louisa.

"Hey, sweetie," I say when I find her and Henrietta playing with dolls in the living room. "It seems like it was rough there, huh? Do you want to tell me about it?"

She sighs, smoothing down the hair of the doll in her lap.

"At first, it was fine. They sang songs and told us stories that weren't too bad for being so old."

I laugh a little at her joke, but still, her smile fades.

"But then they had us introduce ourselves and say one thing about us. I said that I'm Louisa and I like to read. But Charles . . . He said he's a girl." She looks at me with big, scared eyes as she says it.

"Have you heard him say that before?" I ask as casually as I can.

"Yeah, he's been saying that since he was two and started to talk," she answers without a pause. "But today, he was mad when the lady corrected him. He told her that she didn't know best. And the lady got so mad, dragged him into the corner, and sat there with her hands on him saying some prayer or something. It scared me, Mom." She crumples into tears, and I wrap my arms around her, taking deep breaths in and out until she joins me.

"It sounds like this morning was terrifying for both of you. I'm sorry that had to happen. We won't be going back there," I tell her, and she nods, wiping tears from her face.

"Why is everyone so mean to him? I have all these shirts that say 'Be Yourself,' but Charles keeps trying, and everyone says he's doing it wrong."

"What do you think about Charles wearing girl stuff?"

"I don't even care, especially if it isn't my clothes that fit me now." I smile. "But maybe he doesn't fit in because he isn't like us. I think he's different. But I don't think that's bad. It's just different."

"I think that too," I say, suddenly aware that we tell the kids not to keep secrets from us, which means Louisa may say all this to Matt. I'm so mad at him for calling the church and dragging us there that I'm not sure I care what he thinks.

"Have you ever heard the word 'transgender'?" I ask her.

She contemplates for a minute, then answers, "I've heard the word, but I can't define it."

I motion to the couch, and we sit down together. Matt would go apeshit if he knew I was talking to Louisa about this. As mad as I am, I know I'm risking making Matt very angry. Still, I want her to understand. She sees too much.

"Transgender is when someone doesn't identify with the gender they were given at birth."

She contemplates this and says, "Like, give me an example."

I swallow hard. "Like maybe someone is born, and they have a penis, so everyone automatically thinks they are a boy, but inside their brain and heart, they are a girl. And they know they are a girl just like you and I know that we are girls. It's wired in and can't be changed."

"Mom, I think that's what Charles is." She says this with big tears in her hopeful eyes. "Did you tell him? He's going to be so happy! He thinks that he's crazy."

She starts to cry hard, and I lean over and pull her in. She's too big for my lap, but she's almost in it. I let her cry it out until she is done.

When she pulls away, she asks, "Why can't we just let him be transgender? It's because of Daddy, right?"

Fuck. I sigh hard. "Some people don't believe that being transgender is real. Almost all doctors, psychiatrists, and experts believe it to be real because there are many more people like Charles. But you're right about your dad. He . . . he just isn't ready to see it yet."

It's the nicest way I can say it. We sit like that for a while, just cuddled up in our feelings. I smooth Louisa's hair and kiss her forehead. "You are always such a big helper to me, and sometimes you seem so grown up that it can be easy to forget you're a kid and you're dealing with all of this too. But this is big stuff, even for me, and I'm a grown-up, and I want you to know that it's okay to have big feelings and to talk to me about everything. I'm here for you too," I tell her. She looks up at me and nods, then settles back into our hug.

Louisa looks fried, so I tell her she can have an hour to play video games. I collect Henrietta and a few toys and carry her to the kitchen so she's safe in the high chair while I make lunch. I've just gotten her settled with a snack and am starting lunch when Matt comes in the back door.

"Hey," he says as if he's had a great morning. I glare at him, hating who he is becoming.

"Do you have any idea what they did to Charles?" I spit. I'm too mad to come at this conversation calmly.

"They prayed with him. They tried to help him understand where he fits in. For crap's sake, Jane. The kid is off the rails. You said that yourself. He needs guidance. What better place than a church?"

"That's the problem, Matt. I don't think this is something you can pray away. We don't get to pick who Charles turns out to be. It won't change it. The only choice is whether we fully support him or not. And you are making it very clear that you will only support him if he fits into your box."

"My box? No. This isn't my box. This is our society. Man or woman, boy or girl. That literally is all there is."

"No, that isn't all there is. Gender is a spectrum. There are so many more ways to be than just boy or girl."

He puts his hands on his hips like he's done with this.

Fine. So am I. No matter how much we fight, we can't get the other one to hear us.

Chapter Thirty-Four

I skipped the December PTA meeting because it was too hectic getting ready for Matt's family to arrive and to make Christmas happen for all of them, but Matt is encouraging me to keep going to the PTA meetings. He offered to come home early and watch the kids so I could attend the January meeting.

I don't have the best attitude going in, and all I can think of when I get to the meeting is how many of these moms were cheering at what Erv Budde said at the "gender meeting." I'm currently competing with Libby for infamous-level gossip in this town.

Of course, all eyes are on me since it all started with my family, and everyone knows it.

Libby couldn't make the meeting because she had mediation about custody with Jason. It would be much easier to ignore the stares and the whispers if Libby were here to make me laugh and feel protected. I am thankful to see Rebecca Darling and choose to sit by her. Kelsey looks at me like I am choosing war by doing this, but I need friends who don't stab me in the back. Fake friends are also fake at supporting you. And who needs that?

I think back to the melee of the "gender meeting," but I only remember pieces. How sick I felt watching Jillie and Kelsey cheer at Erv Budde's words. Libby and Rebecca defending Charles, and Matt staying silent except for when he asked for a vote. The snippets of memories from that awful night remind me that Rebecca was one of the only sane voices I heard in that room.

Rebecca smiles as I sit down beside her.

"Hi, Jane." She seems happy to see me sit with her. "I've been meaning to reach out since the meeting, but with the chaos of the holidays, I lost track of time. I hope you know I'm here for you and so sorry about how all that went down." Rebecca is calm, collected, and makes me feel better, even if it's all crappy, and I can't change any of it.

The meeting starts, and more than half of the conversation is about uniforms or, rather, what options for accessories the school should offer based on gender. The whole thing makes my stomach turn, and I can't sit through it. Halfway through the meeting, I whisper to Rebecca that I need to head out, and leave the meeting. I turn to see Kelsey glare at me as Jillie talks, and I don't even care if the mean girls are mad. Sitting through the meeting makes me feel like an accomplice. The cute barrettes make me think about how much Charles will love them and want them for his long brown curls, and I feel awful because he can't have them. Is the world always going to be a never-ending place Charles doesn't fit into? Is there ever going to be a day he can be himself without anyone hating him?

I walk the block back home in the cold, my winter jacket zipped up as far as it will go. When I get home, I notice the van is missing. Matt finally bought a car, which is parked in the driveway. What was worth leaving the warm house and bundling and buckling up three kids? I make myself some tea and sit down to read a book. It's close to bedtime, and I am getting worried. Where could they have gone?

I text Matt. Hey. I'm home. Where are you all at?

He answers me back. It's a surprise. Be home very soon. I feel myself getting excited. It reminds me of back in the day, when he would bring me home flowers or a plant or a small chocolate bar. I try to think of what he could've gotten and why he chose to go out now. It warms my heart that he's trying to improve things with me. I wait with a slight smile for them to get home with my surprise.

When Matt unlocks the door, Louisa walks in first, and the look on her face tells me immediately that this is not a happy surprise. She looks almost traumatized, and my heart drops to my stomach.

I can't even wrap my brain around what it might be, but as Louisa steps out of the way, I see Charles with very short hair. His long curls are gone, replaced with a buzz cut so short that it makes him almost look sickly. His face is set in a pout, with tearstains on his cheeks and his eyes red from crying.

"Surprise!" Matt yells, and I cannot figure out how he can still think this is a good thing. Can he not see his child?

It takes everything I have not to break down crying. I walk to Charles, but he covers his head with his hands and runs up the stairs to his room. I hear the door slam when I turn to face Matt. He's holding Henrietta on his hip. She's the only one who looks happy, because he gave her a sucker that probably belonged to Charles.

"Matt—" I start, not knowing how to talk without screaming, but Matt interrupts me.

"Look, before you get all upset, I know you and my mom talked, and you agreed to try this out. We've let him be whoever he wanted; now we must show him how to be a boy. And yeah, he might not like it right away. But trust me, he will figure it out and be a normal kid. I know it. He needs a little more help figuring it out."

I can't think of anything friendly or reasonable to say and nothing to fix things, so I shake my head at him and go upstairs to try and comfort Charles.

After his impromptu haircut, Charles stops talking for a week. Matt calls it "acting out," but regardless, Charles has turned off like a light switch.

Chapter Thirty-Five

The Atwood Prep Snowflake Father-Daughter Dance is a bunch of bullshit.

I've been listening to all the PTA moms glow and gush about how sweet their girls are with their daddies and how nice it is for them to have quality time together. The girls dress in fancy dresses, the dads wear suits, and the whole thing is patriarchal and princess themed. I hate it because I know Charles wants to go with his daddy and cannot.

I wouldn't even be at the stupid dance if I had my way. Matt signed me up without asking, so I'm filling cups with juice from a big plastic cooler in the gym. Mrs. Driscoll had bingo, so Charles is sitting next to me, his new signature beanie hat over his head and his thumb in his mouth. He sits silently watching Matt dance with Louisa, twirling her around the gym floor as she smiles. Henrietta is fast asleep in the stroller and will probably not sleep tonight. I am not in a good mood.

This is the last place Charles needs to be right now, I text Libby.

Is he okay? she asks with a sad-face emoji.

He's staring into space as if he's not even there. I seriously don't know how to reach him anymore, I tell her.

I keep looking at Charles and his permanently sad face, and I think of the photo of little Virginia Wellington looking so unhappy, and I wonder what pushed her so far into her reclusive life that she never ventured out again. I can't help but worry that Charles might never crawl back out of himself either.

Maybe I'm being dramatic, but I look back at my child and don't think I am.

"Come on, Charles. Let's go get some pizza," I tell him.

He looks up at me, maybe interested, then shakes his head. "We're supposed to hand out the juice," he says with no tone or care in his voice.

"I know, but we filled enough cups for everyone to have three. Let's at least get out of here for a bit, okay? It's loud."

Charles nods and takes my hand as we make our way out of the gymnasium, and he helps me push his sister's stroller down the hallway, which is covered in a long red carpet with a photo backdrop. I watch Charles scowl at the dad and daughter posing for a photo.

"Buddy," I start, but Charles interrupts me.

"I hate being called 'buddy,'" Charles exclaims with more vigor than I've seen in a while.

"I know. I'm sorry. It slipped out." I stop in the middle of the red carpet and get down to Charles's level. I fix his cockeyed hat, sitting it on top of his head.

"I know this is hard, and I'm here. I can't fix it all, but I swear to you, I am trying to change things to make them better. Do you know that?" I look into his wide brown eyes, searching for desperately needed answers.

"I know, Mama," he says, hugging me right then and there, patting me on the back as if I'm the one who is struggling. And I am. We both are. I feel like E.T. and Elliott. This sadness has spread through Charles, and somehow it has also gotten to me. Neither of us is okay.

We head into the kitchen to get pizza and find it almost deserted, a few daddies and daughters at tables taking a break from the most important part of the night to all the girls—the dancing.

Charles and I head to the lunch counter and get a slice of pizza for him and a fruit cup for me. I contemplate trying to wake Henrietta so that she will sleep tonight, but the peace of the moment is too good to interrupt. We wheel her over to one of the tables near the kitchen, and as Charles and I start to eat, I hear Jillie's voice.

"And did you see the silly hat she puts on him, like, *constantly*? She can't help herself from screwing up that poor kid."

"Between you and me, Matt has been confiding in me more and more, and he has some real concerns about Jane's ability to mother. He said she's always been . . . difficult and antisocial, but he's concerned she's trying to wreck his chances here on purpose. He thinks she may be . . . unstable."

"Jeez. No wonder she gets along with Libby. They are a disastrous match made in heaven. It's how they operate."

I cough loud and hard enough to startle Charles and the people at the nearest table. It also stops the laughter in the kitchen.

Jillie and Kelsey peek through the wide kitchen windows toward us. I stare them both down until they crack.

"I didn't see you there," Jillie says, sounding small and nervous.

"Yeah, no shit. Otherwise, maybe you wouldn't discuss my kids and marriage at a school event? Or is that how you operate?"

Charles puts a hand on my arm.

"It's okay, Mama. People always talk about me too. I know how it feels."

Charles is so full of love despite being told he's wrong at every turn. I hug him and kiss his head, then turn back to Kelsey and Jillie in the kitchen with a glare.

"Maybe people wouldn't talk about you if you weren't freaks," I hear Jillie mutter to Kelsey with a laugh.

"Just like Virginia Wellington. Maybe that house really is haunted," Kelsey says to spark another round of laughter.

I stand up and look at her, and Jillie cowers back.

"You're literally gossiping about a dead woman. How petty are you?" They both look shocked, as if they aren't used to being confronted. "And you gossip about me as I sit here with my child. I'm not sure why you can't help yourselves from being so mean to everyone who isn't the same as you, but it does make you the backstabbing bitches everyone says you are."

Kelsey outright gasps, as if no one has ever told her what a cruel person she is, and Jillie stands there open-mouthed, so I turn around and take Charles's hand.

"Thanks for the pizza," he calls out to them as we leave. I hold back tears because my kid feels compelled to thank the adult bullies at his school. Maybe this place isn't any better than Browning. Perhaps it's the same as soon as you scratch the surface.

Charles and I abandon our post at the drink station and head to the library. We sit silently in the giant beanbags in the quiet corner, looking through books, with Henrietta still fast asleep in her stroller.

It's obvious my popularity is waning here. I think of how Libby says popularity isn't real; it's an illusion, a magic trick. The only real part is how much you believe it.

Either way, I'm on the wrong side of the cool kids. Maybe I feel such empathy for Charles because he's on the wrong side too. And if moving across the country and having more money hasn't solved the problem, then what will? How can I make it right? For Charles and me?

After I calm down, I am less mad about them being hateful gossips than I am about Matt giving them the goddamn ammunition. I can't believe he confided in the Plastics and the school's biggest gossip about our private life. Although, at this point, who hasn't he talked to about me?

Chapter Thirty-Six

I am in the middle of making dinner when the doorbell rings.

I open the front door, expecting maybe an Amazon package, and instead, I find my mother and Mickey standing on my front porch.

"Surprise!" Mickey and Mom yell. Mom has some cheap plastic kazoo she starts blowing into to make the whole thing more festive. Despite the deep, dark feeling that this will not end well, I am smiling anyway.

They are my family. I do love them.

"Oh my gosh, you two. Come in. It's so cold right now. We are having a lovely February cold spell. It's awful."

"We get cold in South Dakota too. Colder than this, even," Mickey says, like everything is some competition. I do not want to fight with them before they even get into the house.

"I can't believe you're here," I say, helping my mom remove her coat and boots. "It's such a great surprise. Sorry about the mess. I didn't know you were coming, and, you know, kids."

"No worries, dear. That's what moms are for. I can help you get this place into shape."

My mom pats my arm, surveying the toys, dust, and big house I can't seem to keep clean. I can finish one floor, but it's all undone when I move to the next. If my mom wants to take a swipe at it, I'll let her.

"So, to what do I owe this great surprise? Is everything all right?" It suddenly occurs to me that this may not be a good visit. My mom partakes in smoking and drinking daily. "Are you okay, Mom?" I ask, wondering if her years of smoky bars have caught up with her and feeling more worried than I would've thought.

"Oh, no. Nothing bad. We came for you. Matt said you might need some help and some encouragement. It sounds like everyone has had a hard time adjusting, and he thought you could use some time with family to help you get settled and help you sort it all out."

"We got here seven months ago. We're pretty settled," I say, watching them survey the room cluttered with clothes and books.

"Well, we can help with everything." Mom is being unusually nice to me based on all her past behaviors. I am too tired to pick a fight, so I will see how it all plays out. They are here, and there is nothing to do now.

"Where is everyone?" Mom asks.

"The kids and Matt are at school but will be home in a few hours. Henrietta is taking her nap."

I head to Henrietta's room when Mickey and Mom run to the liquor store to get what they need. Her bedroom is enormous, so I make up the extra bed to bunk the kids together. I strip the kids' sheets, put new ones on, and give my mom and Mickey each a bedroom. I'll be damned if they get to go in my attic. Besides, except for the kids' beds, the attic is where I'm sleeping these days.

They return from the store with their drinks and head to the kitchen to find glasses while I call Matt.

"Did you get your surprise?" I can hear the smile on his face as he asks.

"Uh, yes. Way to warn me to clean the house, bud." There is some snark to my voice because I don't like surprises.

"I thought it would be nice for you to have some support and family here. I know things have been rough, but I hope we're on the right road now. I was trying to be nice."

If anything, Mickey and my mom are taking Matt's side regarding Charles, so I want to ask him if the support is for him. But he sounds sincere. Even if he's doing it wrong, he is trying to help.

It could be easy to wonder if I'm the one who is off her rocker.

When Matt comes home with the kids, I can tell my mom and Mickey are trying to be friendly and not say anything to pick a fight. I can tell they are on their best behavior. They play board games with the kids, beer and gin and tonics in hand. They pause the games to go out for smoke breaks and come in complaining about the cold. Maybe it's my newfound determination to find peace or my family's best behavior, but we have a lovely first night. No one brings up anything divisive, and we enjoy our time together. I even get a few smiles out of Charles.

While the older kids and Matt are at school the next day, Mickey and my mom take Henrietta to her weekly playgroup and story time. After school, Mickey takes Louisa to the mall so the two of them can have some girl time and go shopping. About an hour after they leave, Mickey video calls me, but it's Louisa's face that pops on the screen.

"Hey, Mom! Aunt Mickey said she will get my ears pierced for me! Can I? Can I please? I know you said I could do it soon, and I'm almost eleven already. All my friends have them done already. Please!"

I take a deep breath, wishing that Mickey would have discussed this with me. Louisa looks so excited that I don't want to say no, but I had hoped it would be something we'd do together.

Mickey's face leans into the screen beside Louisa's. "Come on, Jane! Let me get the girl's ears pierced. I don't have any girls, and it'll be a nice way for her to remember my visit."

It warms me, Mickey taking this trip and giving Louisa some special attention. I'm apprehensive, but I say yes anyway. I don't want to be the one to say no on their special day.

"Okay, yes. You can get your ears pierced," I tell her, and they both whoop with joy. "Just make sure to get all the supplies we need and the instructions on how to care for them so that we know how."

"Will do!" Mickey says. "And let Charles know that I have a surprise for him too. Can you have him all ready to go when we get home in a bit? Me and the boy are going on our own adventure." With that, she ends the call before I can ask any details of what they are going to do. Mickey taking Charles on an adventure makes me more nervous than her getting Louisa's ears pierced.

I let Charles know that he's going to be going on his own adventure with Mickey. He nods at me but doesn't say anything. I let him know that if he doesn't have fun, he can just call me or ask to come home. I do appreciate Mickey making an effort with the kids, but I can't help but be nervous that she won't pick an activity that Charles will enjoy.

Mickey and Louisa arrive home an hour later with a few shopping bags full of cute shirts and dresses, and Louisa instantly hugs me and shows me her pink little ears with the small sparkly studs.

"She's a brave one, Jane. She didn't cry or nothing! She was all smiles the whole time."

I thank Mickey for taking Louisa, and she waves me off, calling into the living room for Charles.

"You ready, my boy? It's Aunt Mickey and Charles night! And boy, do I have a surprise for you. You're gonna love it! Grab your coat. We're hitting the road."

Charles climbs off the couch, looking at me with big eyes before coming to hug me.

"Where are you going?" I ask Mickey, hoping to allay my fears as well as Charles's.

"It's a surprise, Jane! But don't worry. We're going to have a fun time. We might be a little late!"

"You call me if you need anything," I say to Charles as I help him with his winter coat and hat, and they head out the door.

I finish dinner and feed everyone, and Matt disappears to the office to work while my mom and I play with the baby. Louisa tries on all her new clothes for us, stopping in between to admire her ears as she passes the mirror in the hallway.

I've already tucked Henrietta into bed and read a chapter with Louisa when I hear Mickey and Charles come home. I walk out to the entryway to greet them and find Charles holding a big red toy truck with humungous wheels and wearing a baseball hat with a similar truck embroidered on the front.

"We went to the monster truck show!" Mickey says with a grin. I look down at Charles, who gives a small polite smile.

"You did?" I ask. "Wow! What a cool surprise. What did you think, Charles?" I ask, and he shrugs.

"It was loud," he says, and Mickey laughs.

"Yeah, it sure was, my boy! But we had a great time. We had hot dogs and soda for dinner and got some souvenirs. I planned our trip for this week so I could take my only nephew to the monster truck show. I told him that my boys always loved it so much. I had to be the first one to take him."

Charles does not look particularly impressed, and I'm not surprised that monster trucks are not his thing. Still, Mickey made a huge effort, so I say, "What do you say, Charles?"

He looks up at her. "Thanks, Aunt Mickey, for dinner and my truck and hat."

Mickey pats him on the head, and I tell him he should go brush his teeth and get ready for bed. He heads up the stairs carrying his new truck, and I turn to Mickey.

"That was really nice of you to do all this for the kids," I tell her.

"I don't get much time with them. I wanted to make it special, you know? Charles is a quiet guy, not rowdy like my boys. But I still think he had fun. I'm heading to the kitchen for a beer. You want anything, Jane?"

I tell her I'm good and that I need to help Charles get ready for bed. I feel a glimmer of hope that maybe, finally, my relationship with my family is taking a turn for the better.

❧

The following evening, though, after Mickey and my mom return from happy hour, Mickey asks Charles why he isn't wearing his new hat the second she enters the door.

Charles just shrugs, looking at the floor.

"Don't you like it, Charles? Didn't you have fun at the monster truck show with Aunt Mickey?" she asks.

Charles shrugs again, but he nods.

"I thought we had fun," Mickey says with an edge to her voice that I don't like.

"I just think we are all different, and maybe Charles would have enjoyed something else more. But we are both thankful you took him," I say, trying to defuse what I can tell is building.

"Is that true, Charles? Did you want to do something else?" Mickey asks, leaning down close to him. Charles looks up at her and then at me, silent.

"It's okay, Charles. You can be honest with us about the things you like and don't like," I tell him.

Charles draws with his foot for a few seconds before mumbling, "I wanted my ears pierced like Louisa."

"What?" Mickey barks. "Speak up, boy. You wanted your ears pierced, you said?"

Charles nods, finally looking up at her, and Mickey rears her head back with a low whistle before she starts to laugh. "Damn, Jane. Matt was right. You've got some problems."

"Charles," I say, trying to keep my voice steady. "Please go upstairs and play for me." I don't have to say it again. Charles races up the stairs like he's on a mission.

"So, tell me, Jane, why I gotta side with Matt, who is trying to help the child, and you are insistent on making him into some freak. I took him to the truck show because someone needs to show that child how to be a man. Why do you insist on dressing him like he's a girl?" She smiles as she says it, but it's clear she isn't being friendly.

My sister has a way of dragging an argument around with her, like a shadow or a handbag.

"In case you haven't noticed, he isn't dressing like a girl these days, yet you keep bringing it up. I am not discussing this with you," I say, having already decided.

"What do you mean, you aren't discussing it with us? Why the fuck do you think we're here? To play some stupid board games with a bunch of brats?"

I gasp. Sometimes, I forget how awful my family can be. Mickey is just mean.

"Yes, Mickey. I was dumb enough to believe you came to see your family because you love us. Stupid Jane, right?"

"Jane. Mickey. Girls, don't fight." These are the words of wisdom my mother has for us. No wonder I don't have shit for coping skills.

"Fight? I was in here reading, and she starts yelling at me about *my* child, who is *my* business. No matter what kind of special relationship you two have with Matt, Charles is still my child. So back off. I'm not asking."

I walk out of the room to make dinner and leave them to ponder what kind of assholes they are.

Matt looks just as broken down as I feel by the end of Mom and Mickey's visit, which included many late-night arrivals after going to the bars and days with all of us tiptoeing around while they slept it off. And, of course, Mom's constant worry of "What you are playing with is the kind of thing that lands a person in hell."

By some miracle, my mother never seems to feel the same about her sins as she does about mine or everyone else's.

Matt won't come out and say inviting them was a bad idea, but he is also ready to be rid of them. Two days before they're supposed to leave, we're all trying to go through the motions and get along for the kids' sake.

We all sit in the living room on the two couches, watching *Mrs. Doubtfire*. Matt and I love watching old movies with the kids, and Mickey suggested this one. It isn't until about a third of the way through that I realize why.

Mickey has her laser focus on Charles, who is sitting on the floor with his legs crossed and his thumb in his mouth. The short haircut makes him look frail to me, not boyish. He looks hurt. As usual, he's wearing one of my hats on his head as a stylish slouchy beanie. Instead of eating popcorn like the rest of us, he sucks his thumb in silence.

"Hey, Charles," Mickey says or almost yells. Charles startles. Everything Mickey says comes out like she's a football coach barking orders.

He turns to her quickly with big eyes. He's afraid of Aunt Mickey. He told me so, in those exact words, when I put him to bed last night. He also asked me, "What if she tried to kill me for being a freak?"

"What? Charles, no. She would never. And you aren't a freak. Who said that?" I asked, but he turned away, unwilling to say more.

"Charles, are you the same as Mrs. Doubtfire?" she asks him. Her voice, for once, is not harsh. He stares her down for a few moments.

"No, I'm not," he says as he returns to the movie, but Mickey pauses the television.

"Why not? Don't you both like to dress up?"

Charles sighs hard, as if Mickey doesn't get it.

"He dresses up because he wants to see his kids. I wear girl clothes because I am a girl." He says this so casually that it almost makes me worry. He puts his thumb back into his mouth like the moment is over.

I know this is the moment Mickey has been waiting for the whole visit.

She starts to laugh so hard she begins coughing, and Mom has to help her get up off the couch. She stands up to tower over Charles before I know what's happening.

"You're a girl? A *girl*? What do you mean, you *are* a girl? That don't make no sense."

Charles sits blinking at her silently.

"Why do you think you're a girl?" she asks as I interrupt. I don't know exactly what Mickey is trying to accomplish, but all the hairs on my body are standing straight up like lightning is about to strike.

"Hey, no. This isn't okay. It's not trivia night with Charles and gender. No." I start to get up.

"Why can't we talk about it? If it is no big deal and we're all supposed to be honest, what can it hurt for all of us to talk about it?" Mickey asks calmly.

Trying to think when I'm put on the spot is not my best quality. I suppose it would be reasonable to have a conversation, even if it's with Mickey and Mom. I look to Matt, who opens his mouth and then closes it as if he's about to say something but changes his mind. He gives a small shrug of indifference.

"It is up to Charles if he wants to talk or not," I say, changing my gaze to Charles. He nods.

"So, Charles, my boy," she says, and I see Charles straighten. "We need to talk about what makes a boy and what makes a girl, and it's a penis and a vagina. You have a penis, right?" she asks, all slow, as if he's not very smart.

Charles nods at her and doesn't say a word.

"Well, that automatically makes you a boy." I can tell even she believes this.

"No, that isn't true," I say, and Charles looks at me as if his whole world is crumbling. I want to reach across the void and stop it from happening, but I don't know how. It's not just Mickey; it's the whole thing, coming apart at the seams.

"Jane," Mickey interrupts me, "this is basic biology. As old as the Bible and still as true. It's time Junior here understood that the thing between his legs means he's a boy and will eventually be a man. There ain't no way to change that."

"That isn't true. There is no right way to be a boy or a girl. Gender is in the brain and heart, not the body parts." I say this, but Charles is sitting there with tears rolling down his face, defeated.

"Jane, stop. You are so brainwashed by this new 'transgenderism' trend. You think if you pretend, it makes it real. It isn't real. You act like he's some magical unicorn who should be celebrated when you're turning him into the freaky girl-boy with a penis. It's not a good way to win popularity or help poor Matt keep his job."

I get up to take Charles out of there, but it's too late. He races up the stairs so fast that he's out of sight by the time I get to Mickey. I look to Matt, who is staring at his hands in his lap, and I glare at him for staying silent through all this, and then I turn to Mickey.

"How dare you come here into my house with your ignorant terms and biology lessons and traumatize my kid. Get the hell out of my house. You can find a hotel until your flight or fly home early. I don't give a shit. But I want you out." I say it defeated because all the mad is used up. I am done with Charles and me being their punching bags.

I stare at Matt until he nods at me, because I mean it. I want them gone. I head up the stairs to see how Charles is doing and find him in the upstairs bathroom, throwing up into the garbage can.

"Honey, are you okay?" I touch his forehead and say, "You aren't hot. Is anyone in your class sick?" as I go to the cupboard to get him a washcloth.

"I'm okay," he says, leaning away from the can.

"Did you feel sick earlier?"

He shakes his head. "I just felt sick when Aunt Mickey said all that."

He's so honest and vulnerable that I push back tears. And his calling her "Aunt" breaks me. She does not deserve the title.

"What she said was awful, and she was *wrong*. I know things are a mess, but we will find a way to get them to listen, okay? Do you know how much I love you exactly as you are?"

Charles nods at me in his usual way, as if he isn't sure of anything. He's tethered to us all by a dwindling string, and I am afraid I will lose him.

Mickey and my mom are nowhere to be found when I return downstairs after putting the kids to bed.

"I got them rooms at the American Inn because they wanted a hotel with a bar." He seems to think it's a cute joke, but I don't find my family's alcoholism any funnier than their bigotry. I try to head to the kitchen to avoid him, but he follows me.

"I'm sorry I invited them. I didn't know . . ." Matt starts and doesn't finish. I stare him down.

"Matt, I don't think you listen to me. I've told you *for years* that my mom and Mickey *don't* support me. They don't listen to me. They let me suffer for years when I was sick and thought I was faking it for attention. They have not been good to me, family or not. They have been toxic to even borderline abusive. You keep forcing them onto me, and it's hurtful. Stop pushing them into my life. I'd also appreciate it if you'd stop inviting them into yours since we can choose who the other associates with now. Because I don't think they are a healthy relationship for anyone in this family."

"I didn't know they would be so awful, Jane. The way she talked to Charles. I'm sorry. I'm sorry I didn't listen. I . . ."

"You thought you knew what was best for me. Just like you think you know what's best for Charles. I hope you aren't so wrong about that too."

I grab the baby monitor, climb the creaky attic steps, and head to the bedroom. Turning on the small light on the bedside table, I reach for my phone to text Libby.

I sent my mom and sister packing because they are hateful assholes.

I hit send with an emoji of a girl doing a cartwheel.

Libby texts back:

Great job! Fuck them and their hating. You rock.

Chapter Thirty-Seven

It's been a few weeks since my mom and sister left, and things are quiet between Matt and me. He's sorry about inviting my family and disapproves of how they talked to Charles, but he still thinks I am somehow pushing Charles into this. It's almost funny since I can barely get the kid to eat these days. As if I have so much power over my children.

I get an email from Charles's teacher, Ms. Keaton, moments before I pick up the kids. The subject line reads "Concerns about Charles."

My heart begins to race in my chest. "Will there ever be an easy day where I'm not screwing anyone up?" I ask Henrietta, who stares me down, giggles, and toddles off to find some choking hazard I've left behind.

> Dear Dr. and Mrs. Zander,
>
> I am writing to express some concerns about your child, Charles. I noticed some changes in him starting at the beginning of the spring semester, which, unfortunately, escalated. My biggest concern is a handful of accidents where Charles has wet his pants. I suggest you take him to a physician to rule out anything medical.

> I am also concerned about Charles's mental health. He has been very withdrawn and has hardly spoken this month.

I nod as I read the email. He's also barely spoken at home since Matt cut his hair.

> I hope you can schedule a time to speak with me, but I highly recommend speaking with medical professionals to assess what is going on with your child. I am here if I can be of any assistance,
>
> Ms. Keaton

As soon as I read the email, I call Libby, even though she's at work. It didn't occur to me that I called her first until she asks, "What did Matt say?"

"I don't know. I called you without even thinking about it," I say with a smile that turns into laughter.

"Jane, I love how you laugh at things that aren't funny. You are wonderful."

I find myself laughing again.

"I suppose I should call Matt. Not that it'll do any good."

"Maybe one of these times he will surprise you?" she suggests.

"Eh. I think I've gone dark. All I do is worry about what terrible thing will have to happen for my husband to understand our child is hurting."

⁂

Matt looks spooked when we get another email from the school a few weeks later, this time requesting an in-person meeting with the school psychiatrist. He ignored the first email and kept blowing off a meeting with Charles's teacher. I followed Ms. Keaton's advice and got Charles in to see his pediatrician, who was more concerned about Charles's mood and thought we should discuss antidepressants if he doesn't improve in a few months. Matt was all for meds, as if there is some pill to get yourself a socially acceptable child.

Ms. Keaton insisted she had immediate concerns that required us to meet in person. Matt sits on the small chair, bouncing his knee in uncharacteristic nervousness. I pick at my cuticles and try to slow down my breathing.

"Dr. and Mrs. Zander," Ms. Keaton says to us. "Mrs. Klinger." She nods in the direction of the psychiatrist. "I'm sure you have all met."

I haven't met her but decide against saying anything yet. Matt sabotaged us at the last meeting at school, so I'll see what is going on before I chime in and put a target on my head.

"We've brought you all in today because we have serious concerns about your child. I know you took Charles to his pediatrician, and they found no medical reason for the wetting accidents at school, correct?"

I nod, and Matt adds, "Nope, no medical issues at all. He told us that Charles is shipshape. I was thinking about this and wondered if the problem might be long bathroom lines or him not being allowed to go in time?"

Ms. Keaton looks at the psychiatrist, who gives a nod of support. Oh brother.

"We believe the behavior may result from the new rules instituted in the school about 'gendered bathrooms.' I think your son does not feel comfortable in the boys' bathroom. The accidents may be a result of bathroom avoidance.

"I also think Mrs. Zander agrees and sees what is happening with your child, but I think you are still in denial, Dr. Zander. I worry for my job saying this," she says as Matt turns bright red and looks ready to blow, "but I still feel your child's health and safety are more important. Charles is depressed, despondent, and a shell of the child I met in

September, who scampered in here singing 'good morning' to me in a little pink shirt."

"You pulled us in here because my kid won't sing to you in the morning anymore?" Matt says.

I roll my eyes. I hate when he takes one stupid piece of an argument and makes it the whole thing when it isn't even close to the point. It's his most annoying trait ever.

"No, Dr. Zander. I brought you in here because your son has had periods where he's gone mute, and if your child's behaviors become more erratic, the school will have no choice but to report the situation to the authorities."

I feel my mouth go dry, and all the air gets sucked out of my lungs. Are they going to take my kid?

"No," I almost yell, without even meaning to. But it's my worst fear, coming true. My whole family is unraveling. They all spin to look at me.

"I do see how sad Charles is. We've talked with his doctor about it, who will evaluate in a few months to see if Charles may need some mental health meds. We also have an appointment for him at the gender clinic at Children's Hospital, but they can't get us in until October. Matt and I don't . . . agree on what to do, but we are trying here. Matt has been hesitant but agrees that the clinic can help us figure out what's happening."

I can see Ms. Keaton and the psychiatrist thinking about this. They didn't expect it. They ask to meet up again after our appointment with the clinic to tell the school how we will proceed the following year. In the meantime, they will offer Charles the option of using the staff bathroom in the office.

Matt thanks me as we leave. "You saved the day in there, Jane," he says, but I whip around and face him.

"I didn't do that for you. That was for Charles and for our kids, who I will not allow to be parceled off like furniture. I'm trying to save our family, and so help me, God, Matt, you better start helping me too. I'm trying to save our asses, not yours."

When I try to talk to Charles about school and the bathrooms, his answers come in shrugs.

"What about using the bathroom in the office? I mean, that's kind of cool. You are pretty much the only kid cool enough to use it," I tell him.

He shrugs and says, "I wish I was like everyone else."

I hug him to my chest. "I know that feeling all too well, my friend."

Chapter Thirty-Eight

Louisa has her Tuesday-afternoon STEM club, so just Charles comes home from school with me. We head upstairs, and I tuck Henrietta in for her afternoon nap while Charles washes his hands. I tell him he can come down and help me make muffins or play outside once he changes out of his school clothes.

It's our routine every day. He does not sashay around asking if he's beautiful anymore. Instead, sometimes, he asks me if he would be allowed to be a girl if he were born at another time. The bathroom accidents have lessened since he's been allowed to use the one in the office, and he is talking more, but all in a sad little monotone voice. My happy child has disappeared.

Despite this, I'm trying to feel hope for no particular reason except spring has sprung. The windows are cracked for fresh air, making the world feel fresh and new.

I work on making dinner with muffins as a treat. Charles typically comes down right away for some Julia Child and a snack after changing clothes. *Probably playing nicely,* I tell myself.

I pull the first batch of muffins out of the oven, the warm scent of cinnamon and apples stretching through my kitchen. I set the muffins on cooling racks on my kitchen table one by one. I don't bother to remove a glass dancer figurine with a windup music box that Charles likes to carry around. I leave it in the middle of the table and place the muffins around her, smiling at how the dancer looks ready to perform in the middle of an audience of muffins. I put the hot pan on the stove and return to the counter to start the next batch, humming as I work.

I've scooped half of the batter into muffin cups when Charles's dancer chimes a few notes out randomly, and a cold fear creeps through me. Something isn't right. I realize it's too quiet as I hear a muffled cry from upstairs.

I race up the servants' steps, two at a time, praying I'm not too late.

I head straight for the shared bathroom and find Charles sitting naked on the white bathroom counter, with scissors still in his hand.

"Charles!" I scream in a voice that doesn't sound like my own when I see a few drops of blood on the counter. There isn't much blood. *He's okay,* I think, but he barely looks up at me.

He's mumbling, "Am I a girl? I tried, but I can't. I can't be a girl," over and over.

I stare down at the scissors in his hand and the small cut he made. Was he going to cut off his penis to be a girl?

A sob escapes my mouth as I grab a towel and try to take a deep breath before checking the tiny wound. He's no longer bleeding, so I grab some Neosporin and the Band-Aids from the medicine cabinet. I'm shaking like a leaf but don't want Charles to know. I scoop him up and carry him to his room.

Physically, he's fine. But he isn't okay. I get him dressed and hope he will talk to me.

"Charles, we need to talk about this. What happened?" I ask, kneeling on the ground in front of where he sits on the bed.

"Nothing happened. Maybe I'm not a girl. Maybe I'm crazy." He turns to me as he says this, almost seeming hopeful that it would improve things.

"You aren't crazy. I don't even like that word, but you aren't."

"Then how come no one believes except me and you and Libby?"

"I don't know. But I will do what I can to find people to listen to us, okay?" But Charles retreats into his silence, a world away, where I can't protect him from anything, even himself.

Calling Matt immediately was not the best choice because I was scared and hysterical. He came home to talk to me, which he was less than thrilled about, especially when he found out "nothing happened." His words.

"What if I hadn't gotten to him in time? I almost started another batch of muffins. I would've stayed in the kitchen another thirty minutes. Who knows what he might've done?" I tell him. I'm not even giving the illusion of calm. I'm too worked up.

"Jane. Stop being so dramatic. Regardless of the situation, you don't seem to have a level head regarding Charles. The pediatrician said he's fine, and nothing is wrong with him, but you're still harping on his 'gender.' That probably confuses him even more than anything. But it's our job, as his parents, to show him how to be a boy."

"No," I tell him. "He sees examples of typical boys all day long. But he's telling us that's *not who he is*. And the statistics of him harming himself eventually if we don't support him are very high."

Matt shakes his head and runs his hand over his hair. "He is a little boy. That's all he is." His voice nearly reaches a shout, and I pull away from him and try to take deep breaths.

"Matt. I think he needs some therapy. How can you not see this as a cry for help?"

"First of all, he didn't hurt himself. It's barely a paper cut."

"Yeah, on his penis. The one you keep telling him means he's a boy. You don't see the connection here?"

"No, I don't. Because kids do stupid stuff like play with sharp scissors."

"Naked?"

"He also runs around in just underwear in the summer. Is that supposed to mean something too? I don't see why you're trying to make such a big deal out of this. It's not like he hurt himself. Clearly, we need to review the rules on sharp objects, but mostly . . ." He trails off like he doesn't want to say.

"What, Matt?"

"Mostly, you need to keep a better eye on him."

I stop dead like I've been slapped. "You're saying this was my fault?" I swallow hard to push away the nausea. "Now you're blaming *me*?"

"I'm not saying you're to blame. But yes, you've been so busy lately with your friend Libby and your constant research on our hypothetical trans kid that you've neglected to watch our actual kid."

I think of at least three ways to respond, but in the end, I settle on one.

"What's it going to take, Matt? What catastrophic thing will have to happen to get you to listen?" He stares me down, and we remain, as always, at an impasse.

Chapter Thirty-Nine

Libby told me to be ready to go at ten a.m. because she was bringing over a sitter, and we were going out of town for an adventure. I don't want to do anything, but I will try for Libby. It will be nice to get out of the house for a bit.

When Libby drops Mrs. Driscoll off at my house, I head out into the cold spring morning and jump into Libby's SUV.

"Hello. It's cold as hell today. I hope our adventure is indoors."

"Absolutely. And I turned on your heated seat, so you'll be sweating in no time. We can crank the heat and pretend we're in Florida. It's the closest we have seen to a vacation in a while, huh?"

I laugh despite not wanting to come. It feels good to be out and about with my best friend.

We head toward Madison, chatting about our kids and what we've been up to, and I'm so glad to be away from my worries. We pull into the parking lot of a small coffee shop on Madison's East Side.

"Okay, so this is where some local parents of trans kids meet up to talk once a month. It's no pressure. We can turn around and hit the mall instead."

I look at her with pursed lips, half excited to go in and half petrified.

"Look, we can both go in if you want. We don't even have to say which one of us is the parent of a trans kid. We can talk to them, listen, or bail if you want to. You tug on your ear as a signal, and I'll have you out of there in thirty seconds flat." I can't help but laugh at Libby. She makes everything more fun. "But you keep saying you need to talk to someone who gets it. Well, these people are the ones who get it."

I gather my phone and my purse to head in.

"Thank you for this," I say softly. I'm a little amazed she did this for me. "I think I need to do this on my own."

Walking into the coffeehouse, I feel excited and nervous all at once. Libby is right. These people can answer my questions because they've lived through it.

I find the group without a problem once I'm inside. A small rainbow flag sits on one of the tables, with a group of about a dozen people sitting around talking. The coffee shop is quiet, so they have the back corner to themselves.

I suddenly wish I'd let Libby come in with me and scope it out, but I told her to head to her favorite big-box store.

"Are you looking for the parents of trans kids group?" one of the people at the table asks me.

"I am. I'm Jane."

"Hi, Jane. I'm Mel, and my pronouns are 'she/her,'" says a woman with bright-green eyes as she gets up to welcome me. She introduces me to the women sitting near her, and they invite me to sit down.

"We're so glad you could join us today. We're pretty casual here, so if you have any questions, we're happy to answer them. Or you can hang out and listen to the challenges and triumphs we are having lately." I glance around the table and realize a big laundry basket full of kittens is on one of the chairs.

"Also, Susan's cat gets knocked up like twice a year, so we always have a batch of extra kittens if you want one." I laugh, imagining Matt's face if I come home with a kitten from my adventure with Libby.

I instantly feel welcomed. They all seem so down to earth and chill.

"Well, I'm here because my son is . . . well, I don't know for sure. I think he may be transgender, but his doctor wouldn't even consider that. We have an appointment at MPTC, but not until autumn. I'm just struggling with what to do. My husband doesn't . . . He isn't . . . I mean, he's supportive of us, but not in this. He thinks it's something I put in our child's head."

I can't believe how it all rattles out of me.

They all nod knowingly.

"My husband and I split over our child. He couldn't accept it, but I think it was more about what other people thought. He doesn't see our son right now," the woman at the end of the table tells me.

"My husband has always been such a good dad and husband. But now, he's so adamant that he can change Charles."

"I think we all have stories of people in our lives who aren't accepting. I lost friends and have family I no longer speak to because they cannot respect my child and honor their wishes," Mel tells me.

"How did you know your child was transgender? I think that's the part I struggle with. And people seem to want me to prove it somehow. Especially my husband. How do you know for sure?"

"Well, only your child can know for sure. But the consensus on a child being trans is that they are insistent, persistent, and consistent about who they are."

"Well, that's definitely Charles. He's been all those things for years."

"Does Charles have any dysphoria? Does he hate his body or talk about being in the wrong one?"

I nod. "Charles told me he wishes he didn't have a penis since he could talk. And he's been . . ."

I sigh, looking around at the faces of these strangers who seem to get it.

"His teacher worries about him because he's suddenly having bathroom accidents at school. He had this weird situation with a pair of scissors . . ." The woman across from me raises her eyebrows at me, but I can't bring myself to tell them what I think Charles was trying to do. "He's a good kid. He's never been anything but a good kid, but it's like he's off the rails."

"What can you do to support your child?"

"My husband runs our school and voted for gendered bathrooms and uniforms. He also took Charles to cut his hair when I wasn't there. I feel like for all the support I give, there is someone else just tearing him down right behind me. I'm waiting for my husband to understand and get on board."

"With all due respect, your husband sounds intelligent enough to understand what the medical experts say. If he's still not believing at this point, it's willful. And it is dangerous to your child. Trans kids who aren't supported have very high self-harm rates, especially as they age and their bodies start to change. It sounds like they may need a therapist to help them through this."

"Matt doesn't want a therapist putting anything into Charles's head. Up until now, he's been a hard no on therapy. I feel so stuck."

Before I know it, I'm crying. I feel a hand rest gently on my shoulder, and then I feel something soft on my lap. When I look up, I find a kitten someone put there. As soon as I pet it, it starts to purr and settles in for a nap.

"Thank you all for listening and talking to me."

"I swear this is the hardest part, that in-between phase when you are still trying to figure it all out and have all the resistance. Just listen to your kiddo and get them all the support and resources you can," Mel says.

She adds me to a couple of online groups for parents of trans kids, one of them a group that gets together with the kids too. I walk out toward Libby's vehicle with the kitten I couldn't put down, feeling weepy.

❧

"The trans group gives out kittens? No fair!" Libby says as she takes the tiny cat from my hands as I get in.

"How did it go?" she asks right away. "I was thinking about you the whole time. I know you're having a hard time, and I'm unsure how to help except to be here and help you find your answers."

"I got so many answers. Some were easier to take than others," I say, telling her all about what I learned on the way home. She listens to me, and I realize again how much I wish I had this kind of relationship with Matt when it comes to Charles, but I'm so happy to have the support I do have from Libby.

❧

The kids were all so excited when I brought the kitten home. She is so tolerant of the kids and loves to nap on anyone. She brings some much-needed comic relief into our home and someone small and sweet for all of us to seek out and cuddle. Of course, Matt disapproves since it has something to do with Libby.

"You should've consulted with me first," he says about the kitten. I try to explain to him that it wasn't an option so much as something that happened, but it's yet another part of our lives where we can't seem to agree.

Matt is upstairs helping the kids brush their teeth while I make lunches for the next day. I hear a lot of yelling, primarily from Charles, and I assume Henrietta is bothering him and Matt will take care of it. When it doesn't stop and gets louder, I head upstairs to see what's up.

Matt is frozen at the sink, looking at Charles, who is yelling, "I'm not a boy! I'm a girl!" at the top of his lungs, over and over at Matt, who seems incapable of moving. Poor Henrietta is standing there watching, covering her ears. Charles is at full wail by the time Louisa joins us. Charles's yelling has brought everyone.

"What happened?" I yell.

"Nothing. I just said to be a good boy and finish brushing his teeth. I swear that's all I said."

Matt and I almost have to shout to hear each other over Charles, still yelling that he's a girl, not a boy.

"Matt, you have to say he's a girl. I think that's what he wants," I yell over Charles's yelling.

Matt looks at me as if we've both gone mad.

"Charles," I say, but he doesn't hear me, so I yell his name loudly. "Charles!"

"CHARLES!" Matt screams at the top of his lungs. "That's enough!" He leans over fast and swats Charles on the bottom hard three times. Charles winces and starts to cry. Louisa gasps and runs off as the room goes silent. We don't hit in our house ever. It's Matt's fucking rule. He said getting spanked as a kid traumatized him. My life growing up was more abject poverty and neglect, but Matt and I vowed when we got married that we wouldn't hurt our kids the way our parents hurt us. We were going to break that cycle.

"I'm a girl," Charles says quietly as he uncurls himself and puts his toothbrush back. "Either I'm a girl, or my brain is broken," he says, shuffling out of the room.

Matt used to be my shining light in the dark. Now he's disappointed in me, and the feeling is mutual. He approaches me in the doorway to leave the room.

"Matt," I say, blocking the door. "Seriously, you just hit our child. What the hell makes you think that's okay?"

I'm livid, trying to keep my voice from cracking, looking at him in utter shock and sadness.

"I knew things were bad," I tell Matt with a lump in my throat, "but I seriously don't even recognize you anymore. Go cool off somewhere away from the kids and me."

He storms out of the room, down the stairs, and out the front door so fast that I wonder if he remembered the keys.

I look down at my shaking hands, and Henrietta stands close to my leg. I lean down and pick her up. She rests her head on me, and I momentarily stop to calm down and breathe in.

"I'm always trying to please everyone, and somehow, I end up not pleasing anyone. You know what I mean, Henrietta?" She nods her little head at me, so sweet. I kiss her, wishing all this could be just a little bit simpler.

Chapter Forty

Charles is in a funk I can't get him out of. He doesn't care about anything, even screen time, and he hasn't watched Julia Child in weeks. I miss her constant voice in the next room.

Even Louisa can't coax Charles out of his room, so she watches TV with Henrietta while I start dinner. I smell something burning after I put the casserole into the oven and check the stove, ensuring there isn't a cookie remnant or something that dropped onto the bottom of the oven, but I don't find anything.

"Mom! I think Charles started a fire!" Louisa shrieks from the living room just as I leave the kitchen to search elsewhere.

"Where?" I turn back to the pantry to grab the fire extinguisher.

"In the driveway out back."

"Stay in this house, and don't let go of Henrietta," I yell to Louisa, who immediately picks up her baby sister.

"Mom?" Her voice cracks in fear.

"It's okay. I'll be right back."

I race down the stairs to the back door and find a large fire burning in the middle of the driveway, with enormous billows of black smoke blooming out of the fire. Charles has lighter fluid next to him, standing too close to the flames, just watching. He doesn't even look scared.

"Charles!" I yell, and my voice is as high-pitched as I've ever heard it. "Get back. Do you hear me?"

He looks at me and moves slowly backward. He doesn't even seem aware of what's happening.

I blast the fire extinguisher at the fire until it's just a smoldering pile. Charles's clothes, his uniforms for school—all charred. I stand on the driveway, panting.

"Charles. Are you okay?" I ask, wrapping my arms around him. He winces, and I notice the blisters forming on his hands and arms.

"Okay, Charles. We are going to the hospital now. We need to get this checked out."

I carry him as carefully as possible to the house to find Louisa and get my phone and keys.

"Louisa, I need you to call Daddy and tell him we're going to the hospital. Charles is burned."

"I called nine-one-one. They are sending an ambulance and fire truck."

I nod at her, setting Charles down on the entryway bench. Fuck. This will be a big thing now that I'm not sure I can handle.

"Can you call Daddy and tell him to come home now? Tell him . . ." I choke on the words. "Just tell him to come home right now."

The ambulance and fire department come roaring up the block, gathering onlookers as they stop in front of our house.

"The fire is out," I say as they run up the walk. "It was some kind of accident, but I got it out. But my son is burned. He needs to get looked at." The EMT follows me into the house as the fire department heads to the driveway to ensure the fire is out.

I sit with the EMT and Charles. He isn't even crying. He looks like no one is home inside.

"He needs to come in to have these burns looked at. It's a small surface area, but one hand looks deep. Can you ride with us?"

"I can't leave the kids for very long. My husband should be home soon . . ."

"Can we call him for you?" I shake my head.

"My daughter already did." I look down and realize I'm shaking like a leaf.

"Ma'am. Can you tell me what happened here?" a policeman I didn't even notice asks me.

"I don't know. I was making dinner, and we smelled smoke from outside, so I ran out with the fire extinguisher. He was standing right there. He was . . . he was just standing there."

The EMT tells me they need to get Charles to the hospital as soon as possible. I ask Louisa, "Can you watch Henrietta for a few minutes until Daddy gets here?"

She nods, fighting back the tears.

I lean in and hug her. "It's going to be okay. You did everything right, Louisa, but we need to get Charles checked out. Daddy will be here soon."

I leave the house with the paramedics, and Matt pulls up just as we get into the back of the ambulance. He races over to me.

"Louisa is inside with Henrietta. Charles got burned. He . . . he started a fire."

"What? Why? He knows not to play with fire."

"It was his clothes, Matt. All his uniforms. He burned all of his boy clothes."

Matt takes a step backward as if someone has struck him.

The EMT asks me if I'm ready, and I sit down and buckle myself while Matt looks at me, all sad, but I don't have time to hold his hand right now.

"Just go inside and take care of Louisa and Henrietta. I'll call you when I know more. See if you can get a sitter so you can meet me at the hospital."

I sit in the waiting room at the hospital, crying, waiting for word on Charles. I have no idea how long I'm there or what they are doing. I try to push away the horrid thought that this is our life now and that he may never recover one of these times.

Matt rushes in, almost skidding across the floor as he enters the hallway. I look at him, frazzled and wide-eyed, but I feel nothing. Not relief or comfort that he's here. I feel like Charles with his dead-inside eyes. He sees me and stops in his tracks.

He wants me to say it's okay. I can't. Nothing is going to be all right ever again. Charles's behaviors are getting more and more dangerous. How can Matt still not see that?

"Jane . . ." He says my name as he looks at me with hope and sorrow.

"I don't know anything. They said he was in shock, and we are determining the severity of his burns and his chances of smoke inhalation. They said they might have to intubate him as a precaution. Or they may keep a close eye. That's all I know."

A doctor walks out and calls my name. I get up fast, rushing past Matt. The doctor leads us back into the ER room with Charles. He's hooked up to an IV, as well as numerous monitors. He's sleeping, and he looks very pale.

"He was in shock and unable to respond when he came in. His burns are superficial surface burns covering a small percentage of his body, but one portion is quite deep. He will be transported to Children's Hospital in Madison soon for diagnosis and observation. He will be heading down via ambulance when transport is ready."

"Children's? Why does he have to? I mean . . ." Matt asks.

"Mr. Zander, your child's burns, combined with his age and smoke-inhalation risks, mean he will need to be monitored for at least a few days. We aren't set up here for such a thing. We're a small hospital."

Matt sighs like it's more an inconvenience than anything.

"Mr. and Mrs. Zander." His tone and face are serious, and it makes my stomach hurt. "It's a good thing you got to him when you did," he says, and I nod. "It could've been much, much worse. He was wearing fire-retardant pajamas that may have also helped keep the rest of his body safe."

I'll blame myself anyway. I was supposed to be watching him.

"Can you tell me what happened?"

"I don't know. I was making dinner, and he was playing in his room. Or that's what I thought. I don't even know how he got a lighter or matches. He isn't a bad kid. He's so sweet and would never hurt a fly. I think it was because he hates his school uniforms."

Matt reaches out and takes my hand. I realize it's not to comfort me; it's to shut me up.

"Thank you, Doctor," Matt says as he steps forward to shake the doctor's hand. "We appreciate all you've done," he says as if we are done here. I shoot him a glare.

"Mr. Zander, I think getting to the bottom of your child's behavior is pertinent. Starting a fire like this can be a cry for help. You got lucky that the fire was put out this time, and Charles appears to have only suffered minor burns on a small percentage of his body. But this behavior is a big red flag. Please take it seriously. I highly recommend getting your child some help."

With that, he exits the room, leaving Matt and me in silence.

"I suppose you'll try to make this into something about Charles wishing he was a girl. But this is kid stuff. Hell, I started a fire in my room growing up with some small fireworks. We were playing around. I was just smart enough to put it out right away."

I look at him, trying to find some shred of the man I married.

"He burned his boy clothes. All of them. Every uniform, every sock, every shoe and hat and shirt. What does that say to you?"

"He clearly still hasn't figured out that he's a boy because his mother keeps telling him it's okay to live in a fantasyland where gender isn't real and anyone can dress however they want. Jesus, Jane. You blame me for this when you are the one who won't face reality. Charles is a boy. Get over it already."

We retreat to opposite sides of the room while we wait for Charles to be transported to Madison. He's sedated and looks so tiny. I go to hold his hand and realize I can't. They are heavily bandaged, and Charles seems to be asleep.

"He is trying to tell us that he isn't okay, but you won't listen. What will it take for you to listen?" I ask Matt, who sits silently in the corner.

Standing over my child—so broken in so many ways—feels like someone else's life, only it isn't. It's mine.

Chapter Forty-One

Time rolls by in the hospital without my knowing the hour or the day. Libby has been staying with my kids a lot of the time, thank God. Day after day, the burns heal and get redressed, and Charles refuses to talk. I'm as worried about his silence as I am about his hands.

Matt is working and switching off with Libby taking the girls or coming to visit. He paces the floor and spends time on his phone when he is here. Charles watches him with a scowl. It's less stressful when Matt isn't here at all.

A nurse comes in and finds me whispering to Charles. I feel embarrassed that she caught me talking to my sleeping child, but she smiles at me. "It's good to talk to him. It will help him find his way to his own words." I nod at her. "He was talking before the incident, right?"

"Oh, yes, up a storm. Try to shut him up," I say with a laugh, but I pause.

"Well, actually, he used to. He was larger than life. But then . . ." I see it so clearly now: the lines we drew and Charles's reaction to all of them. As if I'm in a helicopter, I can finally see the whole picture. Charles has been showing us all along how troubled he is. Matt wasn't listening, and I was still listening to Matt. I cared so much about building my kid a community that I didn't bother to be his advocate in the place where he needed protection the most.

"My child is transgender," I tell her, testing how it feels to say it out loud.

I've been talking to the therapists and psychiatrists caring for Charles; they all believe that Charles is transgender. But it's him we're waiting to hear from.

"I've never said it out loud like that. My husband has fought me on it at every juncture. But I see it now. How Charles was begging for help, and we weren't listening."

"You were doing your best with what you had. It's a good thing you came here. Have you heard of the Midwest Pediatric Transgender Clinic?"

"Yes. We have our first appointment with them in the fall. I've been anxiously waiting for it."

"Well, let me call down there and see if they can come to you since you're here. I know they are busy, but I'll see what I can do to get you seen sooner than that."

I smile at her, so thankful for some ray of hope in this that I blink back tears.

"It's all gone downhill, and I'm afraid it can't get much worse than this."

The nurse looks back toward the open door and then again at me. "My nephew is transgender, although he's a grown-up now. He tried to tell us when he was in high school, and we didn't believe him. Not until he took way too many pills and had to have his stomach pumped. Then the therapist told us that supporting our trans kid is actually suicide prevention. And not supporting them is the exact opposite."

I look at her, realizing there are many more gender-fluid kids than I thought.

"We weren't ready to hear it, but we got ready because we were scared. You will too."

"But what about my husband?" I ask, trying to fight back the tears. It's so hard to let go of the only life raft I've ever had.

She shrugs. "If your marriage is strong enough, it can carry this."

I contemplate how my marriage feels as fragile as Charles's glass dancer, and I weigh the idea that we might be better off without Matt.

"He was my everything," I say to her in a whisper.

"They always are," she says as she returns to work, heading out into the hall with a wave.

She comes back with a book for me about transgender kids. I thank her, settling into a chair next to Charles to read.

Libby arrives a few hours later, as I'm getting Charles into pajamas.

"Hey you, I bought you coffee. I thought it might be too late."

"It's never not coffee time in here. What time is it, anyway?"

"It's quarter to eight. Matt got home in time to put your girls in bed, and I left Mila with my oldest, who seemed excited to babysit. I'm hoping it goes well. How's this one doing?" She nods her head toward Charles, but I sort of shrug.

Libby uses the wall-mounted hand sanitizer as she enters the room and stands back, rubbing it over her hands. Charles looks up at her and manages a weak smile, the first I've seen since we arrived. Libby goes over to stand by Charles's bedside, reaching into her bag. "How's it going, my small friend? Are they treating you okay here?"

Charles doesn't say anything; he watches her. She pulls out a sparkly tiara from her bag.

"This place is the dumps. I brought you something to brighten it up." Charles's eyes light up at the tiara. She knows his weakness. He looks at me as if for validation. I nod, fighting back the tears as Libby puts the crown on Charles's head. He smiles but still doesn't say a word.

It's his new normal. They have no medical reason for him not talking. They think he was traumatized and needs time, which feels true for all of us.

"You still aren't ready to talk, are you, sweetie? And that's okay."

Charles looks at me and catches my eyes but stays silent. I kiss him before sitting on the couch with Libby and letting Charles fall asleep to cartoons.

"So, what's the word? Anything good to report?" Libby asks.

I shake my head. "Not much. Mostly now, they are worried because he won't talk. We can go home in a day or two. But he just . . . disappeared inside himself."

Libby reaches over and puts her hand on mine. "I know this isn't medical science to pin your hopes on, but I believe he will come back. It was hard and scary, and he needs time to figure out what to say. He will talk when he's ready."

I want to believe her because the alternative is unthinkable.

"Are you okay? You look thin. Are you eating?"

I smile at her. "I'm okay. This whole cafeteria is nothing but freaking gluten, so I seem to be surviving solely on a fruit-and-trail-mix diet." I laugh, but the smile fades.

I glance over to Charles, who is asleep.

"I feel like nowhere is safe, as if there is always something in the wings waiting to take Charles away. And I'm so scared and pissed at Matt and everyone who pushed Charles to think he's broken." I pause, contemplating.

"But mostly, I'm numb. If I feel anything at all, it's a strong sense of protection over my kids. I don't care how Matt is or about wasting my time with those fake bitches at school. There is no silver lining here," I say, looking at my child, so tiny in his hospital bed with his bandaged hands. "But I do know I'm done letting anyone hurt him if I can help it."

"This kid needs you to fight for him until he can find his voice. I am here to help you and be loud and proud. But you are his first line of defense."

"I'm trying to figure out how to make this all work. I am super supportive and not taking a single ounce of the shit anymore, and then mix that with Matt, who is, at best, still in ambiguous land. I don't know how we can live in the same house and parent this kid together."

"You could always move in with me. I'm month to month, so we could find a big house to rent. Our house would be supportive all the time."

I look at her, surprised.

"You'd want to live with me?"

Libby laughs. "Of course I would. You're my best friend, and you're wicked cool. Why wouldn't I want to? I know you have a lot going on, but think about it. You're welcome to come to my house when you need to get out, but I'd be super psyched to look at houses with you and do a single-mom tag-team parenting thing."

"Thinking about not being with Matt used to be my worst nightmare. But now I know what my worst nightmare is, and I don't know how I can forgive Matt for not listening to me and fighting us every step of the way. How do I get over it?"

"With time. Maybe. I don't know. But I'm here for you, whatever you decide. You aren't alone, Jane."

❧

In the first light of day, Charles and I sit on his bed, and I talk.

"I did a lot of things wrong, kiddo. I made mistakes and I want you to know how sorry I am for how long it has taken me to hear you. I thought I could go along with things and still protect you, and I couldn't." I hold his little leg instead of his bandaged hands, and he turns his head toward me.

"I also wanted so much to fit in and make friends that I wasn't doing what I could to show you I love you as you are. I love your cooking, how you dress, how you sing, and how you smile. I love you exactly as you are, and I will make sure you are safe and loved. No more hiding. No more making you be someone you aren't. Okay?"

He nods at me.

"Okay, Mama," he says, and the tears start to flow from his eyes. I cry too, because it's the first time he's talked since the fire.

"I don't want you to be like everyone else. You are perfect just the way you are," I tell him, sliding into the bed beside him to curl my body around his.

"Even if I'm a girl?" he asks, looking up at me with big, wet eyes.

"No matter who you are. I'll always love you exactly as you are."

We sit together in a long hug. I can't change the past, but I can make sure he always knows he's loved as he is. That I can do.

Chapter Forty-Two

"You have other kids too," Matt reminds me when I call him from the hospital with an update on Charles. Henrietta isn't allowed in Charles's hospital room, and Louisa is afraid. But Charles is the one who needs me right now. Still, Matt is insistent. "We all need you to come home for a night of normalcy, Jane."

I don't have the energy to argue with him. I am fried and need a night's sleep in my own bed and a few hours with my kids. Libby got Mrs. Driscoll to keep Mila for the night and offered to stay with Charles. Matt has not offered to stay with Charles at all, but at least I don't even have to worry about what he might say to him.

Matt and I and the girls sit down and have dinner together. I try to keep the conversation light, but Charles's empty seat and the tension of the past week hang heavy on us all. Libby messages me photos and updates on Charles because she knows I need to know he's okay. I can't think of what would've happened if we hadn't noticed the fire right away. Being home brings it all back.

Henrietta and I read a book together before I put her to bed. Then I sit down with Louisa to catch up with her. She chats with me about a project for school and a sleepover she's been invited to the following weekend. I want so badly to give the kids some regular life amid all this.

"I know you were really scared when Charles got burned," I say to Louisa. She nods, looking down at her hands. "You're a kid too, even if you do seem like a little grown-up sometimes. It's okay to be scared and need us. I know that so much this year has been about Charles. I see how brave you've been, and what an amazing sister and kid you are. I am doing all I can to make things better for everyone. I want you to know that."

Louisa looks up at me and gives me a small smile. "Thanks, Mom. It's hard worrying about Charles all the time, you know? But I want to come see him at the hospital, if that's okay. I miss him, even if he does steal my favorite clothes." A real smile spreads across her face, and it does my heart good to see it.

"You can absolutely come to the hospital if you feel up to that. And we are going to make more time for you and me once I'm home. I want you to know that you are so special and amazing too."

Louisa leans in and hugs me, and I am thankful that I came home and had this time with my oldest.

When the kids finally go to sleep, I sit on the couch, beat.

"You okay?" Matt asks, and I don't know if he's asking about this moment or in general.

"It feels surreal to be here after all that happened. Louisa's so excited about her friend's party, which may as well be on Mars. Everything feels strange, and I'm all disconnected. But no, I'm not okay."

Matt nods in agreement. He isn't okay either. I sigh, not wanting to have any big talk with him because I'm exhausted. I want my bed and an uninterrupted night's sleep, then breakfast with the girls before I head back to Charles.

"Jane," he starts, but he gets cut off by my phone going off. I left the ringer on in case the hospital needed me. But it isn't the hospital. It's Mickey.

I stare at the phone, not wanting to deal with her. I bump the call, looking up at Matt.

"I don't have it in me tonight to fight or anything. I need sleep," I tell him.

The phone rings again, and it's Mickey.

"For fuck's sake," I mutter before I answer Mickey on video chat. Her face is big and too close to the camera, as always.

"Jane. Are you at home?" she barks.

"Yes, but it's not a good time. Things have . . . well. It's been a rough time, and I have to go." I don't even care if she's going to call me rude. I can't handle her hate right now.

"Jane, I'm here. In Atwood. I heard what happened, and I want to see you."

"What? In Atwood? Why?" I look at Matt and realize he called them. I scowl, closing my eyes to take a deep breath so I don't start yelling.

"I have no energy to get into it with you, Mickey."

"I'm not here to fight, Jane. I just want to talk. Can I come over? For a little bit?"

I frown, wanting to say no and go to bed and relax for the first time in days. But she came all this way.

"Fine. We're here," I say, then hang up and turn to Matt. "You called them?"

"I was freaking out when they took Charles to Children's Hospital and said they might have to intubate him. So, yes, I called our families. I felt like people should know. She's genuinely worried, I think—" he explains.

"Oh, she is, is she? How nice. I'm sure she'll be super helpful."

Mickey arrives looking flushed and scattered. She is disturbing without her signature condescending air.

We go into the sitting room and haven't even sat down when Mickey says, "Jane. I am so sorry."

My eyes open wide, and I shake my head because apologizing isn't something Mickey does. Not for real, anyway.

"Okay . . ." I say cautiously. "My trust level for almost everyone is at an all-time low. So I'm not sure what you're doing here, but I can't handle any drama."

Mickey stands up and starts pacing the small room. "I was such a jerk to Charles. And you. It irked me so badly thinking you dressed him that way. Thinking it was you doing it. I never realized how many big feelings he must've been having . . ."

I stare at Mickey, not sure of what to say or how to trust her with so much water under the bridge.

"We were always so different, Jane. I thought when you had Charles that both of us having boys would give us something in common. I love all your kids. I know I don't show it the best, but I do. But when Charles was born, I got so excited to take him to the monster truck show and teach him fishing. I guess I felt like I got cheated, not having that bond with you. And because Charles doesn't really like stuff like that, does he?"

"No, he doesn't. Charles is not like your boys."

Mickey nods, taking a breath before she goes on. "When Matt called and said they might have to intubate him, I got scared. I stayed up all night, thinking what it'd be like to lose one of my own boys. And I sat up praying that if he was okay, he can be whoever he wants to be and wear whatever he wants. I won't say another word. I just want him safe, Jane. Because if anything had happened to him—" She cuts off her sentence and starts to cry—real crying. I stand watching her because I cannot even figure out how to comfort myself.

It's unnerving watching the biggest, meanest woman I know unravel.

"Mickey, many factors led to what happened, and I'm his mother. I should've known. If anyone should've stopped him, it was me." I didn't even realize how much I felt this until I said it out loud. And then I'm crying, big, hard sobs that shake through me.

Mickey comes over, her long, strong arms wrapping around me. "It's okay, Jane. It's okay. Whatever it takes, we won't let anything happen to that kid again, you hear me? No matter what he wears." Her words only make me cry harder, and I stay there in the safety of her arms, like when I was little.

"If anyone was trying to help him, it was you. And we were too busy thinking we were right to even listen to you. I'm so sorry, Jane. I was wrong."

I turn to Matt, shocked by Mickey's about-face. But Matt looks more annoyed than touched, and when our eyes meet, he averts his gaze and heads into the kitchen.

I stay up late talking with Mickey. She apologizes for not being there when I was young and explains how she blamed me for our dad leaving for no reason at all. I tell her what I've learned about gender-fluid kids, about the risks and the reason why it's so important to respect and love them for who they are and not who we want them to be. And for once, she listens, taking it in, being respectful and not argumentative. It feels like the first real conversation I've had with my sister since we were kids, and though I don't know if we've fixed anything, we have found some common ground. She doesn't mention Mom, and I don't ask. Mickey coming around is a big enough miracle for one night.

Chapter Forty-Three

They finally tell us we can go home on our fifth day at Children's Hospital. Libby has taken over my life so I can stay at the hospital, and I'm ready to relieve her of that. Matt has seemed to come and go in shifts like the constantly rotating staff. Truth be told, I have better relationships with the nurses.

The physical wounds are healing, and our child will come home to us, though none of us have recovered in any traditional sense. And there will be a barrage of appointments. Doctors, therapists, physical therapists, and a follow-up with a new pediatrician. It feels all-consuming.

Since it's discharge day, Matt brings Louisa to help entertain Charles while we meet with the doctors. After a few card games with me and Charles, she asks to read her book, and I sit on the hospital bed. Matt promised to come back and attend the big meeting with all the doctors, but I'm not holding my breath.

"So, I want to talk to you about something, my love," I say, sitting on the hospital bed to face Charles.

He looks up at me with wide, concerned eyes. I realize how many of our talks with him have been so traumatic.

"Do you remember the talk you had yesterday with the therapist? She came while I checked on your sisters and Daddy at home and told me you talked to her?"

He smiles. "Yeah, that was nice." He's talking again, but I wouldn't exactly say he's giving words away. Not to us, anyway.

"I had a nice talk with her too. Do you remember her talking about what it means to be transgender?" I ask.

He nods at me with a smile creeping across his face.

"That's me. I'm transgender!" he says with a grin. "Everyone thought I was a boy because of my parts, but they were wrong. All of me is a girl. My heart and brain and even my penis. Did you know that girls can have penises, and it's okay?" he asks, more excited than I've seen him in months. "That's what my doctor said. She said that I am a girl for real." He stares me down like he needs me to understand.

"You are a girl. For real." I try to compose myself as we talk like this. I'm so happy to see my happy kid. "Do you remember what else she said?"

He nods at me, the smile on his face growing into a grin. "They said I can have a new name."

"Yes. And they also said you should pick your pronouns. Do you know what that means?" I ask. All I get is a shake of the head.

"That's when someone refers to you but doesn't use your name. So I might say, 'Louisa is sweet. *She* is a good sister.' Because Louisa is a girl, her pronouns are 'she' and 'her.'"

He looks up at me, nodding like he understands, so I go on. Louisa perks up from behind her book as if the conversation just got interesting.

"Daddy is a man and uses 'he' and 'him' pronouns, so that's what we use for him because we will respect each other when people ask us to use their names and pronouns. And some people aren't boys or girls. Maybe they feel like neither or both. We use 'they' and 'them' pronouns for people when they ask us to."

I search his face, wondering if it's a lot to take in.

"So, have you given any thought to pronouns?" I ask.

He nods at me with a big grin. "Mine is 'she.' I'm a she," Charles exclaims so proudly that I can't help but smile.

"Then that's what I will use from now on. We might make mistakes and need you to be a little patient with us as we get used to it, okay?"

"It's okay, Mama. We just do our best," she says with a smile.

"And you know what? I think *you* should pick your name."

She looks at me with big eyes and then laughs. "Me? I don't even know what name I want. It's hard to pick."

"It is hard to pick. But you don't have to commit to one right away. If you find one you like, we can try it out for a couple of weeks and see how it feels. There are no rules here. And you are in charge of what name you want. I will help if you want, but it will be up to you."

"Really?" she asks like it's too good to be true.

"I did a little research and found that many trans kids name themselves after someone who they love, think is cool, or inspires them. And others pick the name their parents would've picked if we'd known you were a girl all along. There is no right or wrong way to pick your name."

"I wish you knew all along," she says, going sad on me and probably remembering how hard it's been.

"I know, and I'm sorry I didn't. And I'm sorry I couldn't protect you through all of this. But I want you to know that I'm here now. And I'll always be here, no matter what your name or pronouns you use. I love you for you." She curls up on my lap and snuggles in for a long time.

"What about Annabelle? You always loved that name," I suggest.

"Nah. That's Annabelle's name. It'd get confusing." I doubt it would be confusing since we are on opposite ends of the country, but I nod, impressed at her ability to think critically about this.

"What girl name did you pick when I was in your belly?" she asks.

"We were going to name you Eleanor," I tell her, and she scrunches her nose and face in disapproval.

"No, that's not me."

"Okay, then who are you?" I ask.

Louisa comes to sit on the bed and asks, "What are we talking about?"

"We are talking about a new name for your sister here."

I smile as I say it, and so do both of my girls. They look back and forth at each other and then at me.

"You two are sisters," I say as my voice cracks and the tears well up in my eyes.

"Yeah, Louisa, I'm your sister." Charles laughs as she goes in to hug Louisa with bandaged hands.

"Yay for another sister," she exclaims. I could not have asked for a more supportive sister for Charles than Louisa.

"I've got a suggestion for a name," Louisa says quietly.

"What is it?" Charles asks, almost jumping around in her seat.

"How about Julia? You love her so much and always say that's who you want to be when you grow up."

Charles is wide-eyed and starts flapping her bandaged hands. She's so excited.

"Can I, Mom? Can my name be Julia? Because that's who I am. I'm a cook and a lady baker, and I'm going to teach everyone to cook on TV. I'm a Julia!"

I pull her into my arms.

"Yes, you are, my love. You are Julia."

We all end up in a big hug, and for the first time in forever, I feel it will all be okay.

I wipe the tears from my eyes and grab my phone.

"Can I take a picture of my girls?" I ask, and they both agree. I snap a few pictures of them smiling together, looking so happy.

I've received many kind messages asking how we are and if we are okay, and I haven't known how to reply. Our town is small, and everyone saw the ambulance and fire department at our house. Libby has told me that the rumor mills are busier than ever.

"How do you two feel about me sharing a picture of you two sisters on the internet with our friends?" I ask. "I don't want to do that without getting your permission."

My stoic little Louisa nods with a smile, and Julia grins wide. "Tell everyone I'm a girl, okay? So they know before I come home!"

I choose my favorite photo and make a post on my social media account, with the caption "I love my girls. Louisa and Julia."

I take a deep breath and post the photo. Come what may, I refuse to hide who my child is from the world.

⁂

Matt joins us for the discharge meeting with Julia's doctors and the pediatric endocrinologist from the Midwest Pediatric Transgender Clinic. They agree that Julia has been consistent, insistent, and persistent about her gender. Their professional recommendation is to allow our child to socially transition as soon as possible.

"For young children like yours, a social transition is about clothing, hair, and pronouns. This is all completely reversible, should Julia suddenly 'change her mind.' Though I will tell you that kids who are so persistent at this young age very rarely de-transition." I sit scribbling things down in a notebook, knowing I won't remember everything.

"Hormone blockers aren't prescribed until the second stage of puberty, and surgery isn't discussed until adulthood. You have many years before you have to consider anything permanent. This is about honoring what your child is telling you."

Matt stays silent during the meeting until he says, "I thought it was a phase like me being obsessed with space travel as a kid. I wasn't going to let him get picked on for it."

"It's *her*," I tell Matt, staring him down across the table. He looks up at me, surprised.

"We aren't going to sit here in your feelings anymore. Your assumptions are no longer valid because our child tried to hurt herself. *'She/her' pronouns*. Because she is transgender. Are you listening to what all of these experts are telling you?" He doesn't answer me. I need him to know I am serious.

"I was picked on as a kid too, Matt, by my own family. I was gaslit for my constant stomach pains to the point that I believed I was losing my mind. The difference is that I learned from being picked on because I want to ensure my kids know they are loved, no matter what. You use your experience to mold our child into some irrational ideal of normal that doesn't even exist."

Matt stares at me, open-mouthed, no longer looking forlorn but more shocked. I am not even shaking. I am calm, and I have no doubt I am right.

"I have my faults in trying so hard to keep you that I stopped caring about the real goal. I am kicking myself for all the times I said 'It's a phase' and discounted how our child was feeling. I regret all the times I tried to hide Julia away because of the clothes she wears. I regret not listening to her and needing validation from others. I hate that this awful thing had to happen to make me truly support her. But I'm done with that now. From now on, I'm going to be the biggest supporter and ally that I should have been all along. I see my own mistakes, and I want to make them right. Do you?"

Matt opens his mouth like he's going to say something but then looks away so I go on. "I thought that if I could get all this support in this community, they would protect us. But it's you and me that need to support and protect her. And I get that you want her to fit in, but you are asking for an entirely different kid. And I don't want a different kid. I want this one. I want Julia exactly as she is."

"You can't just put a new name and pronouns on him and pretend it changes something. It doesn't." He's almost yelling, and everyone is looking at him.

I straighten my shoulders and realize that I no longer care what he thinks.

"We will let her grow out her hair like she wants. I'm taking her shopping for anything she wants to wear. She's going to therapy and joining some transgender groups to show her there is nothing wrong with her, because she has been sent the wrong message for too long. But I will protect her from your ignorance and assumptions, Matt, even at the cost of our marriage. Because your avoidance issues and your desire to be 'cool' are endangering our child."

All the professionals in the room nod at me. We all look at Matt, who no longer looks confident or sure of himself. His clothes are rumpled and he's in need of a shave and shower. How long has it been since I've looked at him?

"It's taking everything in my power not to tell you this is flat out your fault for fighting me so hard that we ended up here. You always told her she is a boy because she has a penis. And you made her feel awful about the clothes. I don't know why I let you bully us about this for so long. But it is hurting Julia. Because your priority is what other people think. Well, my priority is our children. I'm done with your unsupportive bullshit. Even if it means our marriage is over right here and now. Do you understand me?"

Matt doesn't say a word. He looks like he got hit by a baseball bat and hasn't decided how bad the injury is.

"Did your child self-harm before? Is there an issue you haven't communicated?"

I look at the doctor for the first time. He's young but seems genuinely interested in Julia.

"Our child has been telling us for almost four years—since she could speak—that she's a girl. She only wants to dress in girl clothes and plays with dolls and mini-kitchens. When she grows up, she wants to be a stay-at-home mommy and girl chef. But my husband thinks it's a four-year phase. He has refused to listen to our child or me all this time. He removed Julia's girl clothes this year and cut her hair very short. Julia has been a mess ever since. I found her once with scissors as if she was going to try to . . ." I let the sentence end there, and I watch as one of the doctors makes a note in the chart.

But Matt interjects before I can finish anyway. "I wanted to protect him. I didn't want him to be picked on."

"*Her.* It's *her*. And no, you didn't want to be divisive because you're afraid of ruining your popularity status since you decided you give a shit about what everyone thinks. It's more important to you than your own family."

The doctor watches us argue back and forth before chiming in. "The statistics on self-harm in transgender kids who aren't supported in their homes and environments are staggeringly high. I can tell you from experience that there will be more frightening consequences if you do not support your child exactly as she is."

He tells us he can get us some pamphlets. I want to tell him I already have them and that my husband refused to look at them. The doctor riffles through a binder he brought and hands some papers directly to Matt. He takes them as his shoulders sag even further. I almost feel sorry for him.

The most significant medical obstacle the doctors brought up is keeping Julia calm for a few weeks while she heals, which means preventing her very agile toddler sister from climbing all over her. Her hands will take a while to heal, but my other main goal is to keep Matt away from Julia as much as I can until he can stop deadnaming her and using the wrong pronouns.

"I'll work from home so we can have two sets of hands," Matt offers. "I can keep Henrietta at bay, and you can tend to Charles. Er, um, I mean, Julia."

Everyone in this meeting is here to ensure we provide a safe place for our children. It seems as good a time as any to tell Matt my idea.

"I have thought about this, and based on Julia's medical and mental health needs, I think I'm going to move up to the attic of our home with her for a few weeks until she's healed."

I turn to the doctor. "It's a huge space, all finished with a big playroom, a bedroom, and a bathroom. It will give her space from her toddler sister jumping on her and any influence that might not be in tune with her healing."

I turn to Matt and say, "Since you agreed to watch Henrietta, it should be no big deal. And I need to see you consistently saying Julia's correct name and pronouns before she can be around you full-time. You never say her name as Julia."

All eyes move to Matt, who has the audacity not to say a damn word. He's taken the silent pouting approach to my outburst in front of the doctors. He's mad that I'm blaming him. And I am. He caused it, but I'm also angry at myself because I let him. But not anymore.

I always worried what I would do if I didn't have Matt's hand to hold. But now it's my own hand I'm holding.

After the doctors all leave, Matt looks at me as we pack all the gifts and flowers onto the cart.

"I'm sorry," he says. He sounds sincere, anyway. I stare at him, contemplating.

"You're sorry," I repeat. "But the problem is you're only sorry this happened. You're sorry everyone found out. You're sorry there is gossip and pain. But you haven't changed at all. You're only sorry it turned out this way. You still refuse to see your part in this."

Chapter Forty-Four

When we arrive home, we find numerous bags of "girl" clothes and many gifts for Julia. I open the fridge and find an astounding assortment of casseroles, frozen meals, cupcakes, and cookies that people dropped off. I can't help but get choked up at how many people were willing to show they support us as we are.

"So many people brought food and gifts and stuff for Charles," Matt says.

I glance sideways at him for using her deadname.

"It's Julia," I say, and Matt just nods. "It's ironic how compassionate everyone has been when the whole reason it was supposed to be a secret is for fear of their reactions," I tell him. But he stays silent.

Julia and I move into the attic when we come home, as planned. At first, Julia is quiet and spends most of her days in bed except for a few laps around the attic with me. She gets more energy daily, creeping farther into the attic to play. We all heal a little bit as the days roll by.

Matt and I are polite strangers who pass in the day and night as we hand off kids and catch up on the bare minimum of what we need to discuss. I don't know where he stands because his silence is deafening. We've talked about all this enough. He needs to come to these realizations himself. He needs to decide how much he's going to love us. And if his love will be taken away if we don't fit society's version of normal.

I bring all our favorite things up to the attic, and I tell Louisa she can come up anytime and we will find appropriate times when we can bring Henrietta up.

"What about Daddy?" she asks, my stoic girl sounding teary.

"Of course, Daddy. He will be busy working and caring for Henrietta, so I can care for Julia until she's healed. But we can do some switching off time because I want Daddy to have time with Julia too."

When Matt fought me on us moving up to the attic for a while, I told him the other option was Libby's house for a few weeks.

"I can't describe how much I cannot be around you right now" is all I can say to him. I can't stop thinking about the past nine months here in Atwood and how far the divide between us has grown.

Julia is almost up to speed again and has been putting on fashion shows in the attic with the bags of clothes people have sent. Some are hand-me-downs, and some are from the store. She loves them all, and we've been taking time every afternoon to write thank-you notes to everyone who has been so kind during these challenging weeks.

For all my fears and worries and attempts to fit in, I suddenly realize that I don't have to. I'm amazed at how many people love and support Julia just as she is.

"Are we getting a divorce?" Matt asks me one morning while I'm making our coffee.

"Not that I'm aware of," I say, pouring creamer into my mug.

"Then why are you acting like you hate me?"

I sigh, looking down at the coffee mug in my hand for a long time.

"I don't hate you, Matt. I love you. I'm always going to love you. But you seem to love me only when I agree with you. You seem to love Julia only if she fits into some perfect box. And she doesn't fit into it. And instead of listening to me, you've been gaslighting me for your own agenda."

"Jane, I'm not *gaslighting* you," he says.

"Yes, you are. And you can't even see it, so we need a therapist for all of us. Because this year has been traumatic, we both have blame, and we both need to know how to help Julia. I'm reading the books the hospital recommended. *Are you?* I'm talking to other parents who have been through this. *Are you?* I'm doing all I can to create the most supportive home and school environment for her. *Are you?*"

Matt looks hurt by my outburst, but I've only begun. "I don't think you understand how my priorities have shifted to keeping my kids safe, and everything else has rolled downhill."

"What is that supposed to mean?" Matt has dropped his friendly facade and is flat out scowling at me.

"I would've done anything to keep our family together before because I was so afraid of being alone. And I was terrified that I would be like my mom as a single mother. But I'm not my mom. She couldn't support me when I needed it. If anything, *you* remind me of my mother. You care more about your agenda and how things look than you do about reality. Doing this alone would be better than fighting you to love Julia as she is."

Matt looks stricken, and it's breaking my heart, so I say the rest with tears streaming down my face.

"I am going to go look at public schools for Julia. I will do everything possible to find her the most supportive environment possible. Of course, I'd appreciate your help and support, but I will still do what I feel is best."

I take a deep breath and look straight at him. "I'm also looking for a house to rent with Libby. I'm not saying you and I are over forever, but I can't have Julia living in a house with someone who misgenders and deadnames her."

"Jane, come on. It will take me a while with the name and stuff."

"Sure, but you aren't even trying. You say her deadname every time you come up to see her. And she wilts away again every time."

Matt runs his hands through his hair, frustrated with me.

"I will fight you in court if I have to, and we have a whole team of doctors at Children's Hospital telling me I'm doing the right thing," I say.

Matt looks like someone has sucker punched him.

"I am dedicating the rest of my life to ensuring she never hurts herself again. And you don't seem to take or even see your own responsibility for what happened to her. I can't live with you until you do and support us in the way we deserve."

"Jane, please don't do this. I am trying with the name. It's hard after all these years of thinking of him, er, her as, um, Charles. I mean . . . Julia," he says, his struggles further proving my point. I don't say a word. "And, sure, we can check out schools. We can also have another meeting at Atwood Prep, and I can try to make things better there. I do run the school." He laughs as if it's funny.

I cock my head at him. "Have you lost your mind? Atwood Prep and your 'gender rules' traumatized Julia. *Your* plan traumatized her. It isn't a place where she can heal, not right now, anyway. The public schools I've found in this area have supportive gender plans they make up with parents based on what the child needs. They have all been trained and have numerous other trans or nonbinary kiddos, and they have protections in place for kids like Julia. I hope you'll be able to take a nonbiased look."

Matt stays silent, so I take my coffee and the kids back to the third floor.

Libby arrives with Mila and Vonn an hour later. Vonn goes to Julia's bed and gives her the gift she brought. Libby and I leave them in the bedroom and take the babies to the attic playroom to chat.

"Did Matt say anything to you?" I ask Libby, but she shrugs.

"No. He kind of wordlessly let us in. He's looking pretty pitiful."

"Good," I say without thinking. "I'm just . . ."

"Hey, you don't have to explain to me. He was a class-A shithead. I know. But are you sure you want to leave? It's hard. This whole divorce, custody, mediation, fighting over kids and shit is hard."

"Matt spent the year showing me I can't trust him. He still can't see the big picture. He can't see Julia for who she is, so he can't see his part in harming her. Until he does, how can I trust him with her? This attic has over a thousand square feet and provided an excellent 'apartment' for us this past month, but we can't stay holed up in here forever. I don't want to leave this house, but I doubt Matt would. The most important thing right now is to create a safe place for Julia. That's what all this fight has been for. With or without Matt."

Libby smiles at me. "You know you changed, right? Look at you, fighting for your kid and standing strong. I'm proud of you. You went through the wringer and came out better for it."

"I used to hear people say, 'I couldn't have done it without you,' and I always thought of my marriage. But I could not have gotten through this year without *you*. I'm so excited I get to move forward with you and move in while we tag-team being parents. I think it's going to be good for all of us."

"I am super psyched too. But I also know this is a big decision. What if Matt finally comes around?"

I put my hands on my hips and almost stifle a laugh. "If he gets it now after all this time, it'll be its own little miracle. Sadly, I think I've stopped hoping for it."

"Well, I won't be mad if you change your mind. At least I won't be if we haven't signed a big, expensive lease." She laughs, and we look online at places big enough for us all.

Chapter Forty-Five

In a twist I wasn't expecting, Matt texts that he will join me at the public school for a tour. Mrs. Driscoll has agreed to watch the kids, so I meet him there. We park near each other in the parking lot, and he waits for me so we can walk into the school together.

"Hey," he says as if he doesn't know how to talk to me.

"Hey. I'm glad you came. I figured you wouldn't."

He shrugs, then looks right at me. "I thought it was time I listened to your side."

I appreciate his words, but I scowl at him anyway.

"No offense to you, but it's been a rough year. I hope you're here to find the best option for Julia, but I can't trust you right now."

"I know, Jane. I called . . ." He looks around to make sure no one is near us. "I called the therapist you recommended for all of us, and I've been talking to her. And she's helped me see . . ." Matt coughs as if he's getting choked up. He takes a few seconds and recovers while I watch. "Can we talk about all of this? And I mean talk? I want to hear your thoughts and find a way back to being a team."

I nod at him because something is different. I can see a glimpse of the Matt I fell in love with. The one I almost forgot was even in there.

The principal meets us at the door, and our conversation ends there. We walk the halls, and I can already tell this school is what I want for Julia in every way. They have boys', girls', and gender-neutral bathrooms on each floor, so students may choose what is best for them.

There is an antidiscrimination policy already in place. The district has seen half a dozen trans kids of varying ages, so they are already very familiar with how important it is to support kids however they present and identify.

The very kind principal guides us through a handful of classrooms, where kids raise hands and ask questions. We observe a hands-on science experiment. The kids all look happy with their big safety goggles, and I notice how the teachers use words like "folks" and "friends" instead of "boys and girls." We tour the whole school, checking everything from the gym to the music classes.

"I hope you enjoyed the tour. We think Julia would be a great addition to our school and hope she'd love it here."

I love the school. I love all of it, and I turn to Matt, waiting for him to say he will think about it. Or say no and try to drag me out of there. Instead, he looks choked up again. All he can seem to do is nod.

"Matt?" I ask. "Thoughts?" I don't even care about putting him on the spot. I want Julia in this school.

"Yes," Matt says, too quiet for me to hear, and then again. "Yes. I agree that this is the best fit for Julia. We want to enroll her."

I don't think about the past, blame, or hurt. I reach out and wrap my arms around Matt. Once I get into his arms, I remember how much it feels like home.

Chapter Forty-Six

Things with Matt aren't fixed, but we've been going to therapy together and separately. I joke that it's our family pastime right now, with Louisa and Julia getting turns as well.

We are all better, but the tiptoeing around each other, trying to find our place, hasn't disappeared. Julia and I did move back into the main part of the house, although sleeping next to Matt is something I haven't been able to do yet. I'm sleeping on the extra bed in Julia's room, claiming she needs me close. She doesn't anymore, but I am not ready to leave her side yet, and I'm not sure my place is next to Matt anymore. There is too much to figure out with so much else to do.

Louisa is at school, and Julia is in her room listening to music and playing with her dollhouse. Matt and I agreed it was best not to send her back to school this year. It should be a no-brainer, but I took the win. We will continue to get Julia's work from her teacher so she can finish first grade and move on next year to a new school where she will be accepted by default, not somewhere we have to fight for it.

I'm using Henrietta's nap time to power clean the house. Matt was not a meticulous cleaner while we were in the hospital or upstairs in the attic. The house needs to be vacuumed everywhere, so after I collect all the clutter, I clean all the floors. As I am working on the cat's dust balls under the fainting couch, I hear the repeated ringing of the doorbell.

I turn off the vacuum and cross the room, wondering who is there. When I open the door, an older woman in a suit is holding a briefcase, looking like she wants to sell me something.

"Can I help you?" I ask, dusting my hands off onto my pants.

"Mrs. Zander?" she asks.

"Yes," I answer, wanting to be done with this already. The house is enormous, and if I can't get it vacuumed while the toddler is napping, I won't get it cleaned.

"My name is Elaina Scheel. I'm with Wisconsin's Department of Children and Families. I'm here to investigate a few incidents of self-harm that resulted in the hospitalization of one of your children. May I come in?"

My face and mouth drop at her words. These are the people who can take away your kids. I panic, trying to remind myself to breathe as I think of all the worst-case scenarios.

I nod, letting her in without a word because the Lord knows I can't talk when I'm petrified.

"I realize this feels scary, and it's sudden, but we merely need to understand what happened and what is happening now to ensure this won't happen again. We are all on the same side in trying to protect Charles."

"It's Julia. Charles isn't her name anymore. It's Julia now." The words come out and surprise me.

"Oh," she says, sounding disappointed. "The files here from the hospital say Charles. Is that incorrect?" Now she sounds suspicious, as if I'm trying to pull one over on her.

"No, it says her deadname because she is transgender. That's why she burned her clothes, and . . . she just wanted us to understand that she's a girl." She stares me down without a reaction, so I go on.

"We've been in therapy at the hospital twice a week since, trying to do what's right for her." She nods, but she's frowning, and I'm suddenly worried that maybe she's anti-trans. I feel a second round of panic roll over me and realize I'm shaking like a leaf.

"We were alerted that your child started a fire and was recently hospitalized for burns. There were some notes in the chart about another instance of self-harm. It seems there is much to get to the bottom of."

"Mrs. Scheel, would you mind if I inform my husband that you're here? He's at work a few blocks up, and I think he should join us." Even my damn voice shakes.

She waves me off as if it's okay, and I am still trying to decipher her intentions. She grabs her phone while I grab mine, and I head upstairs to check on the kids while I call Matt.

He has been very agreeable lately and answers my calls and texts immediately.

"Hey, babe. What's up?" He has slid back into this comfortable way of being with me. I'm not sure I'm ready for it, and at this moment, it irritates me.

"Well, social services is here. This woman showed up and wants to talk to us about what happened to Julia. And I'm freaking out. Can you come home?"

"What? Shit. No, I can't. I'm in Madison at the meeting I told you about. I can leave now, but I still won't be home for over an hour. I'm way over on the west side."

I stare at my shaky hand, doubling over and trying not to cry. Matt realizes why I'm silent.

"Jane, it's okay. None of this is your fault. You're doing all you can to protect Julia, and you have been all along. If there is blame, it's mine. Tell her the truth. Make her understand. I've seen you fight for this family, and I know you can do it."

I still feel shaky and scared, but I feel better after talking to Matt. I find Mrs. Scheel pacing my first floor and looking around.

"My husband is in meetings in Madison right now. He won't be home for over an hour." She nods at this as if it's of no consequence. Like we aren't talking about taking away my kids.

"I did verify your child is now going by the name of Julia, so that's been cleared up," she says, but I frown. If she isn't going to believe anything I say, then why is she here?

"Mrs. Zander, could you tell me what happened in your own words?" she asks.

I nod, trying to remember to breathe.

"Julia isn't just a different name. It's like a different kid. Before, there were all these school clothing rules, and our child felt . . . sad and didn't fit in. And I tried to go against my husband, but the whole school got involved. It turned into this change in school clothing policy, so my child had to wear a boy's uniform and use the boys' bathroom, and she stopped talking. She was so unhappy, and no one would listen to me. Certainly not my husband." I don't mean to blame him, but I realize I'm telling the truth.

"Did you try to get your child any medical or mental health resources?"

"Yes, I did make an appointment at the MPTC at Children's Hospital, but our appointment was scheduled for October. They had a ten-month wait list."

She looks at me as if I might be lying, but I stare her down because I'm not.

"Therapy?" she asks, and I shake my head.

"Not until the hospital."

"And why not? You were clearly aware some issues were going on with your child."

I answer her honestly. "My husband wouldn't allow it."

She looks at me again, then writes something down in her notes. She scribbles for a while and then looks back up at me.

"Does your husband hurt you or the kids, Mrs. Zander?" she asks casually, even though it isn't a casual question.

"No. Matt isn't like that. He's very sweet. But he returned to his hometown and suddenly cared more about what everyone thought than anything. He was ill-informed about trans kids and didn't want to believe it about his own child. But he sees it now."

"I'm glad to hear it. I think we will open a file, make some time to talk to all of you, and get to the bottom of this."

I feel my heart beating in my chest.

"I don't think that's necessary," I say, my voice raised in panic. "You can see I'm supporting my child and ensuring she has what she needs."

"Ma'am. I'm going to be blunt. Situations where women completely follow their emotionally abusive husbands' wishes generally end in harm. I don't know your husband, but I know of his complete lack of support for your child, according to Julia's medical file. I know you needed to put aside your fears and your child's needs for your husband's comfort. This dynamic and how blatantly unaccepting he's been of your child make this a continually risky environment. I wonder what kind of support your child will get long-term, when the dust settles and your husband forgets the harm he caused."

"I understand your concerns. I do. But I was leaving him for the same fears you have. Look at this," I say, pulling out a notebook with potential houses I was looking at with Libby. "My very supportive best friend, who ran my house while we were in the hospital, has been looking at us getting a place together. I was leaving my husband because he could not support us emotionally. I will no longer allow that. When we got home from the hospital, we stayed in our finished attic because I didn't want Matt around her unless he would be supportive."

She's staring me down, listening, and trying to decide my fate.

"What's changed?" she asks me, and I falter, looking for the words.

"I know we all have fault here, but we've also all learned something. And I assure you I will walk out of this amazing old house and my previously beautiful marriage if I think it's harming my children to be here. I am not who I was a year ago, when we moved here. I'm not who I was when Julia got hurt. I'm not who my husband married; Julia is different too. People change."

"My concern is, what if your husband reverts backward? The self-harm will return, and statistically, it will get more severe with age."

"I will be out the door immediately. I no longer accept conditional love from my family or friends."

Mrs. Scheel stares me down, but I stare right back. She asks to look around at the kids' rooms and talks to Julia before she leaves, telling us she'll be in touch.

I think it went well. By the time Matt arrives home, I am feeling calmer.

"How did it go with the social worker?"

I can't hug him as he comes in because I resent him for bringing social services to my door and the implied risk of losing my kids.

"I'm trying hard to be a family again, but this feels . . . ugh. I'm so mad about all of it. I assured her that I would leave if you get all unsupportive again. And I meant it. I'm not going to lose my kids. They come first."

He nods at me, looking hurt.

"I don't even know how it went. Good? Maybe? She said she'd be in touch. So now we wait and hope they agree we should keep our kids."

Matt hugs me, gathering me into his arms and trying to make me feel better. I lean into him, trying to believe the world is solid and will be okay.

Chapter Forty-Seven

"Are we going to make it?" Matt asks me one night after we've gotten the kids in bed. There seems to be a reversal of him being the one needing reassurance.

I wait a while to answer because it could go either way.

I shrug. "I'm trying to get through every day. Not anything else right now."

"I thought you would relax after social services dropped their case, but you seem even madder."

I sigh. "I'm not as mad anymore. I'm exhausted and do not tolerate shit that threatens to take my kids away. And you still don't seem to see your part in this."

"Jane, we sleep in separate rooms and live separate lives. You went to look at houses with Libby, but we need to be a family again. If you want to fix it, we need to be together."

"We slept on separate floors for months before the fire. You never minded then."

Matt slouches as if his feelings are hurt, and I feel bad, but I still think of him as the enemy here.

"I'm trying here, Jane. What else do you want me to do?"

"I want you to mean it. I get the feeling you are only going along with Julia's transition, but secretly, you have real problems with it."

"I don't," he says, but I can hear the hesitation in his voice. I look at him until he continues. "I wouldn't say that. I wonder . . ." I scowl, already sure I will hate what he says.

"Go ahead," I say, trying to keep my cool. "Please say what you have to say."

"I wonder about him changing his mind. I mean, in the future. He's *so* young. And here we are going to do all this stuff to him."

"Her. It's *her*," I almost yell at him because he can't get her pronouns right *at all*.

He sighs loudly like he's frustrated, either at me for stating facts or maybe at his mistake in pronouns, as if it's annoying to remember.

I stand in silence, glaring at him. This is just an act. The social services lady was right too. Matt is waiting in the wings to pick this fight back up.

"Our child was exhibiting dangerous behavior just to be heard and validated for who she is. Kids who identify as transgender this young rarely de-transition. Their transitions are normally permanent. And the transition for her is merely letting her pick her hair and clothes and respecting her pronouns. We are not 'doing anything to her.' No meds are involved until the second stage of puberty, which is years away. Are you reading books about trans kids? We're allowing her to be herself so she doesn't need to hurt herself again."

Matt nods as if he half agrees with me.

"I see you trying. I do. But I also see you so deep in denial that you still aren't facing what this is. And I can't settle for half of your support. Not anymore."

"So, what? Are we through? Do you move back into the attic, or one of us move out? I mean, what is happening here, Jane?" His voice shakes as he says it, and I want to feel the old safety of his arms. But I can't until he's a safe place for all of us.

"I don't know, but I need you to have your come-to-Jesus moment about Julia, and I don't think you have. And half of your support almost killed her. I will do everything possible to ensure she never feels like that again."

I look at him, and tears well up in my eyes. "The thing I feared most in the world was losing you. I've built my life around that fear. But now, my only job is to keep our kids safe. I wish I could tell you our future, but I don't know right now."

Matt looks at me with kind eyes, and I think of the old Matt, whom I once believed didn't care what everyone thought. But maybe other people's opinions always mattered to him, and he was only able to love us conditionally. Maybe he truly never was a safe place.

Chapter Forty-Eight

Libby gifted me a journal when Julia was still in the hospital. She told me I could use it as a place for my feelings or to find my voice and tell my story to other parents who might need to hear it. The words wouldn't come to me in the hospital. I'd stare at the empty page because I felt like I knew nothing. But now, I am enjoying my daily journaling. I think of sharing my words with the world someday for someone to find when they need a friend.

> *All of our planning about perfect names for our perfectly normal family was in vain. There is no normal, no perfection to strive for. Not because it's too hard but because it does not exist. We are mere mortals, doing our best, no matter how it may look from the street.*
>
> *I now have three daughters, two I named myself and one who named herself after going through hell and back to be heard. After such a quest, how could I do anything except let her choose what to call herself?*
>
> *Today, we are throwing her the biggest seven-year-old birthday party we can muster. It feels like her coming-out party. How lucky I am to be Julia's mama.*

Libby helped me plan the party, assuring me guests would attend.

"You aren't that woman anymore, Jane. You came into this town, and you made friends. People care about you and your family. And so many people care about Julia."

Planning a big birthday party for Julia became a two-family event, with Libby doing more organizing than me. She even rented a bouncy house for the backyard. Julia and Louisa picked out princess wands and crowns for us to make. I saw more light return to my daughter with every sparkly item we glued. Every time we used her new name, I saw a little bit of her return to me.

I worried it was too soon and too much. We are all barely back on our feet. Libby reminded me how long it had been since we'd had something to celebrate. She said we needed to go above and beyond to show Julia she has complete support from all of us.

Libby was right about attendance. This year's backyard party is full of kids and adults. The atmosphere is light and fun, and Julia races around in her pink party dress and the sparkly crown Libby gave her in the hospital. Julia has never looked happier to me. You'd never know all she has gone through.

Even Julia's therapist has said her progress is remarkable. I have my child back. Only now, she talks to everyone and doesn't need to hang on my leg, and her smile is so bright you'd never guess we had such a traumatic spring. Like the gardens around my house that the girls and I have been out planting every day, Julia is thriving with our love and support. It feels like she has come back to life.

The onslaught of gifts, balloons, craft projects, and cards for Julia is fantastic. The community may have seemed dark and scary before Julia's injury, but it came pouring out with love when she was hurt. It warms my heart to see how much people care about her and want to see her doing well as her true self.

The party is full of families from Atwood Prep who have shown support and kindness. Rebecca Darling arrives and hands me a gift bag for Julia.

"Thank you so much for donating the food for the party," I say. "We were so surprised to find it paid for at the deli when we went to pick it up. That was really nice of you."

"You all have had a rough year. It's the least we can do to show our support." I hug her, overwhelmed by all the love. Rebecca runs off after one of her kids, and Libby comes over and stands beside me.

"It looks like I'm not the only friend you made here," Libby says as she hands me a bottle of water. "And I'm glad for you. You deserve it."

"I always thought I couldn't make friends because I have such a hard time talking to people I don't know, but now I think I just never found the right friends."

"It's not that you can't talk; you just can't talk about bullshit and rumors. You talk about real stuff all day," she says as we stand eating fruit at the food table, watching the kids run while the parents mill around my backyard. We have music and a table with food and punch set up in the great room in the attic, more food in the dining room, and kids chasing each other around the backyard and porch, making it seem like five parties going on instead of one.

"I can't believe how wonderful everyone has been to us," I tell Libby. "It's amazing how I gained friends from the thing we were most afraid to discuss."

"I think we find fake friends when we show everyone who we think we are supposed to be. We only find the real ones when we show who we really are."

I raise a hand to high-five her, which always makes her laugh at me. Maybe the point isn't to stop doing dorky eighth-grader stuff. Perhaps the point is to find someone who loves you as you are.

"Do you ever miss Jillie and Kelsey?" I wonder what it would be like to have friends since childhood and then lose them.

"No. I think I outgrew them long ago, but I had no idea how to move on until I was forced out. I'm grateful to you because you loved me for me. I love who I am now. I'm not fake anymore."

I feel tears start to come at her words and try to look away, but she takes my hand.

"You were my friend even when I was a total hot mess and everyone said to stay away from me. You never judged me. You don't waste your precious time on fake people or bullshit. You see yourself as this boring 'plain Jane' type, but you're wicked interesting and super funny. You name your kids after cool-ass women I've never even heard of before. You read Einstein and know your kid is trans before she does. You are a good mom for standing up for your family. I keep thinking about the widow Wellington, and how she hid out in this house when the rumors started flying. But you're brave, Jane. Instead, you found your voice and made it safe for Julia to be herself."

I start to cry, and she squeezes my hand.

"You are a real friend, Jane. Maybe the first one I've ever had."

I reach out and hug Libby. "You're my best friend. The first one I've ever had. It's been a shit year, but I'm glad you were by my side through it all," I tell her, but when I pull out of our hug, I keep her hand in mine.

"Libby, I wanted to wait to talk to you about moving in together until the party was done. It's been hectic, and I wanted to give it the real thought it deserves." I take a deep breath, and I see her straighten.

"Hey, it's okay. I told you I was fine with you getting back together with Matt. I will find a cool place for me and my kids. It's all good."

I smile at her. "I'm so thankful to have such a kind and easygoing friend. Because I decided I'm not ready to live with Matt full-time. I know he's trying, but I'm still unsure about him. The whole social services thing shook me. And I handled it. *I* did it on my own. And I trust in myself. And you trust in me. But Matt . . . as much as I love him, he makes me doubt me."

Libby looks at me blankly. She was not expecting me to say I want to move in with her.

"I want you to move in with me here. It's so big, so there is plenty of room. And Matt agreed, at least for now, that he'd take over the old apartment they had for the nuns, so it's got space for him to take the kids sometimes. He works so much anyways. I think it's best."

Libby is still quiet, so I say, "Libby. Say something. Do you want to live with me or what?"

She nods, getting all teary-eyed. "Yes, so much. But I was all set up to be brave and happy for you about your marriage working out. I didn't plan for this."

We both burst out laughing. When we stop, we survey the yard. Matt gives us a tip of his hat from his spot at the grill as our kids join Libby and me in the dwindling light.

"They look like they're on a mission," I tell Libby, who nods.

"Mom, can they sleep over?" Louisa asks, her little hands folded like in prayer. Libby's little ones join in on the begging.

I look at Libby, who raises her eyebrows at me. "I don't see why not. Might as well get used to it, right?"

"Yes, you can all sleep over," I tell our kids. Julia makes a beeline to Libby for a hug as Louisa comes in to hug me. Pretty soon, we are all in one big group hug.

I lean my head on Libby's shoulder through all the giggles; I whisper, "Welcome home."

Author's Note

I probably could not have accurately defined the word "transgender" when our child began telling us who she truly is. Like many people, I was ill-informed and mostly in the dark about gender. So I started reading and researching. I sought help from doctors, therapists, and experts, but most importantly, I listened to my child because I believe she knows herself far better than I ever could.

I will never know what it is like to be transgender, but I do know what it's like to be a confused mom in a world that isn't always very understanding. In my research, I connected with other parents and heard some heartbreaking stories about trans kids being the targets of bullying and violence. I didn't realize how exceedingly dangerous the world is for kids like mine. But just as scary was the high rate of self-harm in trans kids who are not supported *as they are*. I want to make this clear: Trans kids don't hurt themselves because they are trans. It's because they are not accepted or respected for who they are. Trans kids who are fully supported have the same low self-harm rates as the rest of the population. We *all* just want to be accepted as we are.

I know that transgender kids are a hot topic right now, yet for my family, it's simply our life. I wrote this book hoping to bridge some of the space between all of us. We are all far more alike than we are different, and when it comes down to it, we are all doing our best for our families and trying to find our way through a world full of change.

This story is not our story, but it represents families like mine and the struggles we face in a world that views gender as binary or only two-sided. But nothing in this world is black and white. All of life is a combination of varying shades, and no two are identical. We are like snowflakes, alike but intricately different.

I hope you find compassion and connection in these words and characters. I hope it brings us all closer together instead of dragging us further apart.

Be kind out there.

Acknowledgments

Writing a book is an organic process. Although these words and ideas are mine, the inspiration came from so many people along the way. I do not believe one writes a book alone. Instead, the stories we create are all the things we carry in our hearts, coming out in pieces to make something new.

I want to thank my amazing agent, Tina Schwartz, for her tireless efforts in bringing this book to the world. As soon as we met, she believed in me and my stories. Tina has been a joyful and enthusiastic cheerleader throughout the long process of rewrites, editing, and pitching, and I count myself lucky to call her my agent and my friend.

I'm also so thankful to Lake Union Publishing and my editors. To Chantelle Aimée Osman, for her excitement in acquiring this book and her belief in the power of this story. And to Laura Van der Veer, for her amazing suggestions and notes that made this book so much better, and for the opportunity she has given me to release it into the world.

I could not have written this novel without my husband Steve's support and help. He read more drafts than I can count, always willing to support my desire to make it the best it could be. He helped me find the time and energy to keep going and cheered me on every step of the way. I couldn't ask for a better partner to walk through the world with.

I want to thank my children, who show me the meaning of unconditional love in varying ways daily. They continue to teach me far more than I have taught them and fill my life with such happiness and wonder. They inspire me to change the world in whatever small way I can.

A huge thank-you to John Galligan, who has inspired me, given me mountains of feedback, and encouraged me whenever writing life felt impossible. I would not be the writer I am without his faithful help all these years.

And to my amazing beta readers and friends who have helped me through numerous edits of this book and years of rewrites: Jess Engle, Nikki Michele, Laura Beth Goral, Bobbi Hague, Ellen Huck, Melody Jones, Loreta K., Sam Panetti, Cat Pippitt, and Jennifer Casey-Sekel. Your feedback, support, and honesty were instrumental in this book's process, and I'm so thankful for all of you.

Book Club Questions

Throughout these questions, we will refer to Julia by her name, not her deadname.

1. Jane is uneducated about gender and goes through her own process of learning what it means for a person to be transgender. Did you have a set perspective about trans kids before reading this book? Has anything in this book altered your perception?
2. How did you feel when Jane let Julia dress how she wanted for the school carnival? What would you have done? Did you find yourself siding with Jane or siding with Matt?
3. Did this book make you question how you would react if Julia were your child? What do you think you would do if your child expressed gender fluidity?
4. Jane always struggled with friendships and finally found a best friend in Libby. Have you had friends that you clicked with immediately? Would you end a friendship if your partner had a problem with it?
5. Do you know women like Jillie and Kelsey? What role have they played in your life and the lives of those around you?
6. When Jane attends the meeting at the school about bathrooms and uniforms, she freezes and can't say a word. Did you relate to this? Or do you think you'd have the courage to speak up

in front of all those people? What would you have said if you were there?

7. When Jane's mother-in-law, Barbara, visits, she talks with Jane about showing her child how to be a boy. She convinces an exhausted Jane to try it, and Jane agrees because she feels she has no choice. Did you think Barbara was right? Would you have listened as well?
8. Louisa is a big supporter of Julia throughout the book. It never occurs to her to want to change Julia in any way. In what ways could siblings of trans kids help (or hurt) them in their transition? Can you see how siblings of trans kids might live in the shadows of their siblings' needs?
9. Jane has insecurities that make her more likely to follow her husband's wishes and attempt to conform to society's idea of normal. Do you see the consequences of believing that we should all strive to be normal when, truly, none of us fit that description?
10. Jane's sister, Mickey, has never had Jane's back. How much of this behavior would you tolerate in the name of family? Do you think the onslaught of influence from others played a part in Jane's reluctance to stand up for her child?
11. When Julia tries to harm herself in the bathroom with the scissors to "be a girl," what would you have done? Would you do things differently as a wife or a mother? Would you have considered this a major cry for help or "a paper cut," as Matt called it?
12. Would you be able to stay married to someone who would not support your child as they are? Do you think that Jane was right to split up with Matt?
13. Jane starts as an anxious, insecure mother and grows into a strong woman, intent on protecting her daughter. Where would your line as a mother be in deciding to support your child completely? Did Jane wait too long to listen to her

young child? If you feel able, please share times when you've struggled to find your voice to stand up for your child or the people in your life.

14. What kind of role did Matt's past and the Zander family legacy play in why Matt was so adamant about not accepting Julia as she is?
15. Trans kids are real and all around us, whether we know it or not. Has this book changed how you view this population? What can you do to show your support for this marginalized community? Are there ways that you can make this world a safer place for all people?

About the Author

Photo © 2022 Stephen Baade

Elle Baade is the author of book club fiction about empowering women that features relatable characters who shed light on the universal human condition. She writes about unique family dynamics to show that we are all more alike than we are different and that there is no such thing as normal. Elle opens pathways for communication around hard things where women have historically been encouraged to stay silent. She is the mother of four children, one of whom is transgender. For more information, visit www.ellebaade.com.